☞ **W9-BRP-113**

"Tired of glamorous private investigators so svelte they could be fashion models? Has author Selma Eichler got a heroine for you."
—*South Florida Sun-Sentinel*

**Raves for Selma Eichler and the Desiree Shapiro mysteries . . .**

*Murder Can Botch Up Your Birthday*
"A highly engrossing read that shouldn't be missed."
—*Rendezvous*

*Murder Can Rain On Your Shower*
"An exciting private investigator tale that is fun to read . . . delightful."          —*Midwest Book Review*

*Murder Can Cool Off Your Affair*
"A laugh-out-loud riot. I love Desiree's sense of humor."                                      —*Mystery News*

*Murder Can Upset Your Mother*
"Eichler scores again. . . . [A] delicious cozy."
—*Publishers Weekly*

*Murder Can Spoil Your Appetite*
"Desiree Shapiro is a shining creation."
—*Romantic Times*

*continued . . .*

***Murder Can Singe Your Old Flame***
"Witty dialogue . . . hilarious characters."
—*Publishers Weekly*

***Murder Can Spook Your Cat***
"Queen-sized entertainment!"   —Barbara D'Amato

***Murder Can Wreck Your Reunion***
"Witty repartee, lots of possible suspects, and even an intriguing subplot will keep you turning the pages to find out who done it—and why."
—*Baldwin City Ledger* (KS)

***Murder Can Stunt Your Growth***
"Poignant and satisfying. . . . Just plain fun to read."
—I Love a Mystery

***Murder Can Ruin Your Looks***
"Dez is a delightful character with a quirky, distinctive voice, and I'd love to go to dinner with her."
—Sue Feder's Magical Mystery Tour

***Murder Can Kill Your Social Life***
"Humor, food, and just plain good writing."
—Tamar Myers

# MURDER CAN MESS UP YOUR MASCARA

### A Desiree Shapiro Mystery

## Selma Eichler

A SIGNET BOOK

SIGNET
Published by New American Library, a division of
Penguin Group (USA) Inc., 375 Hudson Street,
New York, New York 10014, USA
Penguin Group (Canada), 10 Alcorn Avenue, Toronto,
Ontario M4V 3B2, Canada (a division of Pearson Penguin Canada Inc.)
Penguin Books Ltd., 80 Strand, London WC2R 0RL, England
Penguin Ireland, 25 St. Stephen's Green, Dublin 2,
Ireland (a division of Penguin Books Ltd.)
Penguin Group (Australia), 250 Camberwell Road, Camberwell, Victoria 3124,
Australia (a division of Pearson Australia Group Pty. Ltd.)
Penguin Books India Pvt. Ltd., 11 Community Centre, Panchsheel Park,
New Delhi - 110 017, India
Penguin Group (NZ), cnr Airborne and Rosedale Roads, Albany,
Auckland 1310, New Zealand (a division of Pearson New Zealand Ltd.)
Penguin Books (South Africa) (Pty.) Ltd., 24 Sturdee Avenue,
Rosebank, Johannesburg 2196, South Africa

Penguin Books Ltd., Registered Offices:
80 Strand, London WC2R 0RL, England

First published by Signet, an imprint of New American Library,
a division of Penguin Group (USA) Inc.

First Printing, February 2005
10  9  8  7  6  5  4  3  2  1

Copyright © Selma Eichler, 2005
All rights reserved

 REGISTERED TRADEMARK—MARCA REGISTRADA

Printed in the United States of America

Without limiting the rights under copyright reserved above, no part of this
publication may be reproduced, stored in or introduced into a retrieval system, or transmitted, in any form, or by any means (electronic, mechanical,
photocopying, recording, or otherwise), without the prior written permission
of both the copyright owner and the above publisher of this book.

PUBLISHER'S NOTE
This is a work of fiction. Names, characters, places, and incidents either are
the product of the author's imagination or are used fictitiously, and any resemblance to actual persons, living or dead, business establishments, events, or
locales is entirely coincidental.

If you purchased this book without a cover you should be aware that this
book is stolen property. It was reported as "unsold and destroyed" to the
publisher and neither the author nor the publisher has received any payment
for this "stripped book."

The scanning, uploading, and distribution of this book via the Internet or via
any other means without the permission of the publisher is illegal and punish-
able by law. Please purchase only authorized electronic editions, and do not
participate in or encourage electronic piracy of copyrighted materials. Your
support of the author's rights is appreciated.

To my husband, Lloyd Eichler,
for all of his help, encouragement,
and love.

# ACKNOWLEDGMENTS

Many thanks to—

Detective Kevin Czartoryski of the New York City Police Department, for providing crucial information on police procedure.

Alego A. Bartolacci of Dunkelbergers Outfitters in Stroudsburg, Pennsylvania, who so graciously answered all of my questions on deer hunting in that area.

My friend and fellow author Camilla Crespi, for helping me over a plot hurdle.

My talented editor, Ellen Edwards, for (as usual) picking up on what I should—and should not—have put down.

My copy editor, Michele Alpern, who did such a terrific job.

My agent, Stuart Krichevsky, for his help and support.

And last, but definitely not least, my cousin Sid Kay, of All City Insurance, who enabled me to put the killer in the right car.

# Chapter 1

"Desiree Shapiro."

"No kidding. And I thought I was dialing the queen of England."

"Mrs. Goody?" It wasn't really a question. That low, raspy voice delivering its usual measure of sarcasm couldn't possibly belong to anyone else. And if this wasn't enough for me to make a positive identification, just then the woman began to cough. Suddenly I had this mental picture of Blossom Goody—an attorney I'd had some brief contact with in the course of an investigation I'd completed only that month—sitting in her smoke-filled office, the ever-present cigarette momentarily removed from her lips so she could hack away.

"There's no pulling the wool over *your* eyes, Shapiro," she said tartly—once she was able to say anything at all.

"How are you, Mrs. Goody?" I inquired politely.

"Not bad. But never mind the 'making nice' business. I'm calling to do you a favor. I got a client for you. Cousin of mine."

"Oh. Thanks. Your cousin needs the services of a private investigator?"

"No, he needs a chiropractor; that's why I got on the horn to *you*." (Blossom herself, as you can see, doesn't stoop to "making nice.") "Gordie's certain somebody's trying to kill him."

"Why does he think that?" I was beginning to squirm.

"Christ, Shapiro! Why're you asking *me*? Gordie can explain everything a helluva lot better than I can."

Now, I'm not one to sneeze at a paying job—particularly at a time when most of my income seems to be going out. But I had once accepted a case that necessitated my investigating something that hadn't occurred yet. And believe me, I went through some pretty frightening moments before arriving at the truth. This was when I promised myself that from then on I wouldn't get involved unless the jewels had *already* been pilfered from the safe, or—and I feel a thousand percent more strongly about this—the body had *already* been carted away. It's a matter of self-preservation. I mean, not only was I a nervous wreck during that earlier experience, but I'd put myself in the position where, when the crime eventually did take place, I wound up heaping a large portion of the blame on myself for allowing it to happen.

"Has your cousin been to the police about this?" I asked timidly.

"With what?" Blossom snapped. "He's got no evidence. If he did, you and I wouldn't be having this conversation. Look, I told Gordie about your solving that ten-year-old stabbing. He was very impressed."

"I'm pleased to hear that, but—"

"I said how I'd helped you out and that in appreciation you'd be happy to help *him*."

"But—"

"Stop with the 'but's,' all right? Without the information you got from me, you'd be futzing around till this day trying to figure out who did that murder."

Well, this was something I could definitely dispute. The truth is, Blossom hadn't provided me with anything except the most basic facts, facts I could certainly have gotten elsewhere. (I admit this might have taken a little extra work, but still . . .) I didn't see myself as coming out a winner here, however—not against THE MOUTH. "All right, have your cousin get in touch with me. Um, I should tell you, though, that I'm extremely busy just now, so I can't promise that I'll be able to work with him personally. But let me see what's involved. And if I feel that the investigation requires more time than I can devote to it, I'll recommend a really top PI for the job."

Blossom took a few seconds out at this point to allow for some serious coughing, after which she let me have it. "You can cut the crap. A little birdie told me your office doesn't see any more traffic than mine does. In other words, Shapiro, you're as much in demand as a hooker who can stuff 'em into an A-cup."

The uncharitable comparison aside, at least there was a grain of truth to *this* remark. I can't deny that I have my share of dry spells. Nevertheless, I had no intention of acquiring Blossom Goody's cousin as a client. But in deference to the woman's tenacity (and also her tongue), I elected not to protest any longer. When I met with the man, I'd simply wriggle out of taking his case, that's all.

"Look, I'm not going to try and figure out why you're so anxious to turn this down," she went on. "If I had to guess, though, I'd say you're scared silly you won't be able to prevent something's happening to Gordie. But it seems I've got more faith in you than you do, kiddo."

"You have it all wrong," I lied. "I—"

"He'll call you this afternoon." And with this, Blossom hung up the phone in my ear.

*God! You have no idea how much I hate that!*

# Chapter 2

True to Blossom's word, Gordie—full name Gordon Curry—contacted me at the office that Friday afternoon. It was just after two.

His voice was deep and pleasant—sort of sexy, actually. "I understand you spoke to Blossom earlier and that you've agreed to look into something for me."

"Well . . . um . . . not exactly. The thing is, I have a pretty hectic schedule at present, so first I want to make certain I can give your investigation the time it should have. But listen, why don't we set up a meeting, and once I know what's involved we can take it from there."

"Fine. Any chance of our getting together today?"

"Sure," I said too quickly. I mean, wasn't I supposed to be inundated with work?

"How's five o'clock?"

"I'll, er, check my appointment book." I rustled the pages (most of them blank) close enough to the phone for Cousin Gordie to hear. Then I got back on the line. "That could present a problem. I'm expecting a client at four thirty, and I'm not certain I'll be free by five. Would five thirty be convenient for you?"

"I'll see you then."

Go ahead. Call me paranoid. But a gander at me, and I fully expected my visitor's eyebrows to shoot up to his hairline. The truth is, I've almost gotten used to that kind of a reaction by now. Thanks to those geniuses out in La-la Land, when people think "female private investigator" they invariably seem to conjure up somebody with long legs, blond hair, a svelte shape, and a bust that extends practically into the next county.

Well, I have a downstairs neighbor whose Afghan hound, Esmerelda, bears more of a resemblance to that Hollywood tootsie than I do. (Not counting the bust, that is.)

Let's start with my legs. Frequently, when I'm sitting on a sofa, they don't even make it to the floor. Also, there isn't a blond hair on my entire head; I have red hair—*glorious* red hair, to be a hundred percent accurate—courtesy of Egyptian henna. And my body comes with its own natural padding. (Everywhere—with my luck—except in the chest area.)

But if this guy was surprised by my appearance, to his credit, it didn't show.

As to *his* appearance, Blossom's cousin isn't easy to describe. What I mean is, you couldn't call him handsome. Or even particularly good-looking. Yet there was something really charismatic about him. And to this day I can't pinpoint just why this was. All I can tell you is that he was ten times more appealing in the flesh than he is on paper.

I judged the man to be in the neighborhood of fifty—not exactly fresh off the vine, right? He wasn't more than medium height, either; plus, he was ever so slightly chunky. His face was rather angular, his nose a shade too long. And while he was still far from bald, I don't imagine there were many women who'd been inspired to run their fingers through his gray and thinning hair.

On the other hand, though, Gordon Curry had these

blue eyes that seemed to peer into your soul. (Sounds silly, I know, and it's not like me to wax poetic. But this is what I found myself thinking that afternoon.) What's more, his smile could turn your knees to jelly. (Provided, of course, you were into men who appeared to be well nourished and self-assured. Which—being that I have a thing for the skinny, needy-looking type—I'm not.)

Whatever it was he had, though, Cousin Gordie was aware that he had it.

Anyhow, we quickly introduced ourselves. After which he removed his velvet-soft tan suede jacket, and I hung it on the back of the door while managing to continue my appraisal of him without skipping a beat.

He was casually but, I gauged, expensively dressed in well-fitting navy wool slacks and a crisp blue-and-yellow sport shirt, the first and second buttons of which had been (calculatingly?) left open to reveal a dense mat of black and silver curls.

"I understand you were responsible for solving a murder dating back fifteen years," he remarked, placing his flattish tush on the chair alongside my desk—the only available seat in that cigar box I call an office. "I'm impressed."

I didn't bother to apprise him that he was giving me too much credit, that the crime had been committed *ten* years ago, not fifteen. "I got lucky," was all I said—and damned if I didn't feel myself blushing! (I admit it; I'm not exactly immune to flattery.)

He fixed those piercing eyes of his on my face, then threw in an ingratiating little grin for good measure. "I wouldn't put it all on luck if I were you. That's quite an accomplishment."

"Um, tell me, Mr. Curry—"

"It's Gordon," he corrected. And now reaching across the desk to where my right arm rested, he placed his hand on my forearm for a moment. "May I call you Desiree?"

"Yes, of . . . of course," I sputtered.

I informed myself that I couldn't attribute Gordon's coming on to me—which is exactly what he was doing—to his finding me so devastatingly attractive. It was inspired, I strongly suspected, by the mere fact that I was of the female gender. Nevertheless, my cheeks were burning.

"I imagine you were on the verge of asking what leads me to believe that somebody is trying to kill me."

*Probably an irate husband* instantly popped into my head. But I limited my response to, "That's right."

"Well, I'm reasonably certain there have already been two attempts on my life. I was in denial at first—it's not easy to accept that anyone wants you dead. But I finally faced the truth. That's when I decided I had to talk to someone about what had occurred, and Blossom got the nod. I called her yesterday, and we had dinner together last night and—"

"She suggested you see me," I finished for him.

He flashed me a boyish smile. "Uh-uh. *Insisted* I see you."

"You said a moment ago that you were *reasonably* certain there were attempts on your life," I put to him.

"Apparently I didn't phrase it right. I don't have any doubt this is true."

"Just what is it that's happened?"

Abruptly, the man's entire demeanor changed. He chewed on his lower lip for a few seconds, then scrunched up his forehead and, with long, slim fingers, began a nervous rat-a-tat on the desktop.

"Every fall my wife and I vacation in Pennsylvania for two weeks—in the Pocono Mountains. We have a cabin right on the lake. This year we arrived on a Sunday—September twenty-ninth, it was—to find that this incredible, Indian summer kind of weather had set in up there; it lasted until midweek, too. Well, for the next couple of mornings I could barely wait to get into that lake. My wife thought I was crazy—while the air was warm, the water was pretty frigid. I didn't consider this a deterrent, though; to me, the cold water is invigorating. But as things turned out, I should have listened to Rhonda—my wife—and read a book or something, at least on that second day." A rueful expression here.

"At any rate, on Tuesday morning I was swimming a good distance from shore—I'm a strong swimmer—when I heard a motorboat close behind me. I took a quick glance over my shoulder, and it seemed to be coming straight at me. I dove out of the way just in time."

The desktop drumming stopped, and Gordon returned his hands to his lap. But his forehead was still pleated like an accordion. "Then I realized that the boat was turning in my direction again. At about this same instant I spotted a second motorboat approaching—it was maybe a hundred feet away at the time. Evidently the driver of the first boat saw it, too, because he immediately reversed his course and sped away." And now the forehead smoothed. "And that, I'm pleased to report, was the end of *that* little episode."

"I don't suppose you caught a glimpse of who was in the boat," I said, none too hopefully.

Gordon shook his head. "It all happened in a flash. Besides, I was underwater most of that time—I couldn't even describe the boat to you, much less its occupants. Anyhow, at first I attributed the incident to someone with a snootful's being at the wheel. And then I speculated that it could have been some high school kids horsing around."

"You've since changed your mind?"

"Definitely."

"But it's conceivable, isn't it," I ventured, "that whoever was driving that thing got closer to you than he'd meant to and that he was heading back to see if you were okay?"

Gordon shook his head again. "This is exactly what I told myself. But in retrospect, the explanation doesn't really hold water—no pun intended."

"Why not?"

"Because if that near-fatal encounter had been truly accidental, another motorboat's heading in that direction wouldn't have stopped the driver from returning to check on me."

I conceded to myself that he might have a valid point.

"Still, for a long time," Gordon continued, "this escaped me. Even in light of what occurred a week later."

"Which was?"

"The following Monday I went deer hunting with one of our neighbors up there, and—" He broke off. "I gather you don't approve of hunting, Desiree."

*Damn!* I had no idea what gave me away. Maybe I'd wrinkled my nose or something. Or could be I'd just turned a little green. Whatever my reaction was, I wasn't the least bit pleased about revealing my feelings like that. I mean, it's not a large plus for someone in my profession to be so transparent. And the fact is, I'm normally an excellent actress. A regular Meryl Streep—I swear. "I can't say that I do," I told him. (Listen, I wanted to get out of handling this case anyhow.)

"Most of the women I know feel the same way," Gordon responded amiably. "I won't attempt to change your mind about hunting, Desiree, but, well, my father started taking me with him when I was only a youngster, and it turned out to be a real bonding experience for us. Could be that has a lot to do with why I love the sport so much."

*Shooting a defenseless animal is a sport?* The way I see it, killing for food is one thing—but *for fun*? Gordon Curry had, in my eyes, just morphed from a potential victim into a damn murderer himself! And I imagine that I was now looking at the man with distaste—and not really attempting to hide it, either.

"I can see I've alienated you," he murmured with obvious concern.

Well, I wasn't anxious to get into any big discussion on the subject, so I said tersely, "You haven't. Go on, please."

He nodded. "As I told you, this took place at the beginning of the second week of the vacation. Noel— my neighbor—and I couldn't have been in the woods for more than half an hour, if that, when we heard the explosion of a rifle. And all of a sudden there was a good-sized hole in the trunk of this tree not even a foot away from me."

In spite of the man's rotten idea of recreation, I found myself regarding him as the potential victim again. "God! That was a close call!"

"*Too* close. Anyhow, Noel tackled me, and the two of us hit the ground. For a minute or so I couldn't utter a single word, but Noel did the honors for us both, shouting out a few very colorful expletives. There was no response. We thought maybe the shooter had already moved on, not even realizing he'd barely missed killing somebody. Or, if he *was* aware of it, that he might have been too mortified to come forward. I didn't consider that I might have been deliberately targeted; evidently I wasn't ready to deal with something like that. And, after all, that sort of thing has been known to happen during hunting season. Still, both Noel and I were badly shaken, and a few minutes later we scrambled to our feet and high-tailed it out of there."

"What made you finally acknowledge that your life was in danger?"

"I suppose I reached the point where I could no longer kid myself. It's become tougher and tougher for me to function, Desiree. I have difficulty sleeping.

I can barely eat. And I'm constantly looking behind me."

"Did you cut short your vacation after that second episode?"

"No, I decided to stick it out for the remainder of the week—Rhonda loves it up there. Accident or not, though, I had no desire to do any more hunting. So I gave her the excuse that I'd wrenched my shoulder."

"Your wife accepted the explanation?"

"There was no reason for her not to. She even tried to persuade me to see a doctor, but I assured her it wasn't serious and that a couple of Advil were relieving the pain. We left it that I'd visit an orthopedist if the shoulder wasn't any better by the time we got back to Manhattan. So that was no problem. The *real* problem was that my nerves began acting up.

"Well, I wasn't able to control my anxiety, and Rhonda was demanding to know what was troubling me. So I finally said that I was facing a dilemma at work, one I wasn't anxious to return to. I concocted this story about some salesman I'd hired a couple of months earlier, claiming that this nonexistent person had not only failed to generate even a minimally acceptable number of orders but appeared to be purposely causing friction among the other members of the staff, as well. Nevertheless, I hesitated to fire him, I told Rhonda, because he was related to one of the company's directors.

"Later on, once I was back at work, every so often I'd create another disturbing scenario involving this phantom salesman in order to account for my state of mind."

"Your wife still doesn't know the truth?"

"I mentioned the boating thing to her the morning it happened, when I was still thinking high school kids or some drunk. But to this day, I haven't said a word about the shooting business."

"Why is that?"

Gordon appeared to turn the question over in his mind for a moment. "Initially, I thought it was because I didn't want to upset her. But I'm now certain that subconsciously my main concern was that Rhonda would regard what had transpired in the Poconos as part of a single, concerted effort to murder me—and that her reaction would force me to do the same. And, as I've said, I was in denial." Gordon shook his head slowly, almost wonderingly, a kind of ironic grin on his face. "Somehow I'd been able to convince myself—on a superficial level, at least—that as frightening as those incidents had been, they were totally independent of each other; therefore, they had to be *accidents*. Brainwashing, I believe it's called." He chuckled softly. "I even faulted myself for being so edgy. I've since come to the conclusion, however, that if I have any desire to remain among the living, I'd better take some action—before my nemesis tries for third time lucky." He favored me with a megawatt smile. "And that—hopefully—is where you come in, Desiree."

He was looking at me expectantly, but in place of the response he wanted to hear, I posed another question. "Who knew you'd be in the Poconos at that time, Gordon?"

"Well, we've had the cabin for years, and we always head up there in the fall for the early muzzle-loading season. But hold on a second. Apparently Blossom didn't explain."

"Explain what?"

"That I don't want you to find out who's been trying to murder me."

"You don't?" As I recall, this was accompanied by a gasp.

"Absolutely not. I'm here to tell *you* who it is."

# Chapter 3

"Would you mind repeating that?" I couldn't believe he'd said what I thought he'd said.

"Look, Desiree, I know who's trying to murder me. But I have absolutely no proof of it."

"And you want me to—"

"—uncover some evidence against him," Gordon finished for me. "Something I can take to the police."

Well, this was my chance.

"I'd really like to help you, but you have to understand that finding this evidence—assuming there's anything *to* find—could be a very time-consuming project. And as I explained earlier, I'm up to my ears right now." I could see he was about to respond, so I put in hurriedly, "Listen, Gordon, the truth is, I'd never forgive myself if something happened to you because this jammed-up calendar of mine didn't allow me to follow through quickly enough."

"Blossom told me there was a possibility that you might not want to handle the investigation. She has this idea that you'd consider yourself responsible if you took me on as a client and I was then thoughtless enough to get myself killed."

"That's not it at all. I—"

And now I was treated to the full measure of Gordon's persuasive powers. And let me tell you, this guy had charm to spare. "I can understand your feeling the way you do," he said in a voice that could make you melt. After which he reached across the desk for my arm again and gave it an almost imperceptible little squeeze. "Actually, I appreciate your having that sort of sensitivity—I say this in all sincerity. I can't imagine very many people in your line of work turning down a case because of the possible loss of a client. Don't misunderstand me. I'm not suggesting that if another investigator was looking into this for me, he wouldn't be genuinely sorry in the event I wound up dead. What I *am* saying is that if, in spite of his best efforts, I *did* become a homicide victim, he'd manage to derive a degree of comfort from the handsome fee he'd been paid."

"If you think the money will have any influence on me, you're wrong," I responded huffily.

"I didn't mean to imply that it would. I'm—"

"My advice is to hire a PI firm that could assign someone to protect you until this character who's trying to do you in is behind bars."

"A *bodyguard*? That's totally out of the question; it would drive me crazy having somebody hanging over me day and night. Look, Desiree, I've come to you because Blossom has faith in your ability. And that's good enough for me." He gave me one of his winning smiles.

"There are plenty of excellent PIs around, Gordon, many of them with a much more enviable record than mine," I told him firmly. "And I'll be happy to supply you with some names."

"You know something? Your refusing to help me can be compared to a doctor who's out driving and comes across a seriously injured man at the side of the road. The doctor doesn't even attempt to do anything for this person because he's not confident that he'll be able to save him, and he doesn't want that death on his conscience. Besides, he figures that some other doctor will almost certainly happen along soon

and that this second physician *might* be more successful in treating the man than he would have been. And
if not . . . well, the way he looks at it, at least he can't
blame himself if the poor fellow expires."

*The nerve of this guy! It wasn't the same thing at all!*
I was about to give him a dose of my redheaded temper (acquired, no doubt, as a result of all that Egyptian henna's seeping into my scalp) when Gordon
dropped the charm stuff. "Are you really too busy to
handle this for me?" he said in this quiet, no-
nonsense tone.

I quickly assessed the situation before answering.

Suppose I did show Gordon the door. And suppose
he hired another PI—but was killed anyway. Would I
allow the idea to fester in my mind that if I'd conducted the investigation myself, I might somehow have
prevented the murder?

Bet on it.

So in the end I conceded, albeit with some reluctance, "I . . . um . . . guess not."

After which Gordon Curry wasted no time in telling
me who was attempting to put a period to his life—
and why.

"The fellow's name, Desiree, is Roger Clyne. His
father, Jay, and I had been good friends back in pharmacy school. After graduation we kept in close touch
for a while, but as the years went by we began seeing
each other less and less frequently. I suppose that sort
of thing happens with college buddies. As fond as you
are of each other, you get busy with advancing your
career, raising a family. . . ." Gordon's voice trailed
off. A second or two later he added sadly, "I kept
meaning to call Jay about getting together—he probably intended to do the same. But it never happened.
And it never will. Unfortunately, my old friend passed
away in 'ninety-one.

"But to get to the point . . . I'm district sales man-

ager for a pharmaceutical company—McReedy and
Emerson—and about a year and a half ago I received
a call from Roger, who's also in pharmaceuticals. In
fact, he graduated from St. John's, our alma mater—
his father's and mine. At any rate, he was looking
for employment, and as it happened, McReedy and
Emerson was planning to add another person to its
sales force at that time. Now, I didn't really know the
boy. Prior to his father's funeral, it had been a very
long while since I'd even set eyes on him. Furthermore, the qualifications of two of the other candidates
for the position were slightly more impressive than
Roger's. But he had one credential the others didn't:
He was Jay's son.

"So I hired him.

"It was only a couple of months later, however, that
I learned something extremely disturbing."

And now Gordon paused; he seemed to be expecting some reaction from me. "What was that?" I
inquired.

"You see, it's the job of our detail people—the men
and women on our sales force—to visit doctors' offices, hospitals, and pharmacies in order to acquaint
them with our products. We provide these detail people with free samples of the medications, which are
meant to be left with the doctors for distribution to
their patients. Well, one day another salesman—a man
who's been with us for over a decade—came to me
and said he had it on good authority that Roger wasn't
handing out all of his product samples; he was *selling*
the bulk of them to pharmacies. Naturally, I didn't
simply take this salesman's word for that. Some phone
calls were made. And they confirmed that most of the
physicians in Roger's assigned area had been getting
few to none of these leave-behinds. So I confronted
the boy.

"At first he proclaimed his innocence. But it didn't

take long before he admitted the truth. He couldn't have been more contrite, either—he was on the verge of tears. He was financially strapped, he told me, and selling these samples had been helping him climb out of the hole. But he should never have so much as considered such a thing, he said—even though he had a wife and infant daughter to support. He swore that if I was willing to overlook what he'd done, nothing like that would ever happen again. 'I'll be the best salesman this company's ever had,' I remember him saying to me.

"I wasn't unsympathetic, Desiree, far from it. But I had no choice; I had to let him go. It was only a matter of time before the people *I* report to would have found out what he'd been up to. If I'd continued to keep him on the payroll, my own position would have been in jeopardy. And rightly so. Think how it would have reflected on the reputation of the company if it got out that one of our representatives had been peddling what were meant to be complimentary samples—and that despite our being aware of such unethical behavior, we hadn't terminated the fellow."

"This took place over a year ago?"

"That's right."

I was a trifle skeptical. "And Roger waited all this time to make these attempts to kill you?"

"You didn't let me finish," Gordon chastised good-naturedly.

"Sorry. Please go on."

"Less than three months back he phoned and asked to see me. I agreed to let him stop by the office the following afternoon—I couldn't bring myself to say no.

"When he walked in, I was shocked. Roger had always been a fastidious dresser; now his clothes hung on him. He must have lost about twenty pounds—and he was hardly robust to begin with. His skin had an unhealthy pallor, too. Also, he was extremely nervous.

When we shook hands, his palms weren't just moist; they were dripping wet. I wouldn't have been surprised to learn that he'd started to drink. Or even that he was into drugs. At any rate, he'd come to beg me to rehire him. It seems that since leaving the company, his life had fallen apart.

"He'd failed to secure other employment. Very likely word had gotten around in the industry as to the reason he was no longer with us. Also, I hadn't, in all conscience, felt that I could furnish him with a reference—and believe me, I really wrestled with myself over that one. In addition, Roger's situation had apparently put a terrible strain on his relationship with his wife, to the extent that recently Brandy had packed her bags and moved out, taking their little girl with her.

"At any rate, Roger put it to me that his only hope of getting his family back was to earn a decent living again. Well, a large part of me wanted to oblige him. But I simply couldn't consider it. Still, I didn't want to just send the boy away like that, so I tried to give him some money to tide him over for a bit. 'It's only a loan,' I said, 'until you land something.'

"Unfortunately, Roger regarded the offer as an insult. He yelled that he resented my patronizing him, that he didn't want charity—particularly from me. And then he started to carry on about how I'd ruined his life. He claimed I'd crucified him for making one little mistake but that now I'd made a mistake, too— because I was going to pay for treating him like this. 'I swear to that on my father's grave!' he screamed at me. And this is when security, alerted by my secretary, came charging in.

"As security was dragging him out of the office, he kept yelling over and over again, 'You'll pay for this! You'll pay for this!' "

"Were you frightened by his behavior?"

"I was more sad than scared. Everything had gone sour for the boy, and I hadn't been able to help. As for the threats, I figured he'd regret acting up like that after he'd had some time to reflect."

"But now you're convinced that it was Roger who tried to kill you?"

"Absolutely."

"Have you any idea whether he knows how to fire a rifle?"

"It's evident that he does."

"But you can't state this as a fact."

"Actually, I can. He shot at me, didn't he?" And now Gordon looked at me intently. "Look, Desiree, I don't have the slightest doubt it was Roger Clyne who made those two attempts on my life. May I tell you why I'm so certain?"

"Of course."

"Because there's no one else it could be."

# Chapter 4

Gordon supplied me with the last address and phone number he had for Roger Clyne.

"This is the apartment he shared with his wife?"

"Yes. Roger said something about Brandy's moving back with her parents. I don't imagine he'd leave, though. If I remember correctly, the place is rent-controlled." And with this, my newly acquired client got to his feet.

A couple of minutes later I walked out to the hall with him.

"Be careful," I admonished as he was stepping into the elevator. "Be *very* careful."

He managed to respond before the door closed and—would you believe it?—with a wink, too. "Don't worry, pretty lady. You'll be seeing me again."

Well, I didn't figure that Gordon had slipped back into his flirtatious mode because he'd succumbed to my indisputable allure. I attributed it to my having accepted the case—it enabled him to relax a little. Besides, the guy had to keep in practice, didn't he?

As soon as I left the office I realized how hungry I was—also, how tired. I mean, it was doubtful I was even up to boiling a pot of water. I figured I'd grab a cab and have something to eat at Jerome's, this little coffee shop near my apartment building.

The problem was that just about every New Yorker and his sister were also attempting to hail a taxi then. Finally, after about five minutes of standing on the curb with my arm raised and my forefinger in the air (I didn't even have the energy to wave), an empty cab screeched to a stop practically in front of me. I actually had my hand on the door handle—only to be pushed aside by some tiny old lady who couldn't have weighed more than eighty-five pounds after a five-course meal. That's when I gave up. Maybe once I took some nourishment, I'd be able to hold my own against the next senior citizen with designs on *my taxi.*

Now, a new deli had opened up in the neighborhood fairly recently, and only a couple of days back my secretary, Jackie, had recommended I try it. Well, maybe "recommended" is an exaggeration. What she actually said, if I recall correctly, was that the food wasn't nearly as bad as you'd assume you'd get at a Jewish delicatessen with an Irish proprietor.

The restaurant turned out to be small and cheerful. The serving staff (sorry, but I can't seem to get used to "waitstaff") consisted of a boy in his late teens or early twenties with a Mohawk haircut and a slight case of acne, and a smiling, middle-aged brunette whose name tag read DILYS. A pretty good indication that she was the owner of the Dilly Deli. Anyway, I ordered a pastrami on rye with fries and a Coke.

The sandwich was really better than I'd expected, but not as good as I'd hoped. Anyhow, I had no intention of allowing my new case to intrude on my dinner. (It's a funny thing, but thoughts of murder don't do very much to stimulate my appetite.) However, in spite of repeated efforts to push today's meeting with Gordon Curry out of my head, it kept sneaking right back in. So eventually I threw in the towel and gave myself permission to go over our conversation. After all, I reasoned, it wasn't as if I was reflecting on an actual homicide; not so much as a single drop of blood had been shed. I even tried to convince myself that it shouldn't be too difficult to ensure that things stayed that way—considering that my client had practically gift wrapped his assassin-in-waiting for me.

Maybe merely being aware that we're on to him will induce Roger Clyne to back off, I mused. Especially if I could also persuade him that Gordon deeply regretted the action he'd taken but that, under the circumstances, he'd had no alternative. A moment later, however, I factored in how out of control Roger had appeared to be when last heard from. And I was less than optimistic. More than likely I'd have to come up with something that would tie the man to those earlier attacks.

Right on the heels of this, however, I countered with, *But what if Gordon is killed before I have a chance to do a thorough job of investigating? Or what if I do conduct an exhaustive investigation but fail to find the requisite proof—and Gordon is subsequently murdered? Or what if I locate the evidence and the police refuse to act on it? Or—*

I cut myself off. Thanks to those what-ifs of mine, I'd become unnerved to the point where I was having trouble finishing my sandwich. Dessert, of course, was now out of the question.

I switched my focus and began to think in less stressful, more practical terms. Like locating my client's former employee.

The thing is, right after Gordon left my office, I dialed the number he'd provided. A recorded voice notified me that it was no longer in service. Well, Roger Clyne had been in this terrible financial bind only two or three months ago, and it was extremely improbable that his situation had improved very dramatically. So, the way I saw it, there were two possibilities: (1) He resided at the same place but lacked the funds to pay his phone bill; (2) he couldn't keep up the apartment—rent-controlled or not—and had made other living arrangements for himself without bothering to give the telephone company his new information.

I didn't anticipate much of a problem in tracking him down, however. Tomorrow morning I'd visit the address I had for him to determine what was what. In any event, I expected to be having a talk with Roger Clyne very soon.

I wound up eating dessert that night after all. (Yes, I remember what I said, but Dilys made it practically impossible for me to get out a no.) "You have to try the coffee cake; it's an old family recipe," she told me, a little quiver in her voice. "It's about the only thing my poor mother was able to leave me, may she rest in peace."

And it was a short time later, over coffee and Dilys's mother's coffee cake (which was suspiciously similar to an Entenmann's I often buy), that I posed a question to myself: *How do you like this new client of yours anyway?*

The first thing to pop into my head was that hunting business. And I shuddered. But returning now to Gordon's explanation that, as a young boy, sharing this experience with his father had fostered a bond between them, I found it *somewhat* easier to understand the pleasure he took in the activity. (I couldn't, even in my mind, refer to it as a "sport.")

When I set that aside, though—which wasn't easy for me to do—Gordon appeared, in other respects, to be a pretty decent human being. It was evident that he was genuinely disturbed about the necessity of firing the son of his old friend and, similarly, of denying Roger his former job back. I also gave Gordon points for that offer to lend the guy money. Particularly in view of how doubtful it was that he'd ever be repaid.

Speaking of money, while not in the same boat as this Roger (thank God), I wasn't exactly rolling in greenbacks myself. I'd recently been nicely compensated for that decade-old murder I'd solved. But that little windfall went to cover not only my current bills, but also my carryovers—these being all the invoices that had landed facedown when I'd tossed the whole bundle into the air the month before. (During those all too frequent times when I'm a little less than solvent, this is a method I sometimes employ for deciding which bills are entitled to immediate payment and which will have to wait their turn.) Anyhow, until this afternoon the only check I could have looked forward to was a small one—compensation for an insurance fraud thing I'd wrapped up a couple of days earlier. And there was no way it would stretch to cover even the barest of necessities. You know, like food, rent, and telephone—not to mention Bloomingdale's. In fact, just thinking about my next batch of statements had had me toying with the idea of fleeing the country. Then along came Gordon, who handed me a very hefty retainer. And, well, you can't hate a person for that.

As for those little come-ons of his, they seemed to be harmless enough. Listen, it wasn't as if he'd tried to get me into bed or anything. I suddenly found myself comparing Gordon Curry to Pavlov's dog. I mean, I had the impression that if you were to put a woman—*any* woman—in Gordon's immediate area, his flirting would be like a conditioned reflex. Or maybe he simply regarded it as a public service to treat every female he encountered as if she were the spitting image of Heather Locklear.

At any rate, all things considered, I realized now that I liked the man. And being that I already knew the identity of his potential murderer, the odds were in my favor that I'd be able to help him—weren't they?

That evening I left the Dilly Deli half convinced that accepting the case hadn't been such a bad idea after all.

# Chapter 5

I got up early (for me) Saturday morning, and by eleven o'clock I was in the outer lobby of a small, well-kept building on East Seventh Street, searching the tenant listing for "Clyne."

No luck.

I pressed the button for the super, then stood there for over a minute. Nothing. Venting my frustration on the silent intercom, I gave the button another, harder push. Again, nothing. Then, just as I was turning away, someone buzzed me in.

When I got to 1C I found the door open—but only a crack. Whoever was peering at me through that narrow slit, however, must have quickly concluded that there was little chance I was Jane the Ripper, because a couple of seconds later the door opened wide. And now I was face-to-face with a stocky Hispanic woman with liquid brown eyes.

"Yes?" she murmured, fidgeting with the skirt of her shapeless housedress.

"I'd like to speak to the superintendent, please."

"He ees no een."

"When do you expect him?"

The woman's smile was tentative, apologetic. "I no spik good Engleesh."

*Crap! Why did I have to waste all those hours in high school Spanish class playing hangman with Charlotte*

*Schultz?* Well, all I could do was give it my best shot. *"Uh, el superintendent—¿quándo está expected returno?"*

The inquiry was received with hunched shoulders and a thoroughly perplexed expression. (Surprise!) *"No comprendo,"* I was informed unnecessarily.

I was trying to determine how to proceed from here when I became aware that we'd been joined by a small, serious-looking child with long dark hair and oversized glasses. Standing slightly to my left and only inches behind me, she was dressed in neatly pressed jeans and a colorful, multistriped T-shirt. She couldn't have been much more than ten years old. "You want Carlos, huh?"

"If he's the super, I do."

"Oh, he's the super."

"Uh, I can't seem to make myself understood. My Spanish is kind of rusty," I admitted sheepishly.

She giggled her response. "Yes, I heard."

"Anyway, I was attempting to ask this lady when the superintendent is expected in."

"Not till Monday. Carlos flew out to Chicago last night. His daughter, Connie—that's short for Consuela—is getting married tomorrow—and to a lawyer, too. So he's probably pretty rich—her fiancé, I mean—don't you think?" I opened my mouth to answer, but evidently the feedback wasn't crucial, because she went on without so much as a pause. "Rosa—she's Carlos's sister-in law"—the little girl indicated the woman in the doorway with a toss of her head—"and her husband, Angel—Carlos's brother—are supposed to be taking care of this place until Carlos gets back. But nobody can get through to Rosa—she came to this country only about a month ago. And Angel . . . well . . . even though he's been living in Brooklyn for over a year and his English isn't bad at all, he's usually passed out in the basement or someplace. Rum," she added for my edification, rolling her eyes.

Now, all during this conversation, Rosa had been standing there mutely, obviously bewildered. I suppose she finally decided that the kid had taken her off the hook, though. Because she gave me another tentative smile, murmured something in Spanish that I didn't catch (and undoubtedly wouldn't have understood if I did), and firmly closed the door—with herself safely on the other side of it.

"Are you a relative, too?" I inquired.

"Nah, I live down the hall. I just went out to the compactor and saw you talking to Rosa. I figured you might need some help."

"Thanks very much. I certainly did."

"What's your name?"

"Desiree."

"Desiree what?"

"Shapiro."

"No way! You're kidding, right? Your name isn't *really* Desiree Shapiro, is it?"

"It really is—and that's the God's honest truth. What do they call you?"

"I'm Priscilla Ramirez." And so saying, she solemnly extended her hand. After shaking it politely, I put a question to her. It wasn't one I actually thought she'd be able to answer, but what did I have to lose? "You wouldn't know what time Monday Carlos is due back, would you?"

"He should be home by noon; he's taking an early plane. What did you want to see Carlos about anyhow? Are you interested in renting an apartment in this building?"

"No, I just need some information from him."

"What kind of information?"

Before I could come up with a diplomatic way of saying, "That's none of your business," Priscilla threw in quickly, "Listen, maybe *I* can help you. Uh, there's an ice-cream parlor only a couple of blocks from here. It might be a good idea to go over there—just so we can sit down and talk. I . . . um . . . can't be on my feet too long—I have weak ankles."

Somehow I was able to suppress a smile. "Good thinking. I'd better walk back to your apartment with you so we can get your mother's permission."

"You don't have to do that. My mother works all day; so does my father. We have a nanny, me and my sister, Pammy—she's two."

"Still, won't the nanny want to know who you're going out with?"

"Of course. But I'll tell her you're my aunt—" Breaking off, Priscilla put her finger to her chin and wrinkled her brow for a moment. "I'll say you're my aunt Sue—she'd never believe 'Aunt Desiree'—and that you drove down from Long Island especially to take me for ice cream. It'll be okay. Janna's new, and besides, she isn't very bright." And now the kid took off down the hall, calling over her shoulder, "Be right back, Desiree!"

I probably should have insisted on going with her and explaining the truth to the nanny. But how much could I actually reveal?

Anyhow, it took no more than three minutes for Priscilla to reappear at the other end of the hall, slipping on a navy down jacket as she hurried toward me. "Wave to her," she hissed as soon as she was within hissing distance. I gathered she was referring to a young woman standing in the doorway of the apartment she'd just exited.

I dutifully obeyed, and the nanny, apparently satisfied, retreated into the flat.

"Are you acquainted with Roger Clyne?" I said after my third spoonful of hot-fudge sundae.

Priscilla got in another slurp of her strawberry ice-cream soda before responding. "Just sort of. We used to say hello when we saw each other, but that's all."

"He's moved out of the building, I take it."

She nodded. "A few months ago. He lost his job last year, see? And he hasn't gotten another one. Some people—my mother, at least—claim that it's because he's too lazy to look for anything. Mrs. Chow in 4A, though, *she* says it's because the job market's so tough. But in my opinion, neither one of them has it right. The reason Roger is still out of work is because he did something bad, maybe stole things or something. Look, with him having this really decent profession, I'm sure *somebody* would have hired him—unless his hands are dirty."

*Unless his hands are dirty?* This kid definitely watched too much TV! And did I say she was only about ten years old? "It's possible," I conceded.

"Betcha."

"Do you have any idea where Mr. Clyne is living now, Priscilla?"

"No, I don't," she responded, her tone slightly bitter. (Apparently, Priscilla here didn't take too kindly to anyone's keeping her in the dark about their plans.) "A couple of months ago he sneaked out in the middle of the night so he wouldn't have to pay his rent. He used to live in apartment 3D with his wife and baby, but then Brandy—his wife—took little Miranda and left. I suppose it was because Roger was indignant."

*Indignant?* Priscilla went back to her soda while I tried to figure that one out. After another spoonful of sundae it occurred to me that she must have meant "indigent," and I was delighted about the mistake. I was beginning to think some know-it-all forty-year-old had invaded the child's body.

Anyway, moments later she popped up with, "It

was his apartment before they got married, though, so
Brandy wasn't on the lease. Which is a break for her,
since that way she isn't responsible for paying the
rent."

*Is there anything—besides "indigent," that is—that
Priscilla doesn't know?*

"I know all sorts of stuff," she apprised me as if
she'd just crept into my head. "My mother says I'm
terribly nosy, but how are you supposed to learn anything if you don't ask questions?"

A girl after my own heart! Although Priscilla appeared to have a success rate I could only aspire to.

"I wonder if Denny ever heard from him," she murmured now, speaking more to herself than to me.

"Denny?"

"He's the only person in the building Roger was
really friendly with. To be truthful, I didn't care much
for him myself. Roger—not Denny; Denny's very
nice."

"What's Denny's apartment number?"

"It's 3A. But it won't do you any good to go up
there. He's in Kenya—that's in Africa—on his
honeymoon."

"Uh, I don't suppose you'd be able to tell me where
he's staying."

Priscilla was plainly irritated. "I never bothered to
find out," she snapped. "There wasn't any point in it
due to the fact that I'm not familiar with that country." Two or three seconds went by before she put in
defensively, "I can't be expected to know *everything,*
Desiree. After all, I *am* only nine and three-quarters
years old." And then, her tone more even: "His
mother could probably help you, but she has a new
name, and Denny never said what it is. She got married again, see—in August, I think—and I'm sure she
uses her husband's last name now. Ladies that age
generally do."

At this juncture we devoted ourselves entirely to our ice cream for a couple of minutes. Then Priscilla took one last, long slurp, pushed away the empty soda glass, and more or less . . . well, *confronted* me. "You haven't told me why you're trying to locate Roger."

I figured she'd get around to that.

"Um, I work at an employment agency, and I have this client who wants to offer him a position but hasn't been able to reach him."

Priscilla eyed me skeptically. "Is that the truth?"

"Certainly it is."

"Swear on your mother's life."

I didn't actually have a problem with that, my mother being long gone. Nevertheless, just to avoid some other dire consequence, I crossed my fingers under the table. "I swear on my mother's life."

"All right, then. I believe you. I think the best thing would be for you to talk to Brandy."

"I would—if I knew where to find her."

"*I* know."

I grinned. How come I wasn't surprised?

"So?" she demanded impatiently. "You want me to tell you or not?"

"I'd really appreciate it, Priscilla."

"Okay. But you'll have to come back to my house with me; I need to check my address book."

"Incidentally, how do you happen to have Mrs. Clyne's address?" I inquired as we were leaving the ice-cream parlor.

Priscilla looked at me almost pityingly, following which she provided the sort of explanation that I suppose makes absolute sense when you're not quite ten years old: "I asked her for it, of course."

# Chapter 6

When I left Priscilla that afternoon, the information on Brandy Clyne was tightly clenched in my chubby little fist.

As soon as I walked out of the building I went about attempting to lay hands on my cell phone. Now, this wasn't as easy as it sounds, since it was buried somewhere in my suitcase-sized handbag, which item is always stuffed to bursting with what I regard as life's little essentials. (After all, you never really know when you'll need a stapler or a flashlight or some cough medicine—although maybe the black shoe polish *is* pushing things a bit.) Plus, making the phone even more difficult to get ahold of, its case had somehow attached itself to one of the spokes on my folding umbrella—or vice versa. Anyhow, when I finally extricated the thing from the depths of my pocketbook, I wasted no time in dialing the number for Roger Clyne's estranged wife—and got a busy signal. So I hopped in a cab, figuring I'd reach her from home.

Once back in my apartment it took four attempts—three of which produced more busy signals—before I had any luck.

"Hello?" said a thin male voice that I assumed—from what Gordon had said about Brandy's moving back with her parents—belonged to the girl's father.

"May I speak to Brandy Clyne, please?"

"Who's this?" It was more of a demand than a question.

"Um, Brandy wouldn't know me, but a mutual friend suggested I call her."

"What friend?"

"Her name is Priscilla. Priscilla Ramirez."

"Are you talkin' about that kid from Brandy's old building?"

"Er, yes, I am."

He cackled. "That little thing's somethin' else, ain't she? A real pistol. Smart as a whip, too."

"She certainly is."

"Me and the wife used to get a big kick out of her. But I don't see why she'd have you telephone my daughter."

"The reason's kind of personal."

There was a pause before Brandy's father said reluctantly, "Okay, have it your own way. But Brandy's not here; she's been stayin' upstate at her girlfriend's this past week. Me and the wife, we persuaded her to get away and maybe clear her head. I hope she didn't pack up those troubles of hers and take them with her is all I can say."

"Uh, when do you think she'll be coming home?"

"Maybe Monday, maybe Tuesday. She could even be returnin' on Wednesday, for all I know."

"Look, sir, it's *urgent* that I get in touch with your daughter. I'd really appreciate it if you could let me have this girlfriend's telephone number."

"I can't do that, 'counta I got no idea what it is."

"Can you tell me the last name, then, and what town she lives in?"

"Don't have no idea about those things, neither."

Now, while I didn't believe this for a second, I was in no position to say so. "Well, do you expect Brandy to call you over the next few days?"

"Maybe, maybe not."

"Listen, if she *does,* please impress upon her that it's *vital* we speak. It could be a matter of life and death."

"*Life and death?* Gettin' a little carried away, ain't you, missy?"

"It happens to be the truth. I—"

"Never mind. You leave me your name and telephone number." Then with a sigh: "I'll give Brandy your message."

I can't express how agitated I was when I hung up that phone.

I mean, who knew when—or *if*—Brandy would be getting back to me? And the circumstances being what they were, I couldn't afford the luxury of just sitting around waiting to hear from her. No. I had to do something *now*—before the creep who was so determined to turn off my client's lights succeeded in doing just that.

It occurred to me then that Gordon himself might be able to help me locate Roger Clyne.

I didn't want to try him at home, since he'd elected to keep his situation a secret from his wife. And this being Saturday, I doubted he'd be at the office. So I dialed his cell phone number, my palms getting a little wetter with every unanswered ring.

*Could Roger already have done his dirty work? Is Gordon at this very moment lying facedown somewhere in a pool of blood? Where did I get the chutzpah to imagine that I could possibly prevent his death anyway? I should never—*

"Hello."

"Gordon?"

"Speaking."

*Thank God!* Evidently I still had a living, breathing client. "It's Desiree."

Chuckling a little, he responded, "Don't tell me you

miss me already!" Which annoyed me no end. I mean, apparently Gordon just couldn't resist being . . . well, Gordon—no matter what. An instant later, however, his voice turned serious. "Are you calling with some news?"

"Roger's no longer at his old address, and so far I've been unable to track him down."

"What about his wife?"

"I have a telephone number for her, but she's out of town until Monday at the earliest. I was wondering if you might know if Roger was friendly with any of his coworkers."

"Hmm," Gordon murmured thoughtfully. "I can't seem to recall his hanging out with any of the other people in the department; the boy kept pretty much to himself." Then, just as I was prepared to say good-bye: "Wait. I did run into him a couple of times when he was with Gene Worth, who's one of our chemists and, incidentally, quite a few years Roger's senior. I don't know that they've kept up with each other, but you could check it out. Gene—Eugene, actually—lives in Queens. Forest Hills, if I'm not mistaken."

"I'll see if Information can give me his number."

"If not, I'll have it for you when I get to the office on Monday. And Desiree? Stop worrying, will you? I fully intend to make it into my golden years."

Information had a listing for a "Eugene Worth" in Forest Hills.

A woman picked up on the first ring.

"Is Mr. Eugene Worth in, please?"

"Which one—junior or senior?"

"The one who's with McReedy and Emerson."

"That would be senior, and you're in luck. He just walked in."

As soon as Eugene Worth Sr. got on the phone, I gave him my name and explained that I was anxious to reach Roger Clyne. "I understand the two of you worked at the same pharmaceutical company."

Eugene was instantly wary. "Rog isn't in any sort of trouble, is he?"

"Not that I know of. Why do you ask?"

"Oh, uh, no reason really. I haven't the slightest idea why I said that."

Of course, I was all but certain the question was prompted by the circumstances under which *Rog*'s employment had been terminated. In all probability, his threats to my client were also no secret to Eugene. I was quick to assure the man that he'd be benefiting his buddy by putting us in touch.

"I'm with an executive search agency," I stated, "and Mr. Clyne registered with us several months ago. The other day I received a call from a major pharmaceutical firm about a position that's recently opened up there—one for which I feel Mr. Clyne would be very well suited. The problem is, he's no longer at the telephone number we have on file for him. Apparently, he's not at that same address, either, and he didn't provide any forwarding information."

"Oh, my. I wish I could help you, but I couldn't tell you where Roger is living now. It's been close to a year since we last spoke. How did you get my name, by the way?"

"Mr. Clyne listed you as a reference on the form he completed for us. I hope that isn't a problem."

"Definitely not."

"Perhaps you can think of someone else who might know his current address."

"Unfortunately, I can't."

I pressed. "There was no one at work he was even the least bit friendly with? Apart from you, I mean."

"No one I'm aware of. But we weren't in the same department, so I'm probably not the right person to ask. To the best of my knowledge, though, he didn't socialize with anyone at McReedy and Emerson other than myself." And then to ensure that I (or, more correctly, my headhunter persona) didn't walk away with a negative impression, Eugene Worth hastened to qualify his words. "But Roger is a personable young man, so it's likely he'd consciously made the decision to keep the professional part of his life strictly business. He's very goal oriented."

"In spite of that, though, you and he appear to have gotten fairly close. Had you known each other before—is that what it was?" Now, I didn't put this to him because it was at all relevant to my investigation. The inquiry was simply a reflection of my being one of the nosiest creatures ever to inhabit this planet.

"We'd never even met until Rog took a job at M and E. The fact is, one day we happened to sit down at the same table in the company cafeteria, and we were both having the veal stew for lunch. That kitchen has never been known for producing any gourmet delights, but this dish was particularly vile. And pretty soon he and I were commiserating with each other about what we were ingesting. Gradually, though, we went on to chat about other things, and I mentioned that I live in Forest Hills. Roger told me that when he was a youngster his family also had a home here. It turned out that in junior high he'd had a crush on my younger daughter. And—I don't know—after that we just seemed to bond. Possibly he subconsciously regarded me as a substitute father—Rog's dad has been dead for a number of years. And by the same token, I might have been temporarily in the market for a replacement son, since at that point my own flesh and blood was going through a particularly horrendous phase. Which included, among other things, his treating us—his mother and me—as if we were lepers."

"But after Mr. Clyne left the company, you didn't keep in touch for very long," I observed.

"No. I called a number of times to invite him and his wife to our house for dinner. But they couldn't make it—or he said they couldn't. And, regretfully, that was that."

"Well, I thank you for your time, Mr. Worth."

"Not at all. I'm just sorry I couldn't be of assistance to you, particularly being as fond of Roger as I am. He's a very fine fellow, Ms.—?"

"It's Shapiro—Desiree Shapiro," I told him again.

"Listen," Eugene concluded, "if I think of anyone he might be in contact with, you can be sure I'll let you know."

"I'd appreciate it. I honestly feel that what I have to tell Mr. Clyne could make a very positive difference in his life." Then silently: *And in my client's, as well.*

# Chapter 7

My niece Ellen's fiancé was working Saturday evening—Mike's an intern at St. Gregory's—so I'd invited Ellen over for dinner.

The second she walked into the room, I could tell that she could tell that something was wrong—if you follow me. (I hope you realize, however, that Ellen's picking up on my state of mind was no reflection on my acting ability. It's simply that I'd let my guard down.) Anyway, she kind of gave me the fish eye, then enclosed me in a hug so perfunctory that, for once, when we separated I didn't have to check all my parts to verify that they were still in working order. (I mean, here's a person who stands five six and wears a size zero—taken in! Yet those matchstick arms of hers have this almost bone-crushing power.)

"Something's happened," she pronounced.

"God! I hope not."

"What does *that* mean?"

"I'll explain in a few minutes. Let's get comfortable first."

I followed Ellen to the sofa, admiring, as usual, how chic she looked. (If that girl doesn't resemble the late Audrey Hepburn, you tell me who does!) Tonight she had on black slacks and a black cashmere turtleneck sweater, the outfit accented with a two-inch-thick black leather belt at her hipline and large gold-disk earrings.

Not unexpectedly, she plunked herself down within easy reach of the hors d'oeuvres: wild-mushroom croustades (shiitake mushrooms and herbs in little toast cups)—a dish that, as a rule, my niece can hardly wait to pounce on—plus a couple of tasty cheeses accompanied by a variety of crackers. Right now, however, she was ignoring the goodies. "Sit," she commanded, patting the cushion next to hers. And when I'd obliged: "Shoot."

I was bursting to unload. I told Ellen about Blossom and Gordon and Roger and the fears I'd had—and I continued to have—about accepting the case. I went on to talk about Priscilla and Brandy's father and Eugene Worth. I finished with, "I feel that if I'm not actively investigating something every single minute, it could prove fatal to Gordon. The problem, though, is that I don't know how I can proceed until Brandy gets home."

"You can't. Not unless you hear from this Eugene. Maybe he'll come up with someone else Roger might be in contact with."

"I'm afraid that's a long shot."

"It's funny about him, isn't it, Aunt Dez?"

"Who? Roger?"

"No, Eugene. He's probably aware of what Roger did with those samples and maybe that he also threatened your client—don't you think?"

"I can't see how he could help it—especially with regard to that sample business. Even if Roger himself didn't reveal the reason he'd lost his job, word gets around. But what's your point?"

"That I'm astonished Eugene's still so loyal to somebody like that."

"I suppose a lot has to do with the fact that their relationship was kind of a father-son thing. And when your kid does something crappy, you don't disown him—not if you're like most parents. You chastise him, he's repentant—or fools you into believing he

is—and sooner or later you forgive him. As for those
threats, by then Roger had been out of work for more
than a year. *And* he was having marital problems, besides. So I can see why Eugene would make excuses
for Roger's verbal attack on the man who'd fired him,
assuming he'd heard about it, that is. Which he almost
certainly did."

Ellen finally helped herself to an hors d'oeuvre, and
after a moment, her mouth full of mushroom, she declared solemnly, "That . . . mmph . . . mks . . . mm . . .
sns." Which I was reasonably sure translated to "That
makes sense."

"Thanks a heap," I mumbled facetiously.

Now, I have no idea what prompted it, but seconds
later I came to a decision. "You know, Ellen, I'm
going to call Brandy's father again tomorrow morning.
And I'll say whatever is necessary to persuade the
man to give me that upstate phone number. Listen,
I'm not above claiming that his daughter's life could
be in danger, if that's what it takes. Actually, it could
very well be true. True or not, though, I can't afford
to just sit around and do nothing—even if it's only for
one more day."

And feeling somewhat relieved by my resolve, I
spread some Brie on a cracker before heading into
the kitchen to see to our dinner.

We had lightly breaded scallops in a white wine
sauce, along with a rice casserole, an enormous salad,
and a nice Pinot Grigio that was Ellen's contribution
to the meal. While we were eating, we spoke—as we
normally do when there's an exchange lasting much
longer than a minute—about Ellen's pending nuptials,
soon to take place at New York's venerable Plaza
Hotel. (She's almost invariably the one to broach the
subject; I know better.)

"It's just a m-matter of weeks," she reminded me,

her pale complexion turning paler, "and my m-mother still hasn't p-p-picked out a dress."

Now, my nervous Nellie of a niece only stutters when she's really, *really* agitated. So I was quick to reassure her. "Don't worry, Ellen. Your mother will find something in plenty of time—something lovely, too." I almost choked getting out that last part. I mean, Ellen's mother and "lovely" definitely do not belong in the same sentence.

To fill you in . . . Ellen and I aren't related by blood. She's a treasured inheritance, courtesy of my late husband, Ed, her mother being Ed's sister, Margot, who gave me *agita* the first day we met—and has been periodically making me ill ever since.

Our frigid relationship was initially a result of the woman's conviction—or, anyway, *former* conviction—that people should marry within their religion. So it did not sit at all well with Margot when her Jewish brother brought home a nice Catholic girl (albeit of the non-practicing variety)—namely me. But there's another, more compelling reason for the animosity between us: We couldn't stand each other on sight. Fortunately, however, Margot and Ellen's father (a very sweet man who has my deepest sympathy) moved to Florida some years ago, and it isn't often that they visit up North. For which I am truly beholden to the powers that be.

I will say one thing for my sister-in-law, though: She's flexible. The fact that Ellen's intended is Protestant doesn't seem to ruffle Margot's feathers one bit. Of course, this hasn't a thing to do with the "MD" after Mike's name, right?

At any rate, I quickly attempted to steer the talk away from THE EVENT. "How's everything at work?" I inquired naïvely. (Ellen's a buyer at Macy's.) It was instantly apparent that I hadn't made too wise a choice.

"B-busy. I can't take off to do any personal s-stuff. And I *desperately* need a few things for Ba-Ba-Barbados." (Ellen and Mike are going there for the honeymoon.)

"Call in sick if you have to," I advised, refilling her still half-full wineglass in an effort to get her to relax a little.

By the time we were having our chocolate mousse and coffee, it was apparent that Ellen was more than relaxed. She was looped. So looped that by then her additional concerns about the wedding were actually uttered calmly. Once that topic was finally exhausted—for the present, anyway—we went on to chat about a number of other things, including *24,* a TV show we were both hooked on. And *Hairspray,* the Broadway musical Ellen and Mike had adored, which she insisted I *must* get Nick to treat me to. (More about Nick later.) Naturally, a good chunk of the conversation was devoted to Mike, who, his bride-to-be declared, was a brilliant and caring physician, as well as an exemplary human being. I'd have had to agree even if I weren't the one who introduced them.

It was past midnight when Ellen got up to leave.

"Are you *positive* I can't help with the dishes?" she asked while we were standing at the door. It was the third time she'd posed the question.

"Yes, I'm positive."

"I don't mind. Honestly."

"Thanks, but I'll manage just fine." By now I was speaking through clenched teeth.

"Well, okay then," Ellen agreed at last, after which she thanked me for a wonderful dinner and bussed me on the cheek. She had one foot in the hall when she turned toward me again. "Listen, Aunt Dez. I'm sure you'll be able to reach Brandy soon—tomorrow, with any luck. And once you have an opportunity to talk to Roger and maybe impress upon him that if anything happens to your client, he'll wind up behind bars, well, that should put an end to those murder attempts.''

It was at this point that I had a really frightening thought. Suppose I did manage to get in touch with Brandy the next day—and she didn't know her estranged husband's whereabouts.

What then?

# Chapter 8

I'm really not non compos mentis. Honestly. I'm aware that Ellen is a Pollyanna—in fact, she's probably the *queen* of Pollyannas. But I desperately wanted to convince myself that everything would turn out just fine. So for a brief time I allowed her words to give me permission to believe this might be so.

When I opened my eyes the next morning, however, the driblet of optimism I'd clung to the night before had evaporated. To give you an idea of how stressed I was, I bolted out of bed before eight a.m.—and this was a *Sunday,* for heaven's sake!

I was hesitant about what could be considered a decent hour to contact Brandy's father. Of course, for all I knew, the man might get up with the chickens. But I didn't think it would be too wise to go on this assumption. Anyhow, I decided that eight o'clock was definitely too early. And nine was pretty iffy, too. Ten seemed reasonably safe, though. Besides, I didn't think I could hold out any longer than that.

In the meantime, I needed to fortify myself for what I anticipated would be an uphill battle to obtain the phone number of Brandy's hostess. So I had a pretty decent breakfast. Then once the dishes were out of the way, I thought I'd take my mind off things by engaging in a little physical activity—a very little. The wielding of a feather duster being what I had in mind.

But I put the duster down five minutes later when I realized I'd absentmindedly gone over the same end table three times. After this, I plopped down on the sofa, put on the TV, and began switching back and forth between channels while glancing at the clock every minute or two.

At last the little hand was on the ten, and the big hand had made it to the twelve. And I reached for the telephone.

I counted seven rings before conceding that no one would be picking up.

For the remainder of the day I dialed that same number at ridiculously frequent intervals with no success. In between tries, I received a few calls of my own.

Harriet Gould, my friend and across-the-hall neighbor, phoned around one thirty to invite me to her place for dinner—her husband, Steve, had suddenly been summoned out of town on business, and she had a few "perfectly gorgeous" porterhouse steaks sitting in the refrigerator.

"Thanks, Harriet. I only wish I could," I told her truthfully, "but I have to work all evening."

"Oh, I'm so sorry you're tied up, Dez. Well, maybe I'll invite Scott and Hyacinth over," she murmured without much enthusiasm, Scott and Hyacinth being her sullen, spoiled-rotten son and her almost inert daughter-in-law. And then, to make the notion more palatable: "At least I'll get to see the baby."

I'd barely put the receiver back in its cradle when it was my niece's turn. "I just wanted to thank you again for that *scrumptious* meal," she raved. Which was nice to hear, although that glowing review might simply have been the result of Ellen's having had her fill of Chinese takeout for the week. You see, while she manages to fry a mean egg, Ellen's aptitude for cooking seems to end with breakfast. Thank God for that Mandarin Joy restaurant in her neighborhood; otherwise, she'd probably die of malnutrition. Ditto for poor Mike, who can count on being up to his ears in paper cartons whenever he eats at Ellen's—as he does quite frequently. All I can say is that it's lucky for them both that the groom-to-be isn't allergic to Chinese food.

At any rate, the two of us chatted for a short while, with Ellen reacting to my agitation with her usual optimism. "You'll be talking to Brandy today; you wait and see." And when this assurance was received with silence, she threw in, "Or, if not, sometime tomorrow."

It was close to three when I heard from Barbara Gleason, who lives right next door. (We share a common wall.) Barbara wanted me to go to the movies with her. "It's the new Mel Gibson picture," she informed me. Now, I would have restrained myself from scurrying over to the coat closet even if it had been the new Tom Selleck picture—Tom being a very recent replacement for Mel, who, in turn, had supplanted Robert Redford in my fantasies. (Listen, I'd been faithful to Robert for years—and received zilch in return—before giving him the boot. And I wasn't about to invest that much emotion in his successor—especially after a friend brought over some tapes of the old *Magnum, P.I.* series.)

"I'm really sorry I can't make it, Barbara. There are some things I have to take care of."

"What sort of things?" she demanded. Barbara isn't one to let a person off the hook—not without a struggle, anyway.

"It's very important I contact some people with regard to a new client of mine. I'll be tied up making telephone calls all evening."

"We'll go early. We can catch the four o'clock show."

"That won't help. I—"

"You'll be back in plenty of time to do your calling. I promise."

I was trying my damnedest to hold my temper. "I—have—to—stay—home—Barbara." The words came out slowly and emphatically.

"No need to get huffy," my friend chastised. "All you had to do was say no."

I didn't give up on Brandy's family until nine thirty that night, figuring it was too late in the evening to phone them after that. I'd just have to start again in the morning, that's all.

But in the morning I would receive a call from Blossom Goody.

A call that changed everything.

# Chapter 9

Jackie raised one eyebrow. "To what do I owe the pleasure of viewing those half-open eyes of yours at nine fifteen in the a.m.?"

Jackie is my sarcastic, overbearing, irritable, prying, generous, loyal, caring, and superefficient secretary. (And I'm sure I've left out a bunch of other pertinent adjectives.) Well, maybe I shouldn't call her *my* secretary, since I share her services with the principals of Gilbert and Sullivan (yes, I'm serious about the name), the law firm that rents me my (minuscule) office space for what is an unbelievably low (for Manhattan) price.

Anyway, whenever I show up at the office a few minutes earlier than I normally do, you'd think from Jackie's reaction that I make a habit of marching into the place at noon. And after a lot of years of putting up with those uncalled-for little remarks of hers, I've finally discovered the proper reply: silence. The one thing that Jackie absolutely cannot stand is being ignored.

My only response to her conception of a welcoming greeting, therefore, was a chilly smile as I walked past her desk. She immediately called out, "Is everything okay, Dez?"

"Everything's peachy," I told her.

\* \* \*

I was sitting at the computer, typing up my notes—after having reluctantly decided to wait until a bit later before trying Brandy's parents—when the phone rang.

"Well, it's happened," somebody announced in a low, strained voice that I couldn't put a face to.

*"What's* happened? Who is this?"

The caller coughed, and of course, I had my answer. "Mrs. Goody?"

"Who the hell did you think it was?" Blossom Goody snapped. And then she laid it on me: "Your client's been murdered, Shapiro."

For a moment I was too stunned, too sick at my soul, to speak. "Oh, God," I mumbled at last, my eyes starting to sting. (My stomach was by this point down around my ankles.) "I'm *so* sorry. I—"

*"You're* sorry! I'm the one who persuaded Gordie to hire you in the first place, remember? What the hell you been up to all this time anyway—getting your nipples pierced or something?"

Considering that the woman was obviously grief stricken, along with the fact that I'd already begun doing penance for failing to avert this terrible tragedy, I elected to ignore Blossom's gross remark. (Although the thought of something like that still makes me cringe.) I did, however, attempt to defend myself. But I have no doubt it was more for my own benefit than for Blossom's.

"I can't even tell you how desperate I was to locate Roger Clyne and, hopefully, prevent something like this from occurring. But what you refer to as 'all this time' was actually only two days, and Roger had moved from his last apartment without leaving a forwarding address. I was finally able to obtain a telephone number for his estranged wife, but she's been visiting someone upstate this past week, and her father couldn't—or wouldn't—tell me how to reach her there."

"That's it?" And she grumbled a barely audible, "Some PI."

"Not quite. I did manage to speak to the only person Roger had palled around with while he was working at McReedy and Emerson. The two of them haven't been in touch for almost a year, though. Believe me, I couldn't feel worse about not having found Roger in . . . in time."

"Yeah, well, I suppose you weren't brought into this till zero hour Gordon." This was followed by something I didn't quite catch. Something that might actually have been an apology.

I steeled myself. "How . . . um . . . did it happen?"

"Gordie and a few of his buddies have—*had*—this Sunday night poker game once a month. Kind of a tradition. Been going on for years. Seems somebody shot Gordie just before midnight as he was leaving for home. That's all I know, Shapiro. Danny called this morning to give me the news, but he was too busted up to do much talking."

"Danny?"

"Gordie's kid. The two of 'em weren't very close. Still, this *was* his father."

At that point the conversation was temporarily put on hold, owing to Blossom's need to hack away. It allowed me a few moments to reach a decision.

"Look, Mrs. Goody," I said when this current coughing fit was over, "Gordon gave me a very generous retainer when I took this on. And in light of his murder, I'd like to return that money to his family."

"You nuts?"

"I didn't do what I was hired for, and—"

"Hey, this isn't because of what I said before, is it? I'm just real shook up about Gordie"—I could have sworn I heard a sob here—"and I was letting off a little steam, that's all. Sometimes my mouth starts spouting a lot of crap before my brain can get it to shut, you know? But you're a smart lady; I woulda thought you'd have figured that out by now."

"My intention has nothing to do with you. It has to do with my not having earned my fee."

"Maybe you haven't, but you will. I want you to continue the investigation. I'll be speaking to Rhonda—Gordie's wife—about it, and I'm sure she'll feel the same way. So go out and dig up the evidence that'll nail that Roger bastard's ass to the wall. You got me?"

"But—"

"Hey, give me a break! You're not starting with those 'but's' again, are you? I'm sick to death of hearing them."

"Okay, Mrs. Goody, I'll stay on the case if that's what you want."

"That's what I want. And it's Blossom, for crissakes! And listen, if it gets to the point where you require more money to keep on with this, *I'll* pick up the rest of the tab."

"I seriously doubt that'll be nec—"

But I got the idea the discussion was already over when Blossom—as appeared to be a custom of hers—hung up the phone in my ear.

# Chapter 10

Blossom's bombshell altered my priorities.

With my client gone now, so was this unyielding sense of desperation I felt to locate Roger Clyne. Plus, I figured I could use a couple of hours off in order to mourn Gordon a little, alternately beat myself up and forgive my failure a little, and maybe even get a little smashed. No. *Definitely* get a little smashed.

I buzzed Jackie on the intercom. (My annoyance with her never lasts very long.) "Are you free for lunch? My treat."

"Today?"

"No, the first Sunday in June." I apologized at once. "Sorry. I just received some terrible news, but I have no business taking it out on you."

"What's wrong?" Jackie asked with evident concern.

"Well, I acquired a new client this past Friday. I was supposed to prevent his being murdered, but unfortunately, I wasn't very successful."

"Are you saying he's been killed?"

"That's exactly what I'm saying. Listen, I need to get out of here for a couple of hours and have a nice lunch and a glass of wine—possibly an entire bottle of wine."

Jackie laughed. "*You?* A whole bottle of wine? I've seen you get sloshed just sniffing the cork. Anyway, what time do you want to go?"

"Around twelve okay?"

"It's good with me."

As soon as I put down the receiver, I cried. And I mean *cried*. I must have gone through half a box of tissues. When I'd finally composed myself, I checked the mirror I keep in my desk.

My mascara, besides leaving a dark trail in its wake as it slithered down my cheeks, had deposited these large smudges under both eyes. I wasn't sure which I resembled more—a raccoon or a panda. So, in an attempt to inject a tiny bit of levity into this horrible morning, I compromised. "You look like a *pancoon*," I informed my image—which glowered back at me.

After this I headed for the ladies' room. It took me a good fifteen minutes to repair the damage. I still wasn't a thing of beauty, but that was okay. I wasn't one *before* I started bawling.


Jackie and I went to an Italian restaurant about three blocks from the office.

The moment we sat down I ordered a carafe of Chianti for us. I was by now determined to get seriously drunk. I'm talking falling-off-the-chair drunk, if I could manage it.

The waitress had no sooner poured the wine and deposited a couple of menus on the table than Jackie raised her glass, preparatory, it was apparent, to making a toast. "Don't say anything. Let's just drink," I instructed, concerned I'd be hearing something sentimental and that I'd wind up getting all weepy again. She nodded, and we both had a sip of the Chianti. Actually, Jackie was the one who sipped. My first swallow qualified as more of a gulp.

Anyway, after a decent interval—and more wine— Jackie commanded, "Tell me what happened."

So I told her.

"Stop punishing yourself, Dez," she scolded when I

was through. "You did everything you could to apprehend the killer—before he *became* a killer, that is. It's not your fault if this guy crept away in the middle of the night in order to stiff his landlord. And are you responsible if the one person who could fill you in on his whereabouts left town to visit a friend for a few days? It was rotten luck, that's all. It had nothing to do with how you conducted the investigation." And to prove she meant it: "Nothing."

"Thanks, Jackie."

*"De nada."* (Jackie took a course in Spanish last year, and those are two of only about a half dozen words she can still remember.) "But listen, I did hear right before, didn't I?"

"About what?"

"You did invite me to lunch today, true?"

"You know I did."

"Well, where I come from, when someone says 'lunch,' food is normally included."

Now, how do you like that! I'd completely forgotten that we were also here to eat! The fact is, this was one of the rare times in my life when the aforementioned food held absolutely no interest for me. But it didn't follow that Jackie's appetite had gone down the drain, too. Plus, it wouldn't do any harm to line my stomach—and at the rate I was tippling, I'd better do it quickly. So I signaled the waitress, and we relayed our order: chicken parmigiana and a salad for Jackie and the veal piccata for me.

We continued to imbibe while waiting for the meal—with me doing most of the imbibing and Jackie mostly scowling in silent protest. And then I began to get maudlin. "He was such a nice guy, Jackie— Gordon, I'm talking about. A bit of a flirt" (there's an understatement for you!), "but he seemed like a really good person. Blossom—his cousin—is just distraught." To my disgust, I felt a tear working its way down my face.

"Listen, Desiree," Jackie warned, "you're doing too much drinking, especially considering how lousy you are at it. You'll get sick if you don't cut it out. Just realize that you did the best you could—no one could have done better, I'm sure—and move on."

"Didn't I mention it? I promised Blossom I'd continue working on the case. She wants me to prove Roger was responsible for Gordon's death."

"Oh."

"Yeah, that's what I say. I only hope I can come up with the evidence to bag that SOB. At least I'll have accomplished *something*." And with this, I reached for the wine carafe again.

Before very long our entrées were set in front of us, but after a couple of bites I put down my fork. The veal tasted like sandpaper to me (although on sampling the dish, Jackie pronounced it "delicious"). Evidently all that Chianti was responsible not only for my head's twirling round and round, but also it had taken its toll on my taste buds, as well.

At any rate, once Jackie had done justice to her main course, I insisted she remain at the restaurant for coffee and a slice of chocolate-chip cheesecake—a house specialty. (There was, of course, no question of my joining her in this indulgence today.) I paid the bill and with profound apologies to my companion—who was attacking that cheesecake with gusto—got out of the restaurant as fast as my wobbly legs would permit.

Luckily, I spotted an empty taxi immediately. I grabbed it and headed for my apartment, where—without even stopping to remove the key from the lock—I made a beeline for the bathroom.

It was maybe a half hour later that I heard from Jackie. "How are you feeling?"

"A little better, thanks. But I am *such* a jerk; I really have no business drinking like that. One glass of wine is all I can handle—and that's on a good day."

Jackie chuckled. "Tell me about it."

"Besides, it was a lousy thing to do to you."

"I admit that watching you turn green isn't exactly my idea of a fun lunch, but that cheesecake made up for a lot."

"Instead of going out and getting blotto, I should have stayed in the office and had another try at contacting Roger's estranged wife," I grumbled.

"Which brings me to the second reason I'm calling. She phoned you while we were at the restaurant—Shelly took the message. The wife's name *is* Brandy, isn't it?"

"That's right."

"That's what I thought. Anyway, Brandy said that she's back in town, but she has to leave the house for a while. She'll give you a ring tonight."

"Damn!"

"Hey, I thought you'd be pleased."

"I suppose I am. I'm just not very happy that I missed her."

"For God's sake, Dez! You'll be speaking to the woman in a few hours."

"I only hope she knows where Roger is," I fretted.

"Of course she'll know," Jackie said confidently. "Betcha a thousand bucks she can tell you exactly where to find him."

Fortunately, I didn't take the bet.

# Chapter 11

I dined on tea and toast that night. Just toast—no cinnamon, no jelly, and only a smidgen of butter. The tea was of the no-frills variety, too. Not one of those fancy-schmantzy designer bags, but plain orange pekoe. And I had a problem swallowing even that meager fare.

After my little repast, I was prepared to spend the rest of the evening staring at the phone. But before I could position myself within watching distance, it rang.

"Ms. Shapiro, please." The voice was soft, girlish.

I could barely eke out a response. "This is Desiree Shapiro."

"I'm Brandy Clyne."

*Hallelujah!* "Oh, thanks so much for getting back to me, Mrs. Clyne."

"My dad tells me you're a friend of Priscilla Ramirez's."

"Uh, yes—a new friend."

"She's quite a little character, isn't she? But why did she have you call me?"

"She didn't actually *have* me call you. She knew I was very anxious to contact you, and she was kind enough to give me your parents' telephone number."

"According to my dad, you feel that it's extremely important we talk."

"That's true."

"Well, why don't you tell me what it is I can do for you."

"The thing is, I've been attempting to get in touch with your husband about a very serious matter, and I'm having difficulty locating him."

Brandy was slow to respond, and when she did, her voice was wary. "What do you mean by 'a very serious matter'?"

"I'm a private detective, Mrs. Clyne. My client is Gordon Curry."

"Roger's ex-boss?"

"That's right. There have been some anonymous threats on Mr. Curry's life recently, and I'd like to be able to rule out your husband."

"You think Roger—" She began to laugh now, but it was obvious she wasn't amused.

"Are you all right, Mrs. Clyne?"

"Sorry. It just struck me funny. I assure you Roger's not responsible for anything like that."

"You're probably right. But I am anxious to speak to him for a few minutes, and I'm hoping you know where I can find him."

"Oh, I know, all right," Brandy told me bitterly. I have no idea what I expected her to say next, but I was totally unprepared for what followed. "He's in the cemetery."

The words didn't immediately register. "You mean he's *dead?*" I stupidly blurted out a couple of seconds later.

"Yes. Since September."

*My God! If Roger is out of the picture—and evidently he is—then who killed Gordon?* I had to remind myself that I was talking to Clyne's widow now. "I'm very sorry for your loss, Mrs. Clyne," I said quietly.

"Don't be. Roger committed suicide—damn him! Excuse me, Ms. Shapiro, but just thinking about it makes me furious. First he messes up his life, *our* life—his, mine, and our daughter's—by engaging in unethical business practices, something I'm certain you're aware of. And then once he gets caught and decides to play it straight, he expects that, by some mystical process, he'll instantly be rewarded for his good intentions with the perfect job."

I figured this to be the extent of what she'd be revealing of a personal nature, but while I was searching my brain for an appropriate response, the woman went on. "The events, however, didn't follow my husband's scenario, so he became more and more depressed, more and more erratic. I strongly suspect that Roger even turned to drugs after a time. At any rate, eventually he . . . he solved his problems the coward's way." And now Brandy began to sniffle.

I spoke quickly, hoping to abort a full-blown crying jag. "You, uh, seem to have cared a great deal for him."

"I did. I'm not certain Roger realized that, though. You see, I walked out on him toward the end, but it was in desperation. I'd been trying to convince him to *do* something about his situation. When things didn't look too promising in his field, I suggested he consider other employment—at least until a job in pharmaceuticals opened up. Roger turned the idea down flat. I also proposed that I reenter the workplace—temporarily, anyway; I have a degree in teaching. He refused to discuss it. And of course, he laughed when I tried to persuade him to get counseling. I finally came up with this ridiculous notion that if the baby and I left, Roger might be motivated to take some positive steps in order to induce us to come back. But on September twenty-fifth I learned how wrong I was."

"You sound as if you're reproaching yourself for what happened."

"In a way I am. I'm terribly angry at him for slashing his wrists—that's how he did it, you know. Still, I can't help feeling that if I'd only stayed with him—" Brandy broke off abruptly. "What's wrong with me, for God's sake! Why am I telling you all this? I don't even *know* you!"

I smiled to myself. "That's precisely the reason you're confiding in me. Who better to unload on than a complete stranger—someone it's unlikely you'll ever be in contact with again?"

"I'm not so sure that's the reason." A self-conscious little titter here. "It's more likely that I'm bending your ear because there aren't too many ears left for me to bend. My parents try to be good listeners, and they were for quite a while—in spite of the fact that my father isn't long on patience and never cared much for Roger to begin with. But dealing with my depression and this feeling of guilt that I can't seem to shake . . . well, it's been an awful drain on them. These days they keep telling me I'll feel better if I stop going over everything again and again." She uttered a short, harsh laugh. "I know *they'll* feel better. And I can't really blame them. Then last week I went upstate to visit my best friend. But she got tired of hearing me carry on, too. By Saturday her eyes had begun to glaze over."

"Um, since you *are* discussing this with me, would you mind some feedback?"

"Go ahead."

And now I found myself giving Brandy Clyne a lecture that wasn't actually too dissimilar from the one I myself had received earlier in the day. "Your husband didn't commit suicide because you walked out on him. You tried everything else you could think of, and this *should have been* his strongest impetus yet to turn things around. You were right about that. But apparently he didn't have the courage or the drive—or whatever it would have taken. It was his choice to end things rather than attempt to fight for the life you'd been building together."

"Thank you," Brandy murmured, her voice barely above a whisper. "I'll have to try to believe that."

"You should—and I hope you will—because it's true. Well, I won't take up any more of your time. And I'm terribly sorry for intruding on your grief."

"The fact is, I feel better having talked to you." I was about to hang up when she added, "I hope your client will be all right, Ms. Shapiro."

"Uh, thanks. I hope so, too."

*I mean, what else could I say?*

# Chapter 12

My conversation with Roger Clyne's wife—widow, that is—left me in trauma. If I hadn't gotten myself so sick boozing it up earlier that day, I'd have reached for the cooking sherry. (This being the only liquid even remotely alcoholic in nature that was in my apartment just then.) Still, I needed *something* to cushion the shock to my system. So I made straight for the refrigerator, *daring* my stomach to start acting up again.

While I was eating my Häagen-Dazs macadamia brittle—and keeping it down nicely, thank you very much—I tried to absorb this latest development.

Gordon had been so certain the person behind those attacks was his former employee that I'd allowed him to convince me of it, too. A big mistake in my line of work—one that may well have cost my client his life. Of course, I'd been on the case only two days when he was killed, I reminded myself. Which helped me a little in dealing with the tragedy. But not much.

Anyway, the thing I had to concern myself with at this juncture was who else could have wanted to see poor Gordon in his grave.

And there was only one person I knew who might be able to answer that for me.

I didn't have Blossom's home phone number and

wasn't that certain she lived in Manhattan. But I checked the Manhattan telephone directory, and there was a "B. Goody" on Christopher Street in the West Village.

The individual who answered the phone didn't say a word. But it didn't matter. The cough informed me that I had the right "B. Goody."

"Goody," the woman confirmed at last.

"It's Desiree Shapiro, Blossom."

What the response lacked in warmth, it made up for in brevity. "Yeah, what?"

"Listen, there's something I have to talk to you about."

"Talk fast. I got a canasta game going on here." She lowered her voice. "And I'm winning." And now I became aware of some chatter in the background.

"It's about Roger Clyne," I said flatly. "He's dead."

"No kidding!" She let loose with what I concede was an admirable whistle, although it was hardly considerate of my eardrums.

"He committed suicide."

"Good for him."

"But the point is, this was back in September—even before those two earlier attempts on Gordon's life."

"Jee-*sus* Christ!" Blossom exploded.

"So it couldn't have been Roger who shot Gordon."

"I can figure that out for myself, Shapiro. But if not Roger—then who?"

"I'll need your help to determine that."

"*My* help?

"You're in the family, aren't you? And you and Gordon were pretty close, correct? Look, I'm assuming that you're as interested in finding out who murdered him as you claim to be. So if you're aware of any unpleasantness between Gordon and any of the other relatives, you have to be straight with me. And

I want to impress on you that you can't disregard *anything*—no matter how trivial it seems. The same goes for whatever problems Gordon might have related to you concerning his friends or the people he worked with."

"Okay, I'll—" Someone shouted to her at this point, and Blossom broke off. "Hold your water, Isabel!" she shouted back. "Be with you in a minute!" Then to me: "Tell you what. Soon as I can hustle these three dried-up old tomatoes outta here, I'll sit down and do some serious thinking. We can meet tomorrow morning for breakfast, and I'll fill you in on what I've come up with."

"Good."

"Twelve o'clock. There's a nice coffee shop around the corner from my apartment."

Now, I enjoy sleeping late as much as the next one. More, probably. But noon on a workday is pushing it even for me. Especially in light of the job that lay ahead of me.

"All right?" Blossom was asking, although I'm quite certain she viewed the question as a mere formality.

I asserted myself. "I think it might be better if we made it a little earlier."

"Okay, okay. Have it your way. Eleven-forty-five. The Yellow Rooster." She rattled off the address.

(Well, I'd said a "little" earlier, hadn't I?)

Before I had a chance to double-check on whether the number of the place was 54 or 45, Blossom was gone, leaving me pressing a dead receiver to my ear.

*So what else is new, right?*

I got in touch with Jackie about ten the next morning—Tuesday—to report that I wouldn't be at the office until early afternoon. I did this not because I'm that conscientious, but because I've never had any strong desire to be hung up by my thumbs. Which I

sincerely believe is a possibility in the event you fail
to obey one of Jackie's cardinal rules: "If you're going
to be late—call."

Anyway, did the woman thank me for notifying her?
Not on your life!

"How come you're taking the morning off?"

"I'm meeting Blossom Goody—Gordon's cousin—
for breakfast at eleven forty-five. And it doesn't pay
to come in for only a couple of hours and then rush
out again."

"A *couple* of hours, you said? Ha!" Jackie threw
back at me. But while I was struggling to produce a
snotty retort, she peppered me with more questions:
"Why are you getting together? Something going on?
Oh, I just remembered. Did you hear from Roger's
wife last night? And was I right about her being able
to tell you where to reach him?"

I didn't have time to address all this—not if I expected to eat breakfast before my next birthday. "I'll
give you a full report when I see you," I responded.
Following which I pulled a Blossom.

I could just picture Jackie cursing the dead
telephone.

Nick called a few minutes after this.

Now, Nick lives in my building, and we've been out
a number of times. I'm not sure, though, whether
there's any chemistry on his part or he simply consid-
ers me a friend. The thing is, he's never so much as
kissed me. (I do not define a kiss as a peck on the
cheek.) As for me, I'm really attracted to the guy. In
fact, appearance-wise, it's as if I'd created Nick
Grainger myself. I mean, he's short and skinny, with
pale skin and thinning hair. *Plus*—be still my heart!—
his teeth are slightly bucked.

I admit that if you took a poll, not too many women
would find those physical characteristics much of a

turn-on. Some friends of mine have suggested that I'm drawn to men who look like that—you know, in dire need of a good home-cooked meal—because I have this nurturing nature. And I guess that could be one way of explaining it.

Of course, it probably seems strange that a person who's so enamored of a bony little fellow like Nick Grainger could have a fantasy life inhabited, respectively, by hunks like Robert Redford, Mel Gibson, and Tom Selleck. To be truthful, I've wondered about that myself. Possibly the reason is that I'd be severely limited if my on-screen crushes had to be consistent with my real-life preferences. Look, he may be a terrific talent and all, but I'll be damned if I'll waste my daydreams on Woody Allen!

All this must sound pretty shallow to you, right? So I should also mention that I like Nick as a person. He's intelligent and easygoing, with a wonderful sense of humor and a kind heart. Listen, how's this for thoughtful? Recently, when I was out of commission with the flu, he even offered to fix a meal for me!

There is, however, one small glitch in my relationship with the man. (That nonkissing business aside, I mean.) And that glitch's name is Derek.

Derek is Nick's nine-year-old son, and merely thinking about this kid makes my glorious hennaed hair stand on end. The trouble began when Derek's mother—Nick's former wife—trotted off to Vegas for a week with her rocker boyfriend, then forgot to come home. So Derek wound up staying with Nick for months. And one memorable Friday the three of us went to dinner. Well, about two seconds after Nick excused himself to go to the men's room, Derek let me in on the fact that he wasn't overly fond of me—only he put it in much stronger terms. Furthermore, I could forget about making it legal with his father; his parents would be getting back together again, he announced. He drove the message home by deliberately pouring his frozen hot chocolate in my lap! And— wouldn't you know it?—Nick returned just in time to hear me curse out his pride and joy.

Derek claimed he'd spilled the dessert by accident, and I decided to let him get away with it. (After all, who was the devoted father going to believe—his only child or the woman he had no inclination to kiss good night?) I actually went so far as to apologize to the little bastard for calling him a little bastard and then squeezed out a few false tears to demonstrate my remorse. Fortunately, Nick didn't appear to be particularly disturbed by my reaction to the "accident." He told me not to be concerned, that it was a reflex and that we all lose our tempers once in a while.

Anyhow, Nick's former wife has finally found her way back to New York (thank you, God), and he and I have spent a couple of lovely evenings together since Derek went to live with his mother again. (Although apparently not lovely enough to induce the man to abandon that peck-on-the-cheek business for something even slightly more lustful.)

But to return to Nick's telephone call that day . . .

"I tried you at your office, Dez, and they told me you wouldn't be in until later. Are you feeling all right?"

"I'm fine. I'm meeting with a client soon, that's all."

"Then I won't keep you. I phoned to find out if you're free Sunday night. I expected that Derek would be with me that entire weekend, but I just heard from Tiffany"—that's his ex—"and she informs me she'll be picking him up around three to take him to some cousin's birthday party. This being the case, I thought you and I might go out to dinner in the evening—if you can make it."

"Um, why don't you come here for dinner instead?"

"That's very nice of you, but I wouldn't want to put you to any trouble."

"Cooking's no trouble for me. It's one of my favorite things."

Nick hesitated. "Are you certain you want to bother?"

"I'm positive," I answered firmly.

Now, while they say that the way to a man's heart is through his stomach, I, personally, have never given that claim much credence. But I *do* love to cook.

And besides, it was worth a shot, wasn't it?

# Chapter 13

The Yellow Rooster wasn't what you'd call bustling, maybe because most people would consider 11:45 a little late for a weekday breakfast and a little early for lunch. When I walked in, there were only two occupied tables other than Blossom's, both of which were about as far away from hers as you could get. Quite possibly the diners—a solitary middle-aged woman at each table—had decided to give my attorney friend (well, *sort of* friend)—and her cigarette—ample room to do their thing.*

On spotting me, Blossom waved a hand in greeting (although I could barely make this out through the gray cloud that stretched across the entire upper half of her not insubstantial torso). "Have a seat, and take a load off," she invited as I approached. Then, after I'd plunked myself down on the chair opposite her: "Don't worry. I know how squeamish you are about a tiny bit of smoke." And so saying, she dropped her cigarette into her water glass (*yecch!*), the sour expression accompanying this concession informing me that she was making it grudgingly.

"Thank you. I appreciate that," I told her, following which—in spite of my efforts to suppress it—I let loose with a cough.

*Note: This mystery is set in 2002—before New York's antismoking laws went into effect.

"My, aren't you the sensitive lady," Blossom grumbled, shaking her yellow Little Orphan Annie-style curls in irritation. It was then I noticed how red her eyes were, but wisely, I refrained from commenting on the fact.

"Sorry," I murmured, when I was coughed out. "Have you been waiting long?"

"No. Listen, you seen yesterday's *Post*?"

"Uh-uh. Why?"

Blossom didn't answer. Instead, she reached into her "I Love New York" tote bag and took out Monday's Late City Final edition of the *New York Post*. Turning to page fourteen, she placed the newspaper on the table. "Here," she said, pointing her finger at a brief article. "Didn't get a chance to read it myself until this morning."

**EXECUTIVE SLAIN, SUSPECT APPREHENDED,** the headline announced.

The story read:

Manhattan resident Gordon Curry, 53, district sales manager for McReedy and Emerson Pharmaceuticals, headquartered in White Plains, New York, was murdered Sunday evening shortly before midnight. The victim and several friends had just exited the West 21st Street brownstone where the group had gathered for its monthly card game, when Curry was struck by three bullets fired from directly across the street. A patrol car dispatched to investigate a domestic violence dispute in the neighborhood happened on the scene within seconds of the shooting, and Officers Ramon Escobar and Greg Flippin apprehended the suspect as he was attempting to flee the area.

The alleged killer, a white male approximately thirty years old, gave his name as John Smith.

"John Smith!" Blossom snorted.

"I wouldn't have figured this to make it into the newspapers so soon."

"They probably didn't put the paper to bed until the early hours on Monday," Blossom responded. "Anyhow, I expect we'll be seeing some expanded coverage today."

"Most likely. Incidentally, are you familiar with any white, thirty-something male who might have had it in for Gordon?"

"Not a one. It's conceivable this Roger Clyne could have filled the bill, but I guess we can scratch him." Then with a sigh: "Well, we should probably order now, kiddo. Our starving to death won't do Gordie any good."

We both settled on the number two breakfast: orange juice, scrambled eggs with bacon and home fries, and coffee or tea—although Blossom made a few adjustments to the menu, switching her orange juice to grape juice, substituting French fries for the home fries, and opting for a hot chocolate in lieu of the beverages listed. Apparently this came as no big surprise to the waitress—Alice, Blossom called her—who reacted with a knowing smile.

As soon as the unflappable Alice left us, Blossom said, "Wondering about that canasta game last night, aren't you?"

Well, considering how fond Blossom was of her cousin, I *had* found it a little odd that she'd be hosting a card game on the heels of his murder. But I certainly wasn't about to admit it. "Why no." I told her. And with a puzzled expression (I hoped): "Why are you even asking me that?"

"Don't bullshit me, lady," she snapped. "Fact is, that arrangement was made before . . . before Gordie was killed. Once I found out what happened, I called one of the girls to cancel, but she talked me out of it.

Insisted that having the group over for a game would take my mind off . . . things. I suppose I let her convince me; I just couldn't face being alone. Turns out she was right, too. I was pretty much okay—at least until everyone left."

"We all have different ways of coping, Blossom. It doesn't mean you grieved any less."

She responded with a nod, and I moved on. "Incidentally, do you believe in coincidence?"

"Do *you?*" Blossom tossed back at me.

"Rarely. And considering that there were two previous tries on Gordon's life, it would be a *huge* coincidence if this turned out to be a random shooting. Or if those bullets had actually been intended for one of the people he was with—particularly since it would mean the shooter hit Gordon by mistake *three times.*"

"Agreed. The fellow was aiming at Gordie, all right. He was a helluva shot, too."

"So, umm, none of the names you're going to suggest to me fit his description?"

"I could only come up with two possibles—two very remotely possibles, I wanna make clear. And they're both women."

"Well, maybe some white, thirty-year-old male was avenging one of them. Anyhow, let me hear who you've got."

"First off, there's Melanie Slater. She was the wife's live-in nurse."

"Rhonda had been ill?"

"I'm talking about Gordie's *first* wife," Blossom said testily, obviously of the opinion that I should have been aware of the existence of such a person.

I bristled. "I had no idea Gordon was married before."

"Well, he was. To the cousin of my former husband, that stinking bastard, may he rot in hell!"

*Amen,* I said to myself.

A mutual acquaintance had clued me in to the fact that about ten years ago Blossom's ex had left her for his secretary—who was practically still in diapers at the time. And apparently the creep's deserting her like that had affected Blossom to the point where she started to drink; she even had to leave the prestigious law firm she was affiliated with in those days. Eventually, though, she pulled herself together and opened a law office of her own. And while people weren't exactly queuing up at her door to clamor for her services, you could say the same about a lot of individuals—including someone with the initials "DS"—who, nevertheless, manage to pay their bills (sooner or later, at any rate) and lead full, relatively satisfying lives.

"She was a nice woman, too—Edie," Blossom remarked. "In spite of being related to that low-life dog."

"So then Gordon was actually your cousin-*in-law*,"

"If you say so, Shapiro."

"What did this Melanie have against him?"

"Gordie was . . . well, kind of a flirt in a way. Couldn't help himself. And if you wanna give credence to the buzz back then, Melanie had gotten it into her head that after Edith passed on—poor Edie was terminal when Melanie was hired to take care of her—she'd be Mrs. Gordon Curry number two."

"If she did have that impression, Gordon must have said or done something besides flirt with her."

There was a brief silence before Blossom admitted, "Maybe they, uh, played footsie for a bit."

"While his wife was *dying?*" I blurted out.

"Hey, I said *maybe*, didn't I? Anyhow, whatever went on between the two of 'em—and who knows if anything actually did?—presumably Melanie wasn't overjoyed about Gordie's tying the knot with her second cousin."

"Rhonda and Melanie are cousins, too?"

"Didn't I just *tell* you that?" the terrible-tempered Blossom barked.

I was about to do some barking of my own—I mean, enough is enough—when Alice reappeared with our food.

For a few minutes we ate in silence, neither of us with much of an appetite. (I noticed that Blossom wasn't even touching her custom order of French fries.) Then I reopened the discussion, which we carried on between very occasional bites of breakfast.

"How long after his first wife's demise did Gordon remarry?"

"Five, six months."

"I see."

"What the hell does *that* mean?"

God! I'd been hoping that whatever nourishment she got would improve the woman's disposition. "Nothing at all," I assured her. "It's just an expression."

"For your information, Edith was ailing during a good part of the marriage—bum heart. And with her gone, well, Gordie was entitled to a little happiness, wasn't he?"

"Of course."

Blossom didn't comment further, leading me to conclude that we'd pretty much exhausted the subject of Melanie. "So who is remotely possible suspect number two?"

"Rhonda." She said it so quietly that I was barely able to make out the name.

"Gordon's appetite for the ladies again?"

"Uh-uh. Not that I ever heard, anyhow. In fact, he and Rhonda got along fine—until this awful tragedy last winter."

"What tragedy?"

"Chip—Rhonda's kid—died. Nice, friendly boy, only around sixteen or seventeen years old."

"And this had an impact on the marriage?"

The Orphan Annie curls bounced up and down in response. "Gordie and the kid were driving to this ski resort in Vermont, see, and there was an accident. Car skidded and smashed into a tree—the road conditions were piss-poor that day. Gordie got off lucky; he wasn't seriously hurt. But Chip had to be hooked up to a life support system."

"And Rhonda blamed Gordon for the crash?"

Blossom shrugged. "Wasn't his fault. Still, he was the one at the wheel."

"They stayed together, though—Gordon and Rhonda."

"True. Everyone expected they'd be splitting up any day. But apparently they were able to work things out."

"You say Chip died of his injuries?"

"Yeah. But not until weeks later."

"Let me ask you something. Chip's father—is he still living?"

"Good thinking," Blossom responded. And I swear I actually detected a trace of admiration in her tone. "I forgot about him. Luke Garber's his name. I understand he was all broken up over what happened to his son. Can't say for sure he holds Gordie responsible, but it makes sense he would, doesn't it?"

"Perfect sense," I agreed after hastily swallowing a scant forkful of food.

It took about thirty seconds for Blossom to declare, "Shit! It's no good."

"What isn't?"

"Rhonda's ex doesn't fit the description of that guy the cops hauled in. Luke's closer to fifty than thirty. And I'll bet my bloomers he's never *seen* a gun—in the flesh, I mean—much less handled one."

"By the way, when did Gordon and Rhonda get married?"

"Five years ago. Maybe a little longer."

"That makes me wonder how Melanie can be viewed as a serious suspect. I mean, would she have stewed about this for five years, then suddenly decided to murder him?"

Blossom opened her mouth and promptly closed it again. I waited her out. "I don't regard this as giving her a whole lot more of an incentive, but I might as well tell you," she said at last. "A coupla months before Edie died, there was talk—and it coulda been just plain bullshit—that Melanie went and had an abortion. And that it was . . . that she was carrying Gordie's child."

Blossom's hesitation in passing on this information confirmed what was already fairly apparent: a reluctance to sully the reputation of the deceased. I mean, I didn't figure that her reticence stemmed from any desire to protect Melanie's good name. I told myself this was something I'd have to bear in mind when questioning the attorney.

At any rate, after I'd digested that last bit of intelligence, I summed up the situation. "We'll be learning John Smith's real identity pretty soon, I'm sure. And from there, I'll have to try to establish a connection between him and Gordon. Failing that, it'll be necessary to find some link between him and one of the others."

"I take it you're referring to the three of them: Melanie, Rhonda, and Luke."

"That's right. Along with anyone else you can think of."

"There *is* nobody else. Not to my knowledge, at least. Listen, I know I gave you her name, but—as I believe I indicated—I was scrounging around for suspects. The truth is, I can't picture Rhonda's getting somebody to kill her husband for her. Or wanting him dead, for that matter. I got the idea that she eventually came to appreciate that Gordie shared her grief, that he was almost as distraught as she was over the boy's death. And it wasn't only because he blamed himself for the accident; he loved that stepson of his. Anyhow, recently the two of them appeared to be closer than ever."

"And your take on Melanie?"

"I feel the way you do. Whatever sort of relationship she may have had with Gordie is history—abortion or no abortion. They hardly ever saw each other anymore."

"What do you mean 'hardly'?"

"Melanie and Rhonda are related, don't forget. So the three of 'em would sometimes show up at the same family function."

"This was the extent of the contact?"

"Between Melanie and Gordie, it was. But when Chip died, Melanie got in touch with Rhonda to offer condolences, and they began meeting for lunch every so often—just Melanie and Rhonda, though. They seem to have gotten pretty tight again, too—once upon a time they'd been very good friends."

"I gather this friendship had originally ended when Gordon elected to make Rhonda his bride."

"Give that woman an A," Blossom muttered in that genial manner she has.

"Let's talk about the ex-husband."

"Okay. I've been in his company on a few occasions, and he appears to be a decent enough guy. But I don't really *know* him. And he *did* have a strong motive—or might have thought he did."

It was then that I recalled an earlier conversation with Blossom. "I got the impression from what you told me yesterday that Gordon and his son weren't on particularly good terms."

"You're suggesting Danny killed *his own father?*"

"It's certainly not unheard of—as someone in your profession must be aware."

"Yeah, but Danny wouldn't harm a soul; take my word for it, Shapiro. I've known him all his life, and even as a young kid he was a sensitive, caring person."

"What was the source of friction between him and Gordon?"

"Danny, uh, didn't always approve of how his father used to treat his mother."

"How *did* he treat her?"

"Don't go jumping to any conclusions. It wasn't that Gordie was unkind to Edie or anything—and he did see to it she got the best of care. But he wasn't as attentive to her as Danny maybe felt he should be. And . . . er . . . there was this rumor he—" The rest of the sentence was lost to me, since Blossom was now speaking into her hot-chocolate mug.

"I didn't get that."

"I *said* there was some rumor about Gordie's wanting a divorce at one point so he could marry somebody else—I don't know who—but then Edie's family stepped in and bought off the woman."

"Was this while Edie was *terminal?*"

"Definitely not. She wasn't well, but she wasn't dying when that *supposedly* occurred. Like I keep telling you, there's no way of determining what's fact and what's just malicious gossip."

"But you think Danny might have heard that gossip and believed it?"

"It's conceivable. But again, we're talking way in the past here."

"True. Was there anything else—anything more recent in origin—that Danny held against his father?"

"No," Blossom answered firmly. But her now bright pink face brought a lie to the denial.

"Look, if you want me to find out who was responsible for your cousin Gordie's death, you're going to have to put everything on the table. And I mean *everything.*"

There was a prolonged silence as Blossom bent her head and fiddled with the remainder of her retailored number two breakfast, most of which was still sitting in front of her. "This isn't exactly current, either," she mumbled at last, while continuing to focus most of her attention on pushing the eggs around on her plate. "But Danny used to be . . . kinda jealous."

"Of what?"

"Of how close his father was to Chip," she answered, glancing up at me with obvious reluctance. "He had this notion Gordie cared more for his stepson than he did for *him*—his own son. Which I seriously doubt. It's just that Danny and Gordie didn't see very much of each other once Gordie and Rhonda made it legal. While Chip, on the other hand, was right there in the house with them."

"Where was Danny?"

"He went off to Yale about eight months after the marriage. Been away the better part of the last four years.

"Listen to me, though. Danny's envy of the relationship between his father and stepbrother began almost the day Gordie and Rhonda marched down the aisle. And since then Danny's become an adult—he's twenty-two years old now. Graduated college this spring and took an apartment uptown with a buddy of his. Then in August he got a job on Wall Street. I ran into Edie's sister at Saks a few weeks ago, and to hear *her* tell it, her nephew's already the cockeyed wonder of the financial world. So why would he strike out at Gordie after so many years—especially with the cause of his resentment dead and gone?"

*Why indeed?* A thought struck me. "What about Gordon's will? Did you handle that for him, by any chance?"

"I'm a criminal lawyer, remember?"

"Right. Well, are you at all familiar with it?"

"Not really. But . . . hold it a minute. Come to

think of it, a coupla years back, Gordie told me that if something happened to him, he could at least be certain that neither Danny or Rhonda would be hurting for money."

"What brought that on?"

"It was right after we attended the funeral of a mutual friend. Shortly before he passed away, this friend had gotten heavily involved in some risky real estate venture, see? Then, to no one's surprise but his, the deal tanked. Well, his death left the man's wife and kid only about a step away from welfare. But if you ask me, when Gordie made that remark, he wasn't referring to any money Rhonda and Danny would be inheriting from him—not by itself, anyhow. The thing is, although Gordie was pulling in a good salary and, besides that, had had this phenomenal luck playing the market, both his wife and son were already knee-deep in the green stuff. Rhonda's an attorney with a booming practice, and her clients are strictly la crème de la crème, don'tcha know." To illustrate this point, Blossom pursed her lips, crooked her pinky, and batted her eyes. "As for Danny, his mother left him her entire estate, so he is one very rich young guy."

"Edie was well-off on her own?"

"Her daddy died a year or so before she did, and the old man had been . . . uh, connected. If you get my meaning."

I got it. "He was involved in organized crime?"

"Right up to his scrawny little neck. And when Papa Charlie was summoned upstairs—or, more likely, downstairs—his two daughters came into a bundle. This I know because my former husband, that son of a bitch, drew up the old coot's will for him.

"Anyway, Dez," Blossom said earnestly, "I hope I've convinced you that Danny had no motive to murder his father."

Now, between the "Dez"—Blossom never calls me

Dez—and the soft, persuasive tone, which for her was almost like speaking in a foreign tongue, I realized how important it was to the woman that I go along with this assessment.

"Oh, you have, Blossom," I assured her in the sincerest voice I own.

And at the same time I mentally added one more name to my suspect list.

# Chapter 14

Blossom was anxious to get to her office. I, on the other hand, was anxious to have my coffee cup refilled—for the third time. (If you'd ever tasted the vile brew that goes under the name of coffee at my place, you'd find this completely understandable.)

At any rate, I was still seated at the table when Blossom got to her feet, providing me with my first full-length view of her that morning.

This woman—who's no taller and no narrower than yours truly—was dressed in bright, *bright* green pants! I mean, when she turned away from me to put on her coat, I immediately thought of somebody's front lawn.

Now, on the one previous occasion I'd been in her company, Blossom had been wearing slacks that were a blazing, fire engine red. So her attire didn't come as any big shock. But (and, granted, many full-figured ladies of my acquaintance disagree with me on this) if she wanted my opinion—which she obviously did not—I'd have told her that all pants should be banned from the closets of individuals whose dimensions are in the neighborhood of hers—and mine.

Still, if she was determined to wear those things, I would have imagined she'd choose a color that was somewhat more subdued.

I reminded myself with a smile that there was nothing about Blossom Goody that was even the least bit subdued.

I spent the next ten minutes or so enjoying more of the Yellow Rooster's excellent coffee and, for a good part of that time, revising my feelings about my deceased client.

For starters, I could no longer label him a harmless flirt. It was now fairly evident that Gordon Curry had been a dedicated womanizer—prior to his marriage to Rhonda, anyway. Perhaps even afterward. And while I would have been willing to tolerate—albeit grudgingly—his randy behavior (sporting of me, wasn't it?), I couldn't excuse his carrying on during poor Edith's illness.

I was also troubled by the man's apparent insensitivity to the feelings of his only son. It seemed to me—

I pulled myself up short. So what if Gordon had faults—even substantial ones? Did that give anyone the right to execute him? (Listen, I have one or two minor imperfections myself.) Besides, Blossom hadn't hired me to give her cousin Gordie my stamp of approval; she expected me to come up with the identity of his assassin. And that's precisely what I intended to do.

I decided to keep my mind blank while I finished my coffee. Which maybe wasn't as difficult as it should have been.

Before hailing a cab to the office, I picked up Tuesday's *New York Post.* Plunking down my twenty-five cents, I quickly riffled through it until I came to page nine. Blossom was right. Today's paper carried expanded coverage on the shooting.

**MURDER IN CHELSEA,** the headline fairly screamed. There was a decent-sized likeness of Gordon, underneath which was the caption, "**GUNNED DOWN:** Pharmaceutical executive Gordon Curry, 53, slain late Sunday evening after monthly poker game with friends." Below that was a second photo, the copy underneath it reading, "**CRIME SCENE:** The victim was shot to death upon leaving this West 21st Street brownstone."

In the taxi I went over the article, searching for additional facts. According to this edition, the two cops had pursued the suspect for more than three blocks before finally catching up with him. After a brief struggle—during which one of the police officers was slightly injured—the man was placed in handcuffs, at which point he claimed that he'd simply been walking down the street when the homicide occurred. " 'I didn't see who fired at the guy,' he insisted, 'but it wasn't me. I ran because I was being chased.' "

The suspect—who carried no identification at the time of his arrest—was continuing to maintain that his name was John Smith. And so far the police had been unable to verify this or to establish a connection between any John Smith and the victim.

The write-up concluded with a quote from a Marvin Cantor, age forty-eight, resident of the brownstone depicted in the photograph, and for the past fifteen years one of the participants in the group's regularly scheduled card games.

" 'You might find a better poker player,' Cantor told this reporter in a choked voice, 'but you'll never find a better friend.' "

That did it. I dabbed at my eyes, following which I began to reassess my feelings about Gordon once again.

I made it to work at just after one thirty. Jackie could barely wait for me to get through the door.

"Some guy called you this morning. Did he reach you at home?"

"Yes, thanks."

"Was it Nick?"

"It was."

"So?" Jackie demanded, leaning halfway across her desk. "What did he want?"

I suppose I'm kind of perverse. But all that eagerness made it hard for me to resist toying with her a bit. "He wanted me to lend him a couple of hundred dollars."

"You're kidding!" an appalled Jackie exclaimed. Then she took another look at my face. "Very funny, Desiree. You're getting to be a regular stand-up comic. Remind me not to take any interest in your life from now on."

Properly chastised, I apologized at once. "Sorry, Jackie. I have no idea what made me say that. Actually, Nick phoned to ask me out to dinner Sunday. I suggested we eat at my place instead."

"Good thinking. What are you going to serve?"

"I'm not sure yet."

"How about that orangey chicken? You know, with the almonds. Bet he'd love that one. Your boeuf bourguignon is very tasty, too—only a little heavier. I'm also partial to that veal scaloppine dish you make, although—"

An incoming telephone call spared me what might well have turned out to be a critique of every entrée I'd ever prepared for this woman—and over the years there have been quite a few of them. As soon as she lifted the receiver I smiled, mouthed, "See you later," and made my escape.

Once I was settled in my cubbyhole, I debated with myself over my next step. It seemed logical to begin the questioning with Gordon's widow. But for decency's sake, I should probably wait another day or two before contacting her. On the other hand, though, the more time I allotted Rhonda for pulling herself together (assuming, that is, she even required pulling together), the less chance I had of discovering her husband's killer. The fact is, it doesn't take long for memories to fade and evidence to become tainted or disappear altogether. Yes, I'd recently solved a ten-year-old homicide. But I had to attribute this mostly to luck—with maybe something of a minor miracle thrown in.

At any rate, I'd pretty much convinced myself to phone Rhonda that very moment to determine when she could see me. But just then a rather significant piece of information finally registered on my addled brain. It was something I'd read in today's *Post*—and possibly yesterday's, too, for all I knew—but had completely failed to absorb.

*Chelsea! Gordon was killed in Chelsea!*

I conjured up this likeness of a middle-aged man with salt-and-pepper hair who was built like a fireplug. And who, on various occasions, had growled at me and lectured me and even, at times, refused to speak to me at all.

Nonetheless, if Sergeant Tim Fielding had been assigned to this case—and it was a good possibility considering that his precinct was located in Manhattan's Chelsea area—well, I might just be getting a break.

# Chapter 15

I immediately dialed the Twelfth Precinct—or the "one-two," as the cops refer to it. And moments later I was listening to a familiar voice.

"Fielding," it growled.

"Shapiro," I purred.

"No, Lord! No!"

"You always manage to say the right thing," I responded sweetly.

Now, I suppose a quick rundown on my relationship with Tim Fielding might be in order here.

You see, years back—before my late husband, Ed, became a PI—he was a member of the force, and the two men had worked out of the same house for a time and become good buddies. On occasion, Ed and I would even socialize with Fielding and his wife, Jo Ann.

Then after Ed died, Tim and I kind of lost touch for a while—until there was this radical change in the nature of my investigations. I mean, I went from chasing after errant spouses and wandering Weimaraners to sniffing out cold-blooded killers. The result being that, these days, every so often Tim and I wind up involved in the same case. In some instances we've actually shared information—when we weren't locking horns, that is.

Anyhow, in spite of the reception I'd just received,

the truth is, we have these nice warm feelings for each other. Only for some reason—and don't ask me to explain it—we choose to conceal these feelings by taking smart-alecky little potshots at each other.

"Your timing stinks, Shapiro," Fielding was bellyaching. "I'm up to my keister in paperwork; I sprained my back last week, and I'm still in pain; and Jo Ann picked this morning to nag me about buying her a Mercedes. A Mercedes! I can't even afford new rims for my ninety-eight Ford, for God's sake! So the last thing I need at this point is to have to contend with a Desiree Shapiro."

"You sure have a talent for making a girl feel welcome."

"A *girl?* That's a good one!"

"Uh, how is everything, Tim?"

"Weren't you paying attention? I just *told* you that." And then grudgingly: "How have *you* been?"

"Not bad."

"Well, now that that's out of the way, enlighten me. What moved you to suddenly remember my phone number this afternoon?"

"I'm looking into a shooting in Chelsea, and it occurred to me you might be handling that same homicide."

"And which homicide would this be?"

"The victim's name is Gordon Curry."

"How come I'm not surprised?" Fielding groused.

"So it *is* your case?"

"Yeah."

"Could I ask you just a couple of things?"

"That depends on what you want to know."

"Well, have you established yet whether John Smith is the real name of the fellow you've arrested?"

"He tells us it is. Says if he wanted to make up a name, he'd pick something a little less obvious."

"I suppose there's some truth in that."

"Unless *he* figures *we* would figure that's what he'd do."

"He must have provided an address, though."

"Must he? According to our Mr. Smith, he can't do that because his mother has a bad heart, and it could kill her if she learned he'd been arrested."

"You took his prints, I suppose."

"No, I didn't want him to get his dainty little fingers dirty," Fielding retorted in this deceptively pleasant voice. After which he bellowed so loudly I had to hold the receiver away from my ear. "Of *course* we took his prints, Shapiro!"

Something about this last exchange had a familiar ring to it, but I couldn't think why. All at once it came to me. It was like listening to a baritone version of Blossom Goody!

I was in no position, however, to put any bite into my response. "Sorry, Tim," I said. "I really don't know what made me ask a stupid question like that." And now pausing only long enough to assure myself that I couldn't possibly be strangled over the telephone, I ventured, "So . . . um . . . this guy isn't in the system, then."

I was poised to hold the receiver at arm's length again, but Fielding's tone, although dripping with sarcasm, was within normal hearing range. "Came to this conclusion all by yourself, did you?"

"This would mean Mr. X isn't a professional hit man or anything."

"Probably not. Unless he's a beginner. Or very careful. Or just plain lucky."

I swallowed a couple of times before forging ahead. "I assume his hands were tested for gunshot residue."

"Nice of you to grant that us dumb cops could be that competent."

"Listen, you *know* I didn't mean it like that. I was simply summing up my thoughts out loud."

"Hey, no offense taken. In fact, because you're giving us that much credit, I'm going to answer your next question before you ask it: It could be weeks before we get that report back."

"Oh."

"Furthermore," Fielding continued, "even if the results should turn out to be negative, that wouldn't prove anything. Could be the guy was wearing gloves when he fired his weapon, then managed to ditch them when our guys were chasing him down."

"I imagine there was a search of the neighborhood."

"Did you think there might not be?" It sounded as if it was said through clenched teeth.

"No, no, of course not. I'm sure there was a very thorough search." And now I *really* pushed my luck. "I suppose you have the gun, though." And when Fielding didn't respond: "Don't you?"

"I'll write you a letter," he snapped. "But at this moment, *I* have a question for *you,* if you don't mind."

"What's that?"

"Curry's body's hardly cold yet, so why would anybody be in such a god-awful hurry to bring in a PI?"

"I was hired by the victim—before somebody gunned him down, naturally."

"To do what?"

"Gordon Curry strongly suspected that his life was in danger; he'd been attacked twice before. And the thing is, he was absolutely convinced he knew the identity of the person responsible for those earlier attempts. He wanted me to uncover some evidence against that party before"—my voice caught in my throat here—" . . . before there was a third—and possibly successful—try at him."

"I gather you didn't deliver," Fielding commented with an insensitivity that was uncharacteristic of him. Which gave me some idea of the extent to which I'd managed to irritate him that afternoon.

"I was only involved in this for two days before Gordon was shot, so there wasn't really—"

"Never mind. I shouldn't have said that. I wanna make certain I've doped this out, though. You didn't have enough time to gather any proof against whoever it was Curry claimed was out to get him. But being the civic-minded citizen you are, you called to give the NYPD a heads-up on John Smith's identity—just in case we haven't been able to ID him yet. Am I warm?"

"Er . . . not exactly."

"Well, then the reason you got on the horn to me was to confirm John Smith's allegation that we've got the wrong individual on ice."

"Um . . . no. He was probably the shooter."

"I give up. Precisely what *did* prompt you to dial this number?"

"Gordon's cousin requested I remain on the case. But I would have done that on my own, because I can't help feeling a responsibility for what happened—I mean, not having been able to prevent the death of my client. At any rate, I've received information that leads me to believe someone might have conspired with your Mr. X to do this murder—someone besides Gordon's own candidate, that is. And since I have no doubt that you're as anxious as I am to see the perpetrator—or perpetrators—behind bars, I think it would make sense for us to pool whatever we've discovered so far. It would almost certainly put us in a better position to achieve our mutual goal."

There was a second or two of silence before Fielding responded. "Let me ask you something. How many times have you performed this same little dance routine for me?"

"I have no idea what you mean."

"Sure you do." Fielding's voice switched to a falsetto in what was obviously intended to be an imitation—a very unkind imitation—of my own.

"Please, Tim, let me come over there. I swear I'll share *everything* I know, and you can share whatever *you* know." And now dropping down a couple of octaves, he resumed his normal tone. "The trouble is, I always wind up giving a lot more than I get. A helluva lot more."

"Oh, that's not true. I—"

"Save your breath, Shapiro. I'm not buying today. You've already wrung too much out of me."

"Look, why don't I stop by the station house later so we can sit down and talk for a—"

"What'd you do, lady—stuff cotton in your ears?"

"Wait. Suppose that right this minute I provide you with the name of the person Gordon was so convinced wanted him dead."

"I have this impression you're not in agreement with the victim's opinion."

"I didn't say that," I answered carefully. "It's only that there are other possibilities, that's all."

"We'll go into those in a little while. For now, I'd be interested in learning who Curry himself suspected."

"If I tell you, will you let me drop by? I'll fill you in then on the additional possibilities I mentioned."

"First, the name of your deceased client's choice. After that I may consider it."

I hesitated. Before I put my bargaining chip on the table, I had to verify that Tim would match it.

"So?" he demanded impatiently.

"Do I have your promise we can get together?"

"What have I done to deserve this?" he groaned. Then after this came a muttered "Jesus Christ," followed by a long, drawn-out sigh. Finally, Fielding gave in. "Okay. Promise."

"Roger Clyne. That's C-l-y-n-e."

"You've spoken to this Clyne?"

"No. It's a long story, Tim. You'll get all the details when I come over. Deal?"

"Yeah, yeah, deal. And I'll also want to hear about those previous attempts to knock off your client."

"Of course."

"Today's bad, though. Make it tomorrow morning."

"Fine."

"I'll see you at eight. Or is that too early for you?"

I had to allow myself a second for a mental shudder. "No, not at all."

"Liar!" Fielding said, chuckling (maliciously, I thought). After which he added, "And make sure you bring the doughnuts I like. The ones with the—"

"—chocolate icing and walnut sprinkles," I finished for him.

# Chapter 16

Ellen phoned about four o'clock.

She didn't bother with any of the amenities, her first words being "Oh, my God!"

I took a guess at what had prompted this fairly unusual greeting. "You've read the *New York Post.*"

"This minute. And I feel just awful about your client."

"So do I," I murmured.

"And the m-murder took place right in my neighborhood, too!" (Ellen lives on West Nineteenth Street.) "Anyhow, would you like to go out for a drink or something after work? I'll t-try to get off early."

"No, thanks, Ellen. I'm sick about what happened, especially when you take into account that Gordon trusted me to keep him alive. But I don't think I need a drink at this point." I elected to keep to myself that I'd already gone that route—and with less than satisfactory results.

"I hope you realize this wasn't your fault, Aunt Dez. You didn't even have time to locate that guy Roger."

"Regardless, I should have handled things differently."

"How, for goodness' sake?"

"For one thing, by not accepting as gospel Gordon's allegation that it was Roger Clyne who was out to get him."

"Roger Clyne wasn't the man arrested by the police?"

"Brandy—Roger's wife—returned my call last night, Ellen."

"And?"

"She told me her husband is dead."

"Dead?"

"Dead," I reiterated.

"Oh, my God," my niece said again, but in a whisper now. "I was so sure that John Smith was an alias for Roger what's 'is name."

"I still consider it likely that's an alias. But obviously not for Roger Clyne. As a matter of fact, Roger wasn't responsible for those previous attacks on Gordon, either. He committed suicide before they occurred."

Ellen took a moment to digest all of this. Then in a soft, sad voice: "And Gordon was so positive he knew who was trying to kill him."

"I imagine he wasn't able to own up to the truth— and I'm talking about even to himself."

"What truth?"

"That he'd screwed up enough in his personal life to give several other people motives for wanting to see him in his grave, as well."

"Including John Smith."

"Maybe. But it's also possible Smith was acting on behalf of someone else."

"You m-mean he's a *hit* m-man?"

"Not necessarily. Perhaps he was avenging a close friend or relative who had it in for Gordon."

"Well, anyhow, I'm glad you're off the case."

"Uh, Ellen? I suppose I should tell you: I'm not."

"Not what?"

"Off the case."

"But with your client dead, I figured—"

"Listen, I wanted to return the retainer Gordon had given me. But Gordon's cousin—the one who sent him to me in the first place—insisted I keep the money and look into the shooting. The truth is, though, I would have investigated my client's death regardless."

"But a *hit* m-man."

"We don't know that yet. Besides, even if John Smith *is* a hit man, there's no reason for you to be concerned. He's in jail, remember?"

"Whoever's behind this could bring in somebody else."

"To do what? The job's already done."

Ellen appeared to have a modicum of uncertainty in accepting this fact. "I guess. . . . Still, swear to me you'll be c-careful."

"I swear."

"No. I mean really."

"Okay. I *really* swear." And now, to spare myself any further instructions of this nature, I broached a topic I should have been savvy enough to avoid like the plague. "By the way, Ellen, has your mother found a dress yet?"

"I wasn't even going to mention *that*—not in view of what just happened to your poor client. But yes, she found a dress yesterday."

"Oh, great!"

"And she's returning it today."

*Not so great.* "What if she is? There's plenty of time for her to get something else."

"Do you honestly think so?"

"Of course. The wedding is weeks away."

"True. But you know how fussy my mother is."

"Fussy or not, she'll get herself a dress. After all, she has to be aware that attending your daughter's wedding stark naked is a definite faux pas."

Ellen giggled politely before presenting me with another worrisome situation. "But suppose she doesn't see anything she likes?"

At this point I cursed myself for changing the subject before. I mean, I actually longed to swear that I'd be really, really, *really* careful in my hunt for Gordon's murderer. But it was too late for that. So after first biting my lip, I assured her wearily, "She will. You wait and see."

I think Ellen came back with, "I hope you're not just saying that."

Although I can't be positive. Because this was when I tuned her out.

# Chapter 17

At around seven thirty that night, my mouth went so dry that I knew my tongue would be clicking like mad when I spoke. I mean, here I was, phoning for an appointment to interrogate someone whose slain husband wasn't even in his grave yet. It was the sort of call I dread making—regardless of the possibility that Rhonda Curry herself might have had a hand in speeding my client off to "a better place."

A woman picked up.

"Mrs. Curry, please."

"Speaking."

"My name is Desiree Shapiro, and—"

"Oh, Ms. Shapiro. Blossom told me you've agreed to look into Gordie's death, and I'm truly grateful." The voice was pleasant and remarkably composed—under the circumstances, I mean. "It isn't that I don't have confidence in the police," she went on, "but according to the newspapers, the man they've arrested denies any involvement in the shooting. He's almost certainly lying, of course. However, '*almost* certainly' isn't quite the same as 'certainly,' is it?"

"No, it's not," I acknowledged.

"I just don't want to be left with any nagging doubts as to whether whoever winds up being sent away for this horrific crime is actually the person—or persons—responsible for it. That's why I'm so relieved that you've taken the case. I'm a real believer in motivation, Ms. Shapiro, and Blossom feels you have a personal interest in discovering the truth. Besides, she has great faith in your ability."

"That's very kind of her. Especially since I wasn't able to prevent what . . . what happened. I'm so sorry about that . . . so terribly sorry. You have my deepest sympathies on your loss, Mrs. Curry."

"It's Leonidas."

"Excuse me?"

"Leonidas is my maiden name. I chose to retain it when Gordie and I married—it's less confusing to my clients that way. You see, I went under Leonidas when I was married to my first husband. But that's not important. What *does* matter is that you recognize you're not to blame for the murder. After all, as it turned out, you had only two days to conduct your investigation. And Gordie's pointing you in the wrong direction wasn't particularly helpful, either."

"Blossom filled you in on that?"

"Yes, and that was the first I heard about the near miss when Gordie was hunting in the Poconos. He did tell me he was almost run over by a motorboat, but this was immediately after it took place. And at that juncture he was convinced it wasn't intentional, that it was just some teenagers fooling around. I myself wasn't altogether positive, however—not initially."

"Are you saying you thought somebody deliberately aimed that boat at your husband?"

"Only at first. Gordie wasn't aware of it, Ms. Shapiro, but I knew about Roger Clyne, knew that he wasn't quite normal and that he had threatened Gordie."

"You *did?*"

"You sound surprised. But not all office gossip is disseminated around the watercooler; the whispering goes on at fancy affairs, too. Less than a week before leaving for the Poconos, Gordie and I attended a big 'do' at the Waldorf. We were all having cocktails and milling around, and I walked over to this group of women I'd met on previous occasions—the wives of some of the other executives. They stopped chattering the instant I joined them; it was as if they'd all been struck mute. Finally, to fill this terribly awkward silence, one of the women explained that they'd been discussing that awful Roger Clyne's vendetta against my husband. She was obviously under the impression I was aware of this, and I didn't disabuse her of the notion—although, actually, until that moment I had no idea the man even existed. By the time I left those ladies, however, I had the entire story. So when that incident occurred at the lake, the first thing to flash through my mind was that this Clyne was at the helm of the boat—don't forget that I'd learned about him only days earlier. A while later, though, I laughed at myself for being so foolish."

"You never told your husband that you knew about Clyne?"

"No. Clearly, he wanted to spare me the worry, and I let him believe that he had. Particularly since I'd come to accept his version about the teenagers.

"At any rate, I hope you understand that the reason Gordie misled you about his attacker's identity was because he was deceiving himself. My husband," Rhonda explained with what I took to be a fond, almost maternal chuckle, "refused to accept that anyone could find him less than completely charming—that former employee of his excepted, of course. Roger Clyne's hostility was, it seems, too blatant for even Gordie to ignore.

"Still, Gordie was *almost* right; the majority of people did respond very positively to him. Unfortunately, however, there was at least one strong dissenter aside from Clyne. Otherwise, my husband would be with us today, wouldn't he?" And now with a short laugh: "All of which, Ms. Shapiro, is my rambling way of attempting to convince you that it would have been impossible for you to prevent what transpired."

"Thank you. I appreciate your saying that," I murmured.

"Why shouldn't I say it? It's a fact. But you must have some things you want to discuss with me."

"I was hoping to sit down with you for a few minutes." *A lot more than a few,* I amended in my head.

"Naturally. When would you like to do it?"

"As soon as you're up to it, Mrs. Cu— I mean, Ms. Leonidas."

"I suppose we shouldn't delay something like that. Hold on for a moment while I check my calendar." She was back on the line in less than a minute. "How about Thursday, my office—say, at noon?"

"That would be fine," I told her, surprised that she'd be returning to work so soon after the loss of her husband.

Apparently the woman read minds. "We're having a private service for Gordie tomorrow," she informed me. "And I decided that if I didn't keep myself busy, I'd spend all of Thursday sitting around and bawling."

Now, I'm not saying I felt that Gordon's widow was lying about this. Well, okay, maybe I am. I mean, regardless of her stated determination to see the perpetrator(s) brought to justice, Rhonda Leonidas appeared to be emotionally removed from the tragedy. And the notion of this curiously contained woman sprawled on her living room sofa, clutching a box of Kleenex to her bosom while almost prostrate with grief, just didn't make it for me.

As soon as I laid down the receiver, I picked it up again. Blossom hadn't been able to supply me with either the home or office number of Luke Garber,

Rhonda's former husband, so I put in a call to Information. There was a listing in Brooklyn—which is where Blossom had advised me the man was living—for a *Lucas* Garber. That was close enough.

"Hello, it's Jennifer," I was apprised by a little girl of indeterminate age.

"Well, hi, Jennifer. How are you?"

"Fine, thank you."

"Um, is Mr. Garber in?"

"My daddy?"

I smiled. "I suppose so."

The next thing I heard was a loud clunk, the phone evidently having been deposited none too gently on some hard surface. Then directly on the heels of this came a high-pitched, almost ear-shattering, "Dad-*dy!*"

An instant later I could make out a masculine voice in the background saying something like, "Aren't you ever going to put that child to sleep?" The woman's response was indistinct, but the shrill wail that followed it became fainter almost at once—a pretty good indication that Jennifer was now being shepherded to dreamland.

Finally, a man spoke into the receiver. "Luke Garber here. Uh, sorry to have kept you waiting."

"That's perfectly all right. Am I speaking to the Luke Garber who was formerly married to Rhonda Leonidas?"

"Yes, you are." He sounded cautious.

"My name is Desiree Shapiro. I'm investigating the murder of Gordon Curry, and I could really use your help."

"Investigating? I'm a little confused. I was under the impression that the fellow who shot Gordon was already in custody."

"His guilt hasn't been definitely established yet."

"But I thought . . . Are you with the police, Ms. Shapiro?"

Now, you wouldn't believe how many people just *assume* that I'm a member of the force on the basis of my little introductory spiel. And while I have to admit that I don't make much of an effort to disabuse them of this conclusion, I back off from responding with an out-and-out lie. (Listen, picture what would happen if it were ever discovered that I went around impersonating a police officer.) "No," I admitted, "I'm a private investigator. I was hired by Gordon Curry himself two days prior to his death because he felt he was in imminent danger."

"Is this true? Gordon actually feared for his life? Oh, I didn't mean to imply—" Garber broke off, flustered. "I'm sure it *is* true. I don't understand why you've contacted *me,* though. Gordon and I weren't much more than nodding acquaintances—we'd run into each other two or three times a year at family celebrations and funerals, that type of thing. And sometimes he'd be around when I went to the house to pick up my son for the weekend, and we'd say a quick hello."

"Nevertheless, there are a couple of matters that I think you may be able to assist me with."

"I can't imagine what they could be. But go ahead. Ask me whatever you like."

"Um, it would be much better if we could do this in person."

"I'm afraid that isn't feasible. I'm extremely busy in the office at present."

"I won't keep you long. And naturally, we'd get together at your convenience."

"I suppose I *might* manage to give you a little time next week."

"Unfortunately, this can't wait, Mr. Garber, and I'd really be grateful for your input."

"But I don't know anything that could possibly be of help to you," he insisted.

"Maybe not. Then again, though, maybe you do. You'd be amazed at how often people are in possession of a piece of information holding no significance for them that subsequently ends up being vital to an investigation."

"I'm sure this doesn't apply in my case."

"That's what everybody thinks. Honestly."

"But—"

"We can make it whenever you say."

Garber caved. "All right," he responded wearily. "But this will have to be a very short meeting."

"I give you my word that it will be."

It turned out that Luke Garber worked in Manhattan, at an office only about five blocks from my own.

"Let's do it tomorrow. I have to be out in the afternoon, anyway—a dental appointment. I could stop by when I'm through. I'd guess that would be around three, three thirty. But remember, Ms. Shapiro, this has to be brief."

"Ten minutes is all I need," I assured him.

And, no, I wasn't the least bit embarrassed to say it, either.


I put up a pot of coffee, then dialed the Manhattan number Blossom had given me for the nurse who'd ministered to Gordon's deceased first wife and—if you chose to believe the rumors—attended to the needs of her husband, as well.

The answering machine picked up.

"This is Melanie Slater. I'm unable to take your call now. Please leave a message, and I'll get back to you soon. Thank you."

Of course, there was a chance that the woman was presently caring for a patient on a live-in basis—although, according to a telephone conversation Blossom had with Rhonda only last week, this was highly unlikely. During their chat, Rhonda happened to mention that her cousin had just come off a particularly draining case and that it was Melanie's intention to stay home and unwind for about a month.

Well, I'd try her again in the morning—and hope she hadn't changed her mind.


And now it was Danny's turn.

He answered on the first ring.

I began with my usual introduction, but I didn't get too far. "My name is Desiree Shapiro, and—"

"You're the private detective my father hired," the boy interjected. (I don't care *what* Blossom says; twenty-two is still a boy to me.)

"That's right. And I'm so sorry I wasn't able to do anything to—"

"It wasn't your fault, Ms. Shapiro. Aunt Blossom filled me in on the circumstances."

*Aunt* Blossom! That really brought back memories. In the very, *very* distant past, when I was a kid growing up in Ohio, my mother used to insist that any adult I came in contact with on an even semiregular basis had to be addressed as "Aunt" or "Uncle." She claimed it was only respectful. Sometimes my putting this edict into practice must have struck strangers as pretty peculiar, though. Especially when they heard me call Mrs. Chang, who owned the hand laundry around the corner, "Aunt Wendy," or Mrs. Washington, our next-door neighbor, "Aunt Leona."

Anyway, I continued to offer my regrets. "Still, I'd have given anything for things to have turned out differently."

"I know," Danny responded simply.

"Look, I'm not certain whether your aunt Blossom mentioned this, but I'm investigating your father's murder now, and I'd like to meet with you to go over a few things."

"Sure. Tomorrow my dad's being cremated." (I

thought I detected a slight quiver in his voice here.) "We could do it anytime on Thursday, though, if that's okay."

Well, it seemed that, unlike his stepmother, Danny wasn't in such a great big hurry to get back to work. I didn't know that this was even worth noting. But I noted it anyway.

"Could we possibly make it in the evening?" I asked, recalling my midday appointment with Rhonda and not having any idea of how long I'd be tied up. (And given a choice, why would I even consider scheduling something earlier than that?)

"No problem."

We arranged that Danny would be at my apartment at eight. And then, just as I was preparing to end the conversation, he said softly, "Ms. Shapiro?"

"Yes?"

"Please don't feel so bad about not being able to save my dad. No one else could have done any better than you did. Listen, with the kind of misinformation you got from him, Hercule Poirot would have flubbed it."

Now, although just a short while ago his stepmother, too, had given me absolution, I was touched by the sincerity of the boy's tone. I mean, he was actually *imploring* me to forgive myself. And it also didn't taint my impression of him to learn that, like me, Danny had the good taste to be an Agatha Christie fan.

*God! I hope he isn't the guilty one!* I thought, hanging up the phone.

# Chapter 18

How early did I have to vacate my nice warm bed on Wednesday? Let's put it this way: If I lived on a farm, I'd have been up in time to wake the rooster.

The thing is, when it comes to getting myself together in the morning (or at any hour of the day, actually), I'm not normally the fastest person in the world. But on those rare occasions when I have an appointment for an obscene eight a.m., well, compared to me, a tortoise is a speed freak. (Listen, it isn't easy to apply mascara when you're still brushing the sleepers from your eyes.) And add to this that I had to make two—count 'em, *two*—separate stops for those damn doughnuts.

But at any rate, I managed to arrive at the station house with a few minutes to spare.

Fielding got to his feet as soon as he spotted me and extended his hand when I reached his desk. Ignoring the hand, I deposited my two bags of goodies on the one small section of desk that was free of manila folders, loose papers, pens, pencils, paper clips, gum wrappers, and other assorted paraphernalia. Then I enveloped him in an enthusiastic hug.

"Christ, Shapiro, you've gotta cut out that kinda stuff; it could land you in trouble," he cautioned, breaking away. It was said in jest, but a pink flush betrayed his embarrassment. (Which I have to admit I enjoyed.)

He jerked his thumb in the direction of the wooden chair alongside the desk. "You may as well sit," was the gracious way he put it. I struggled out of my coat and plunked my derriere where indicated. Then, as he was returning to his own chair, Fielding called out to the fellow occupying the desk directly in front of his, "Hey, Norm, guess who's here."

Detective Norm Melnick swiveled around, grinned, and came over to shake my hand. "It's nice to see you again, Desiree."

Not only is Detective Melnick attractive—around thirty and medium tall, with clean-cut, boyish good looks—but he has lovely manners, besides. Best of all, though, he isn't Walter Corcoran, the guy Fielding was previously paired with. I mean, Corcoran used to make my skin crawl. The only consolation: I had the same effect on him.

"Desiree's brought refreshments," Fielding apprised his partner.

The younger man grinned. "Great!"

I removed three Styrofoam cups from the larger bag. Fielding reached for one with a *B* scrawled on the lid, and I handed the other of these to Melnick. "I don't know how you take your coffee, so I got you a black, with milk and sweeteners on the side."

"Black's fine. If it's good enough for my uncle Tim, here, it's good enough for me."

" 'Uncle Tim,' your ass," Fielding grumbled good-naturedly.

"I recalled your mentioning your favorite kind of doughnut the last time I stopped by," I told Norm, presenting him with the smaller bag. "Here. A few Krispy Kremes—glazed. Plain, no jelly, as specified."

"Gee, thanks," he said, obviously pleased. "This is really nice of you. I can't believe you remembered something like that."

"I warned you once before, Norm; you have to watch out for this woman," Fielding pronounced. "She makes sure she doesn't forget that sort of thing—probably writes it down. Then she uses it to soften you up. And if you're not careful, before you know it she's pumping you dry."

I didn't deign to refute this foul accusation. And Norm Melnick didn't respond to it, either. Very likely because his mouth was so full of Krispy Kreme.

"Anyway, you'd better stick around for a while," Fielding instructed him. "Desiree insists she has something important to share with us, and you should probably hear whatever it is." The young detective nodded (his mouth still otherwise occupied) and went to get his chair. When he rejoined us seconds later, Tim had already dipped into the goody bag himself, predictably fishing out one of the doughnuts with chocolate icing and walnut sprinkles. "Just give us a couple of seconds, huh?" he put to Melnick as he passed me the bag.

And now Fielding and I took time out for a decent-sized sampling of our respective choices (mine was a tasty little number with strawberry icing), and then we both had a couple of healthy swallows of coffee. Following this, Fielding wiped his mouth and focused his eyes on my face. "Am I correct in stating that you don't believe the individual we have in custody is this Roger Clyne you mentioned on the phone?"

"Yes, you are."

"Why is that?"

"As I believe I said on the phone, I've never met Clyne. But the description in the newspaper doesn't match up with how he was described to me." I could only hope this would be enough to satisfy the man—for now, at least.

It wasn't.

"No? In what way?"

Suddenly the back of my neck felt as if it were on

fire, and my palms were so wet that the strawberry doughnut almost slipped from my grasp. The thing is, I hadn't a clue as to Clyne's physical appearance. Even if I did, though, it wouldn't have helped. I had to make it sound as if he bore no resemblance whatsoever to that fellow the police had arrested. Only I had no idea what *he* looked like, either. I mean, the article in the *Post* hadn't gone into that type of detail.

"We-ell . . ." I was frantically rooting around in my brain for some kind of response when Fielding, impatient for more substantive information, unwittingly let me off the hook.

"So how does this guy Clyne fit into things, anyway?" he demanded, right before having another bite of pastry.

*WHEW!* "He worked under Gordon for a short while. At McReedy and Emerson—the pharmaceutical company."

"When was this?"

"A little over a year ago."

"There was some problem between them?"

"Clyne behaved unethically, and Gordon had to fire him."

"And your client believed this was the reason Clyne was trying to waste him?"

"There's more. Roger Clyne went to see Gordon only about three months back. He hadn't been able to find other employment, and he begged to be rehired. You see, since losing his job, Roger's life had pretty much come apart. He was struggling financially. His wife had walked out on him. And it's likely he was also into drugs. All of which he attributed to his having been terminated from McReedy and Emerson.

"At any rate, in light of what had transpired when Roger was previously with the company, Gordon didn't feel he could consider putting him on the payroll again. So he turned him down—very regretfully, I should add. And Clyne went berserk. He screamed that Gordon would be sorry—stuff like that. It wasn't long after this that there were two attempts on Gordon Curry's life."

"Exactly what was the nature of those attempts?"

I told him about the incidents in the Poconos.

Tim frowned. "Curry was sure these weren't accidents?"

"He was positive. Don't forget they occurred within a week of each other."

"But he didn't actually see the perpetrator either time?"

"No."

"Still, he had no doubt that Roger Clyne was responsible in both cases?"

"That's right. I should tell you this about Gordon— and I didn't realize it until after the murder. He was a man who was so used to getting by on his charm that I don't believe he ever gave any serious thought to how an action of his might have affected someone. Don't misunderstand me. It wasn't that he was callous—not from the impression I got of him, anyway. It wasn't that he didn't _care_. The way I see it, he was just so self-absorbed that he tended to be oblivious to other people's responses."

"In other words, he was an ass," Fielding supplied.

"I wouldn't say that," I retorted, astonished at how defensive I sounded. "It's simply that Gordon probably wasn't always as sensitive as he might have been. Anyhow, along comes Roger Clyne. And although in this instance what Gordon did was definitely justified, there was no way he could fail to recognize the fact that Roger held him responsible for his current ills. Not in view of the man's violent behavior that afternoon. Ergo, in Gordon's mind, it had to be Clyne up there in the Poconos."

"All of a sudden we've become a real little psychiatrist, haven't we?" Fielding commented sarcastically.

"Well, it makes sense. Listen, as I've already indicated to you, my client doesn't seem to have produced bitter feelings in his former employee alone. But Gordon chose not to admit—and I'm talking about even to himself—that anybody else might be nurturing the sort of hostility toward him that could result in his death."

"And you're of the opinion that one of the individuals Curry antagonized had some involvement with John Smith."

"I suspect that's a possibility. Let me explain. Gordon and his cousin—the one who requested that I continue with my investigation—were very close. And she's aware of a handful of people who might have had it in for him. But she has no knowledge of Gordon's having alienated a white, thirty-something male. And she's quite sure that if there'd been anything like that, she'd have heard about it. That's what led to our independently arriving at the theory that Mr. X had a collaborator."

Fielding tilted his head to one side. "Then I gather Roger Clyne isn't a white, thirty-something male."

It was a good long moment before I was able to locate my voice. "His cousin was . . . um . . . referring to someone *besides* Roger," I mumbled, feeling as if I were picking my way across a minefield. "She was, uh, satisfied that Roger isn't the guy in the newspaper."

"But she *does* consider him one of that handful you mentioned who might have had something to do with Curry's murder?"

I gave silent thanks to the powers that be that Fielding hadn't asked what had led the cousin to conclude that the man in the article was someone other than Clyne. After which I managed to avoid giving a direct response to the question he *had* put to me. "Roger Clyne wasn't exactly one of Gordon's biggest fans." (Well, it wasn't a lie, was it?)

"I'm ready now for that list of names you said you had for me," Fielding declared at this juncture.

"One minute. We're supposed to pool our information, right? And I've just provided you with the details regarding the dispute between my client and the man he believed was out for his blood. So now it's your turn."

Fielding looked over at his partner, who'd been silent for so long he was almost like a nonpresence. "You've been treated to a classic example of chutzpah, Norm. Desiree here must have forgotten about all the questions she peppered me with over the phone—the majority of which I was obliging enough to answer."

Melnick smiled. "Go easy on her, Tim. She does bring us good doughnuts."

"Christ," Fielding muttered. "All it takes to buy your goodwill is a couple of goddam Krispy Kremes."

Melnick, still smiling, shrugged. "Guilty."

"I apologize, Tim," I put in hurriedly. "You're right. You *were* pretty forthcoming. Only I'd like to know if you've learned anything at all about Mr. X."

"Such as?"

"Well, I don't imagine you've found out his name yet, but—"

"That's your story."

"He finally told you who he is?"

"You've gotta be kidding."

"Then how did you ID him?"

"I don't see any reason for not enlightening you on that one. Maybe you'll learn something. So pay attention, Shapiro.

"Okay. We figured there was at least a fair chance the guy had traveled to the area in a car or truck and that it might be worthwhile to act on that premise. In the event you've never noticed, in Chelsea we're big on parking restrictions. So our guys scoured the neighborhood for violations—just in case. The license plate numbers of any illegally parked autos were passed on to Motor Vehicles, and we had them fax us the driver's licenses of the registrants. The licenses came in late yesterday afternoon."

"And?" I said impatiently.

"We went through the photos. And guess what."

"You've got yourself a match."

"That we do. The owner of a black 2001 Nissan Altima is our Mr. X—as you like to call him—right down to the mole on his cheek. Seems his automobile was occupying a space that had to be vacated by eight a.m. Monday. However, for obvious reasons, Mr. X was in no position to comply." Looking quite pleased (for him), Fielding tilted his chair back now and clasped his hands behind his head.

"Uh, I'd appreciate his name, Tim. Maybe I can help you establish a link between him and Gordon—or else somebody who knew Gordon."

"As my neighbor's kid would say, 'Chill.' We're not prepared to release that information yet."

"I certainly wouldn't give it to the media, if that's what you're concerned about."

Tim's tone was emphatic. "The answer's still no."

I dropped the subject, fully intending to revisit it later and see if I could wear the man down then. In the meantime, I wanted to keep things amiable. "Well, anyway, things seem to be moving along."

In a flash, Fielding's mood changed. "Sure they are—at a crawl." And scowling, he righted his chair.

"What's wrong?"

There was silence for two, maybe three seconds. Then a ray of light entered my dim little brain. "The gun. You don't have the gun." It wasn't a question.

"Bingo," he grunted. "And believe me, we've gone over every inch of that area, from the spot where the weapon was discharged to where the perpetrator was apprehended."

"It'll turn up." It was the kind of Pollyannaish pronouncement worthy of Ellen, but I didn't know what else to say.

"Yeah, when? Right now, we have nothing solid to tie the suspect to the homicide. So far he's behind bars for resisting arrest and assaulting an officer. But Greg Flippin's black-and-blue shin will only keep Mr. X—or whatever you want to call him—out of circulation for ninety days. *Ninety days!*" He shook his head in disgust. "Three effin' months for blasting some guy to kingdom come!"

"I suppose none of the card players was able to ID Mr. X as the shooter?"

"No. The brownstone's outside light was switched on when the group was leaving. So that section was well lit—perfect, in fact, for picking off the victim. But there wasn't much illumination on the other side of the street."

Melnick chimed in here. "Besides, once the bullets began to fly, everyone scrambled for cover. After talking to those men, we didn't have to bother with a lineup."

"Did the suspect ever give you a reason he was in the neighborhood?"

"Oh, sure," Melnick responded. "He says he'd been to a jazz club in Greenwich Village to hear some group called the Low Downs—his favorites. And afterward he thought he'd take a little drive over to West Twenty-first Street and check out the block again. Claims he was considering renting an apartment in a building about six doors away from the brownstone. He was even carrying the *New York Times* classified ad for the place in his jacket pocket."

"You're kidding."

"Most likely he came across the ad in the *Times* and designed his cover story around it—in the highly improbable event he'd need an excuse for being around there. Which, as it turned out, he did."

"This was the only piece of paper on him, too," Fielding interjected, "because he *happened* to leave his wallet at home in his other pants."

"He had everything all worked out, didn't he?" I remarked.

Sucking in his cheeks, Tim nodded. "You bet he did. Right down to filling us in on the numbers the band played that night. But his being at the club then doesn't mean zilch. Who's to say that after a couple of hours of music appreciation he didn't sashay out of there and go plug your client?"

"I read in the *Post* that Mr. X's story is that he only ran from the crime scene because the two police officers were chasing him."

"Yeah. According to him, he heard the shots and witnessed the mayhem across the street, and he was afraid they'd collar him for something he didn't do. Naturally, though, he didn't see the shooter. And—also naturally—he himself doesn't own a weapon and wouldn't know how to fire one if he did. What's more, he'd never so much as *heard* of Gordon Curry before he was accused of murdering him."

Tim's phone rang at this moment. He mumbled an "Excuse me" and lifted the receiver.

Almost as soon as he began talking, I had a question for Melnick. "It was fortunate you were able to identify the perp through his car, Norm. But what if he'd been local and had used the subway Sunday night—or even come to the neighborhood on foot?" I asked this not because I was particularly anxious for the answer—I could have predicted it—but mostly to engage the man in conversation while we waited for Fielding to end his telephone call.

Melnick gave me a boyish grin. "We would have been pot out of luck."

This topic evidently exhausted, I had to reach for another one. I threw out the next thing that occurred to me. "It's a shame Gordon's buddies weren't able to get a good look at the killer."

"Yeah, it would have—"

"Okay, you can lay off my partner," Fielding cut in as he was hanging up the phone. His face was stern, but there was a playfulness in his voice. "What's she been pestering you with, Norm?"

"Nothing, really. She's been remarkably well behaved." (From this little snippet you might have figured they were referring to something on four legs with a tail.)

"Glad to hear it." Immediately following this, Fielding made a show of checking his watch. "Christ! Do you know what time it is?" And now he turned his full attention to me. "As much as we've enjoyed your company, Norm and I do have some other business to take care of. And I'm sure there are a few things you need to attend to yourself. So why don't you tell us about those individuals you allege had a motive for knocking off the victim, and we can call it a day."

And with this, he pulled a lined yellow pad from his top drawer and laid hands on a pen. Then putting pen to paper with a flourish, he said firmly, "Okay, Shapiro. I'm listening."

# Chapter 19

In order to oblige Fielding, I would need my address book, which was buried in my handbag somewhere. Most likely at the bottom. Since there wasn't enough space on Fielding's desk to accommodate even a fraction of the items I tote around with me, I dumped the bag's entire contents on the floor—the stapler landing squarely on my big toe.

When I finally had the address book in hand and had shoveled all the other items back into my pocketbook, I looked up to see my old friend rolling his eyes heavenward. "I was hoping we could get on with this before I took my retirement," he remarked testily. "Now, what have you got for me?"

"Well, according to my source—"

"This is the cousin?"

"Uh-huh. She told me about a tragedy that had occurred this past winter. It seems that Gordon was taking his stepson skiing—both Gordon and his wife had been married before, you know. Anyhow, on the way up to Vermont, they had this horrific accident—the car crashed into a tree. Unfortunately, the boy was critically injured; he died a few weeks later. The crackup wasn't anyone's fault—the road conditions were terrible that day—but Gordon *was* driving. And for a while Rhonda blamed him for her loss. But then she came to appreciate that he was suffering, too, and they worked things out. At least, that's the impression people got. But we can't be sure of how she actually felt, can we?"

"The woman didn't appear to be too shaken up when we broke the news of the shooting to her," Fielding commented as he made some notes on his pad. "But that doesn't really mean anything."

"I imagine you've spoken to Gordon's son, too," I said.

"That's right. Anything about him we should know?"

"Only that for a time Chip—the stepson—was, through no fault of his own, the cause of a strain in the relationship between father and son. Apparently, Danny was under the impression Gordon preferred Chip to him." It was due to a certain fondness for this young man I'd never even met that I immediately threw in, "Of course, that was when Danny was much younger. Most likely he put all that behind him ages ago."

"Maybe," Fielding mumbled, scribbling on the pad again. After which he eyed me expectantly. "What else have you got?"

"Well, there was some gossip that when Gordon was married to wife number one, who'd been seriously ill for years, he was having a thing with her live-in nurse."

"What do you mean, 'a thing'? Spit it out! Nursie and the victim were having an affair. And while his wife was terminally ill, too."

"It was just talk, Tim. Nobody knows this for a fact."

Fielding paid no attention to the disclaimer. "Some caregiver *she* was. And as for your client, he was a real prince, Shapiro."

"Like I keep telling you, it was a *rumor*. But whether it was true or not, from what I understand the nurse was still pretty unhappy when Gordon took himself a new bride five years ago, about six months after Edith—his first wife—passed away."

"Let me ask you something. Was Curry's son close to his mother?"

"I don't really know."

"Well, do you think he was aware of what was being said about his father and this nurse?"

It didn't take a Rhodes scholar to see what Tim was getting at. But while I couldn't deny that it was possible Danny had been convinced his father was playing house during Edith's illness, it just didn't make sense that he'd wait this long to have him shot for it. And I said as much.

"What about the woman your client supposedly threw over?" he put to me. "Does it seem likely to you that that nurse would twiddle her thumbs all this time before taking *her* revenge?" Frowning, he shook his head. "The motives of both these people have whiskers."

Suddenly Norm—who hadn't been heard from in so long that I started at the sound of his voice—made an observation. "Something might have happened fairly recently to set one of them off, though."

"I guess it's not inconceivable," Fielding conceded. And to me: "The woman's name?"

"Umm, there's a small problem. Naturally, I jotted down all the particulars, but I couldn't find my notebook at that moment, so I used a piece of paper. And unfortunately, I've not only misplaced the damn paper, but I can't recall the name."

I felt entirely justified in telling that teeny lie. I mean, whenever it's feasible, I try to conduct my interviews in advance of the police, since people have a tendency to balk when—after they've been thoroughly interrogated by the NYPD—I show up and ask them to rehash all that stuff. (And I can't say I blame them.)

At any rate, there was a certain amount of skepticism on Fielding's face, but he didn't comment.

"It has to be at home somewhere—the paper, that is," I assured him. "I'll give you a call as soon as I find it."

"Never mind. I can get the information from your source. You'd better let me have the name of that cousin of Curry's, while I think of it."

"It's Blossom Goody."

"The lawyer?"

"Do you know her?"

"Only well enough to say that she's the one individual who's got a disposition even sweeter than yours."

I batted my eyelashes. "You're too kind, Tim."

"Her telephone number, if you don't mind?"

It took maybe three seconds for me to decide that I'd supply Tim with Blossom's office number—and only her office number. From what was, granted, my limited experience with the lady in question, I didn't think it too likely that she'd be showing up at work much before noon. In the meantime, I should be able to reach her at her apartment and ask that she tell Fielding I was mistaken, that she wasn't the one who'd provided me with the information on Gordon's former sweetie—*alleged* former sweetie, I mean. That, in fact, she had no idea who I was referring to.

"You have a home telephone number for Goody?" Tim inquired after I'd recited the office number.

"I'm afraid not."

"Okay. Let me have the rest of your suspects."

I instantly made up my mind to refrain from mentioning Luke Garber—for the same reason I wanted to keep Melanie Slater under wraps at present. Besides, I assumed that Tim would get around to questioning the father of Rhonda's dead son without any help from me. I mean, if Chip had a male parent around somewhere—and it should be simple enough for Fielding to ascertain that he did—the father would have the same motive for murder that the boy's mother had.

"There is no 'rest,'" I informed him.

And now came the moment I'd been dreading since I walked into the place. Leaning toward me, Fielding said, "I suppose you realize that you haven't told me yet how I can reach Roger Clyne."

Of course, I'd been expecting that he'd get around to this sooner or later. What I hadn't anticipated was that my throat would begin to constrict when he did. Well, I had no choice now but to own up to my deception before I became completely paralyzed with anxiety. "Uh, the thing is, Tim"—I eked out a sickly smile here—"Roger Clyne is . . . well . . ."—I moistened my lower lip with my tongue—"he's . . . um, not . . . that is, he's dead."

Fielding's eyes narrowed. "When did he die?"

"In September," I responded weakly.

"It was *before* those assaults in the Poconos?"

I could only nod.

I was watching his face, and trust me, purple is definitely not Tim Fielding's color. "I don't believe this!" he roared. "You persuade me to see you by coming up with some cock-and-bull story about the victim's suspecting that this Clyne was out to do him. But after Norm and I give you more than an hour of our time—which, incidentally, is in very short supply—we learn that you left out the punch line. What's the matter, Shapiro? Did you just *forget* to mention that Clyne is now fertilizer?"

I shuddered at the metaphor. "Please try to understand. It was just that I—"

"You *lied* your way in here!"

"I didn't actually lie—I left out something. But that's because I thought it was so important that we talk, and this was the only way I could think of to induce you to meet with me."

"Fine. But you'd better leave now. You've worn out your welcome—permanently."

Standing up, I rested my palms on the desk, mostly because I regarded it as a pretty iffy proposition that my legs would be able to support me. "You can't imagine how bad I feel," I said, close to tears. (It may not be very professional for PIs to cry, but every so often us wimpy ones can't seem to help it.) "Our jobs aside, Tim, I truly value your friendship."

"Bull," he muttered. But I was almost positive his tone had softened a bit.

"I apologize," I went on. I glanced up at Melnick, who had gotten to his feet moments after I did. "And I also apologize to you, Norm. I still say my reason for coming here was a good one—collaborating like this is our best chance to nail Gordon's killer. But I have to admit that my method was a little underhanded."

Fielding nodded. "It sucked."

"You're right. It did."

"Maybe I overreacted, though," he conceded grudgingly. And rising, he gave my arm a couple of awkward pats.

"You're not mad at me anymore?"

"I wouldn't go that far. Just be satisfied that I no longer have designs on your jugular."

This lighter, less threatening tone warmed my heart. And while I still didn't think I'd have the courage (or the nerve, depending on your point of view) to make any kind of request at this point, I managed to make one anyway.

"Uh, before I go, maybe you'll reconsider letting me in on the identity of the man you have in custody. Keep in mind that I spent some time with my client, and he may even have spoken of this man in passing."

"You don't really believe that, do you?" Fielding put to me.

I didn't dare level with him. "It *is* possible."

"Yeah. And so's my winning the lottery. Listen, Shapiro, why don't you drag your tush outta here before I have second thoughts about your jugular."

# Chapter 20

I was feeling so lousy after my meeting with Fielding that I pretty much *slunk* into the office that morning. I was about to pass Jackie's desk with no more than a nod when she looked up.

"Somebody named Luke Garber phoned a few minutes ago." She thrust a pink slip in my direction, then immediately drew it back and, while looking it over, recited the contents. "He won't be able to see you today. He's come down with the flu or something—he even had to cancel his dental appointment. He'll be in touch with you as soon as he's better." And here she finally elected to release the slip to my custody.

Well, call me ungrateful, but I don't exactly feel beholden to Jackie for sparing me the trouble of having to read my messages for myself—which she's liable to do as often as not. And I'm particularly unappreciative when I'm not too crazy about what these messages contain. Like now.

I hissed my thanks.

"Wait," she ordered as I started to turn away. "Sergeant Fielding called, too. He wants you to get back to him."

I ran (well, my version of running, at any rate) to my cubbyhole. I was still breathless when I dialed the number.

"It's me," I told Fielding after he'd barked out his name.

"Yeah. Well, listen, *me*. Norm and I had a talk when you left. He tells me I was too rough on you. Now, considering what you pulled, from where I sit, I wasn't rough enough. In fact, I censored myself—you should have heard what I *wanted* to say. But it's probably better that you didn't.

"Anyhow, Norm reminded me that you did share a couple of leads with us. And that got me thinking. From past experience, I have no doubt that you'll be sticking your nose into the business of everyone connected with the case. And this is where your not being a cop could have its advantages. People are less likely to be guarded when—instead of having to deal with an officer of the law—they're schmoozing with someone who prances around with dimpled knees and dyed red hair."

Believe me, I would have taken exception to this characterization if I'd felt I was in a position to. I mean, I don't go around showing my knees (although they might occasionally be visible when I'm seated—or if I happen to be outside in a strong wind). And my hair certainly isn't dyed. As any reputable colorist can tell you, only Egyptian henna produces such a glorious shade of red. Plus, I definitely do not *prance!*

"So it's possible you'll learn something relevant," Fielding went on. "Maybe you'll even come across the shooter's name."

"If I'm supposed to recognize it, first you'll have to tell me what it is," I pointed out.

"Don't be such a smart-ass; I'm getting to that. The name is Francis Lonergan. Not Frank, mind you—Francis. He's from a small town upstate. He's the brother of Little Jimmy Lonergan, and Big Jim Lonergan's his cousin. Do those last two names ring a bell?"

"Well, no," I had to admit.

"Between them, those beauts have been arrested

for murder on half a dozen occasions. Big Jim was even sent to prison for doing some politician out in Utah, but the conviction was later overturned on a technicality. Little Jimmy was tried twice here in New York and acquitted in both instances—once because this bleeding-heart judge ruled two key pieces of evidence inadmissible."

"So Francis *is* a hit man, then."

"Hit man, professional assassin, whatever you want to call him. Our guy's in the family business, all right."

"Uh, I imagine you informed him that he'd been ID'd."

"You do, do you? That's the last thing we'd want him to know. Obviously, the guy's been trying to conceal his identity. And why is that, do you suppose?" Fielding answered his own question. "Because he's afraid that if we find out who his relatives are, we'll be even less apt to buy into his story about being an innocent passerby than we are now. Which I'm certain is the reason he settled for having a public defender represent him on the assault charge. But once *he's* aware that *we're* aware of who he is, the perp has nothing to lose by bringing in the high-priced mouthpiece who normally represents the members of that upstanding family. And, of course, Grinkoff—that's the attorney's name, Sebastian Grinkoff—would attempt to get the ruling against his client overturned—or at least have that ninety-day sentence reduced."

"What are the chances he could do that?"

"Let's put it this way. I wouldn't want to make book that he couldn't. He might claim, for example, that Lonergan was inadequately represented by his previous counsel. Or that he didn't realize the men chasing him were police officers, because they failed to identify themselves. But I'm no lawyer. Who can predict what Grinkoff could come up with?"

"You feel that he'd probably be successful, though."

"I have no idea. And to tell you the truth, I'd rather not find out. There isn't a doubt in my mind that Lonergan shot Gordon Curry to death. But if Grinkoff appears before the right judge, he might be able to cut down on the time his client has to serve on that assault business. And Lonergan could then head for parts unknown before we've had an opportunity to establish a case against him." I heard a sharp intake of breath now. And when Fielding spoke again, his voice was strained. "Of course, without the murder weapon . . ." The sentence was left unfinished.

"It could still turn up."

"So I've been attempting to convince myself," he muttered.

"Look, Tim, I really appreciate your sharing that name with me."

"Yeah. If you learn anything, though, don't play games. Let me know right away. And keep in mind that this conversation is strictly confidential."

"I will. I promise."

"And Desiree, you watch your back, got me? What I'm saying is, find out what you can, but don't try being a hero—you don't have the build for it. If there's even the slightest chance you might wind up in trouble, call me immediately." (See? And you didn't believe he liked me!)

"Thanks, Tim, I will," I responded, so touched by his concern that I began to feel a little guilty. I mean, in light of what I was about to do next.

# Chapter 21

Blossom's "Hello" was preceded by only one mild little cough into the phone.

"It's Desiree," I told her. "I'm so glad I got you."

"What's up?"

"A few minutes ago I came back from a meeting with the two detectives in charge of Gordon's case, and they asked for your telephone number. I gave them just the office number—I was hoping I could catch you at home before they had a chance to talk to you."

"About what?"

"The thing is, I wanted to find out where the police investigation stood—incidentally they're still floundering around, too. But at any rate, in order to pry anything out of those two, I had to offer something in return. I told them you'd mentioned a rumor concerning an affair between Gordon and Edith's nurse— but I claimed I'd forgotten the woman's name. I'm fairly positive they'll be contacting you about this, and I'd like you to say that you can't remember the name, either. And that, anyhow, you're not aware of any affair, so my information must have come from someone else." And here I went into my rationale for the deception.

"You got a point there, Shapiro," Blossom agreed in a voice that wasn't quite familiar to me. "It would be better if you could be the first to question her."

"Oh, and I also avoided any mention of Luke for the same reason."

"Gotcha. The cops won't hear about him from me."

It was at this moment that, being the perceptive creature I am, I realized for the first time that Blossom was close to tears. "Is anything wrong, Blossom?"

"You could say that. I'm getting dressed right now to attend the memorial service for Gordie, and all of a sudden it's almost like it was when I first got the news he was dead. It's really tough to accept that he's gone for good, Shapiro. He was a true friend. When El Creepo—sometimes referred to as my former husband—took off with his prepubescent little girlfriend, Gordie was there for me. Fact is, I'm not sure he ever spoke to Leonard after that. And the two men were palsy-walsy till then—Leonard was Edie's first cousin."

"Leonard is your ex, I take it."

"Right. Funny, isn't it?" she remarked tremulously—just prior to breaking down in earnest.

It must have been close to a minute before the woman was able to compose herself. "Sorry, kiddo," she murmured, following a brief time-out to blow her nose. "I didn't mean to do that."

"Please. Don't apologize. I know how fond you were of Gordon."

"No, you don't. But what did I want to say before I was so rudely interrupted by me?" She managed a faint little chuckle. "Oh, yeah. I was about to comment on how some people might consider it ironic that Gordie reacted like that to my being dumped. I mean, the ones who believed all the gossip about his not always being Mr. Faithful himself."

"He—"

"Listen, gotta get ready for that damn memorial thing, so I'd better hang up."

And without another word, that's what she did.

\*     \*     \*

Blossom now forewarned, I buzzed Jackie. "If Tim Fielding should call again, I'm not in, and you don't know when I'll be back, but you'll take a message. Okay?"

"Fine. What's going on, though?"

"He wants some information from me that I'm not ready to give him."

"What— Oh, hell. I've got another call. Talk to you later."

Sometimes I do get lucky.

It was well past eleven at this point, so I figured this would probably be a good time to try Melanie Slater. Even if I hadn't been thoroughly occupied before now, I'd have hesitated about phoning her any earlier. If she'd recently wrapped up a particularly grueling case, it was likely that one of her priorities would be catching up on her sleep.

Apparently I figured wrong. There was no one to communicate with at Melanie's apartment this morning but the answering machine—which repeated the same message it had foisted on me yesterday.

I slammed down the receiver.

Except for my frequent attempts to reach the elusive Melanie and the short recess I took to wolf down a BLT at my desk, I spent most of the afternoon typing up my notes. By around twenty to five, though, I'd had it. I could barely see what was on the computer screen anymore. Which is what comes of a person's evacuating her bed at an hour when more social types haven't even hit the pillow yet.

I waved good night as I passed Jackie's desk—but escape wasn't that easy. "So, Desiree," she called out after me, "about Sunday night . . ." And retracing my steps, I foolishly allowed her to draw me into another unwelcome dialogue about what I should be serving Nick for dinner.

It seemed that Jackie had made up her mind to the

orange chicken with almonds, while I was pretty much set on the boeuf bourguignon. In fact, I tried to impress upon her that I'd already planned the rest of the meal around the beef dish. Actually, though, I was simply digging my heels in. The hors d'oeuvres I'd decided on—wild-mushroom croustades (I had made plenty of extras when I prepared them for Ellen's visit the other night), along with a variety of cheeses—went just as well with chicken as they did with meat. Ditto the dessert—which I'd narrowed down to either a chilled lemon soufflé or a chocolate mousse flavored with Grand Marnier. Anyhow, one good thing: Jackie had to content herself with merely putting in her two cents on the entrée. Because Elliot Gilbert summoned her for dictation before she could tackle the rest of the menu.

Immediately after coming home from work, I had a sixth go at reaching Melanie Slater. (And yes, I was counting.)

I was so thrown when I realized the "Hello" on the other end of the line hadn't been produced by a machine that for a moment I had trouble stringing a few coherent words together.

"Hello?" the voice said again, only a little louder now.

"Miss Slater?"

"That's right."

I rattled off the usual introduction. "My name is Desiree Shapiro, Miss Slater. I'm a private investigator, and I've been engaged to look into the murder of Gordon Curry."

"Yes, Rhonda—his wife—told me about that. Is it true that the man who was arrested may have been . . . *hired* to do the shooting?" The question was posed tentatively, in a small, thin voice.

"I can't say anything definite yet. Hopefully, we'll

have a better fix on his involvement once we have a chance to speak to Mr. Curry's family and acquaintances. Which brings me to the purpose of this call, Miss Slater. I'd appreciate it if you could meet with me for a few minutes. There are a couple of details I'd like to check out with you."

"With me? But why? I have no idea what went on in Gordie's life—except for a mention from Rhonda every once in a while. And it was never about anything important."

"Still, you were related to him."

"By marriage, Ms. Shapiro—and just barely, too. Rhonda's only my second cousin."

"I understand you lived with Gordon and his first wife before she died."

"Yes, I was her nurse. But that was years ago. Nowadays—well, I can't remember the last time Gordie and I even had a conversation."

"Nevertheless, I believe you might be able to clarify some matters for me."

"I swear to you, I'd be *eager* to sit down with you if there was the slightest chance I could be of help. But there isn't."

"You can't be sure of that, Miss Slater." And I went through the drill about people often knowing more than they think they do.

"That isn't the case here; take my word for it. And I'm truly not up to being interrogated—not when it wouldn't serve any purpose."

"I wouldn't be 'interrogating' you, as you put it. It's just that I could use your perspective on certain issues."

"Listen, a couple of weeks ago a thirty-three-year-old patient of mine—a wonderful lady I'd been caring for these last ten months—passed away. No one—not even the specialists who were recently brought in to evaluate her condition—expected that. They estimated that Sissy had another year, maybe longer. But now her eight-year-old twins—the cutest little boys you'd ever want to see—are suddenly without their mother.

"I was very fond of Sissy McCann, Ms. Shapiro. The truth is—and this will sound terribly corny—she'd become like a sister to me. And her death really rocked me. Right now I'm as depressed as I've ever been in my life. I'm also totally exhausted. And I'm just not going to be bullied into doing something that doesn't make sense."

"I don't mean to bully you, Miss Slater. And I do sympathize with how you feel, honestly. Nevertheless—"

"I'm sorry, but I'm going to have to turn you down."

Well, I couldn't let her wriggle off the hook like that, could I? So on the spot I came up with a little ruse that I thought might persuade Melanie to reconsider. And while I was relying on a misstatement (okay, lie), I refused to allow this to deter me. Not with so much at stake.

"Look, in view of my professional relationship with Gordon Curry, the police and I are working closely together on this investigation—something, by the way, that happens very infrequently. Anyhow, this means that you'll either have to talk to me or to them." Of course, it wouldn't have been an either-or kind of thing, even in the unprecedented event that this had been a truly cooperative undertaking. Whether she agreed to see me or not, the woman suspected of being Gordon's ex-lover could look forward to a session with the cops. Nonetheless, a threat often works. (Although it's been my experience that at least as often, it doesn't.)

"This is silly," Melanie responded. "Rhonda and I aren't only distantly related; we're also close friends. So you can be certain that if I knew anything that could contribute to solving her husband's murder, you wouldn't have had to contact me; I'd have gotten in touch with *you*."

"I don't doubt that. But as I've been trying to make clear, it's quite possible you have no idea of the relevance of some of the facts in your possession. It's up to you, though. If you'd feel more comfortable speaking to a homicide detective, that's fine, too."

I held my breath. *Would she call my bluff?*

"Can we set up an appointment for Friday?" Melanie asked.

*Gulp.* "Sure. What time would you like to make it?"

"Is two o'clock okay?"

"Perfect." I gave her my office address.

"All right. I'll see you then."

She sounded as if she'd been forced to swallow a heaping spoonful of cod-liver oil.

# Chapter 22

I spent the next few minutes congratulating myself on having wangled Melanie into meeting with me. It meant that in a couple of days I'd have the opportunity to question all of my suspects.

Before long, though, a disturbing thought attempted to strong-arm its way into my head. I closed my mind to it at once. I wasn't going to ruin this rare, if brief, euphoria with some sensible words of caution. Like reminding myself that Gordon's murderer might not even have made it onto my list.

It was close to seven when I started fixing supper, which would feature what Ellen refers to as one of my "refrigerator omelets," so named because it contains virtually every edible item in my refrigerator. (And quite often one or two that might be in dispute.) Tonight's version was going to include some ham, a small piece of red pepper, tomato, scallions, a few mushrooms, and a tiny chunk of Gruyère (which was all that was left after I'd cut away the mold). Anyhow, I was busy chopping and slicing when the phone rang.

"Hi," Nick said.

"Well, hi to you, too," I caught myself simpering. (I hate it when I do that!) Worse yet, though, I realized I was unconsciously patting my hair, besides.

"How are you, Dez?"

"I'm fine. You?"

"I've been pretty busy. But, hey, I'm not complaining; busy's good. And, speaking of that, what about you? Any interesting new cases?"

I groaned. "I do have a new case, but I wouldn't refer to it as 'interesting.' 'Aggravating,' 'nerve-racking,' 'depressing'—even 'mortifying'—would be more like it."

"I'm sorry to hear that. Still, it *does* sound interesting."

"I guess," I conceded.

"Maybe I can convince you to tell me about it on Sunday."

"I'll give you a quick summary."

"Deal. In the meantime, I have a question. What would you like me to bring Sunday night?"

"Yourself will do nicely."

"Well, thanks—thanks very much, in fact—but I can at least supply the wine. Would you prefer red or white?"

"Neither."

"Good. I'll bring both."

"Listen, Nick, I *have* both. Honestly."

"That's no problem. You can save them for another time. And why don't I spare you some trouble and pick something up for dessert?"

"Don't even think about doing that. I already shopped for the ingredients for our dessert." (I threw in an "Honestly" here, too, since I do feel it lends a bit of credence to a lie, don't you?)

"All right. If you're sure . . . By the way, when do you want me there?"

"Whenever you can make it."

"How is seven thirty?"

"Perfect."

"Oh, and Dez?"

"Yes?"

"I'm looking forward to seeing you. I've missed you."

I was seriously considering whether to respond with,

"I've missed you, too." But I required more than the few seconds that remained of our conversation to make up my mind about taking such a courageous step.

So the option was soon moot.

# Chapter 23

On Thursday, at exactly twelve noon, I entered the lobby of a handsome building on Manhattan's Upper East Side. An express elevator whisked me to the thirty-second floor—and the law offices of Leonidas and Associates. After a brief wait in the elegant reception area, I was shown into an inner sanctum that came close to making my eyes pop. I mean, Rhonda Curry's—er, Leonidas's—professional domain might have been a movie set.

She was seated behind a desk at the far end of the very ample space, in front of an entire wall of soaring, floor-to-ceiling windows. No doubt the view was spectacular. However, not being overly comfortable with heights, I was instantly light-headed, even at this distance, my knees turning to rubber. Fortunately, Rhonda rose and walked over to greet me. We got together somewhere around the middle of the room, where she extended a carefully manicured hand adorned with a brilliant emerald-cut diamond. "It's very nice to meet you, Ms. Shapiro," she said in the pleasant voice I recognized from our phone conversation.

The woman was maybe in her mid-forties and large—five eight if she was an inch. And while you couldn't call her fat, she wasn't exactly a flyweight, either. Another thing you'd be unlikely to call her is

beautiful. But she was certainly attractive enough—
striking, even. Her lips were full and well shaped, and
her nose, while rather long, seemed almost made-to-
order for her angular face. She was immaculately
groomed: her makeup skillfully applied, her blond hair
pulled sleekly back into a fashionable chignon. And
the charcoal wool suit she had on was perfectly tai-
lored, very likely by one of those hot, high-ticket de-
signers few of us will ever be able to afford. (Armani
immediately sprang to mind.) But the most arresting
thing about this lady was her eyes—almond shaped,
long-lashed, and a startling turquoise blue.

I shook the proffered hand while searching Rhonda's face for a sign of her newly acquired widowhood.
There wasn't any. At any rate, I told her that it was
nice to meet her, too. "But please. Call me Desiree."

"And I'm Rhonda. Come," she directed. And,
wheeling around, she preceded me to a furniture
grouping positioned—praise the Lord—against an in-
side wall. Here, there was a damask sofa in kind of an
oatmeal color and, on either side of this, two matching
Queen Anne chairs. A low glass coffee table holding
only a telephone, an ashtray, and a box of tissues completed the arrangement.

I sank into the sofa, which was embarrassingly deep.
The thing is, this was one of those instances where, in
order for my feet to reach the floor, I had to place
my posterior on the very edge of the cushion. (I'm
sure I looked as if I were poised to take flight.)
Rhonda sat down gracefully on one of the chairs.

"This is quite an office," I murmured apprecia-
tively, glancing at the lacquered dark chocolate
walls, the thick oatmeal carpeting, and the gleaming
mahogany furniture. I wouldn't have been surprised
to learn that at least some of the pieces were bona
fide antiques.

"I gather that means you like it."

"I love it," I gushed.

"I'm so pleased to hear that," Rhonda told me, beaming. "It was just redone. But never mind that. It's lunchtime. What can we get for you, Desiree?"

"Nothing, thank you. I had a late breakfast. But don't let that keep you from having something yourself."

"Actually, I'm not very hungry, either. So why don't you go ahead and ask your questions."

"Well," I began, "in our conversation the other night you said that Gordon was deceiving himself when he refused to consider that anyone other than Roger Clyne could possibly want to do him harm."

"That's right. My husband was convinced that everyone adored him—and as I also said on the phone, the fact is, most people did. But no one, Desiree—not even Gordie—is *universally* loved."

"I'm going to need the names of any individuals who were less than enthusiastic about him."

"Oh, I didn't have anyone particular in mind when I made that statement. I was merely attempting to point out how, in light of this misperception of Gordie's, it was virtually impossible for you to prevent his murder."

"That was very kind of you. But it's extremely important that I know about the existence of any ill feelings toward your husband. I'm talking about a grudge of any sort—even if it didn't amount to much and no matter how far back it dated."

"If I were aware of something of that nature, I would have brought it to your attention when you called," Rhonda declared, sounding slightly offended.

"I was hoping something might have occurred to you since then."

"I wish it had."

"Um, I understand your cousin Melanie became involved with Gordon when she was caring for his first wife." (I elected not to label this a rumor.)

"They were not 'involved,' Desiree," Rhonda corrected, her voice rising ever so slightly. "This was a very sad, very lonely period in Gordie's life. Edith—his wife—was desperately ill by the time Melanie went to live with them. So every once in a while he and Melanie would go to dinner together—just to leave all that sickness and pain behind them for a couple of hours. But dining out at a restaurant is a far cry from checking into a motel." And adamantly now: "Melanie and Gordie were friends. Nothing more."

"You seem pretty certain of that."

"Maybe this will put things in their proper perspective. Originally, Melanie was hired as a temporary live-in nurse for an aunt of Edith's, who, as I recall, had been badly injured in a fall. In about eighteen months the aunt was fully recovered, and Melanie went to work for Edith's father—the father, like Edith, had a degenerative heart condition. Melanie was with the old man for years. And then, when he expired, she was free to look after his daughter.

"What I'm trying to make clear is that by this point my cousin was almost like a member of that family. She and Gordie had frequently been in each other's company and had developed a nice, easy rapport. *This,* Desiree," Rhonda asserted sarcastically, "was the extent of their so-called involvement."

"It's very possible you're right. However, I was told that after Edith died, Melanie had expectations of becoming the next Mrs. Gordon Curry."

"That's absolutely untrue. It—" The heated denial was cut short by the ringing of the phone.

Plainly irritated at the interruption, Rhonda reached over to the coffee table and pressed the intercom. "Yes, Roberta?" A pause. "I told you to hold my calls." Another, longer pause. "No. Mr. Sanderson can wait. Tell him I'll be back to him shortly."

She replaced the receiver and shrugged. "My secretary interprets the phrase 'Hold my calls' as applying to everyone but ex–football players with blond, curly hair and muscles."

I produced the requisite smile. After which I said, "I believe you were about to tell me why you're so sure that Melanie never contemplated marrying your husband."

"Yes, I was. Listen, it was Melanie who *introduced* me to Gordie—after Edith passed away, of course. Would she have done that if she was interested in him herself?"

"She arranged some kind of blind date for the two of you?"

"Well, no. Not really. Gordie and Melanie kept in touch after Edith's death, of course—I did mention they were old friends—and she phoned me one day to request a favor. Gordie needed clarification on a legal issue, and his attorney was on a month's vacation in Europe. She asked if they—she and Gordie—could stop by the office for a few minutes. The intention being that he'd explain the problem so I would then be in a position to direct him to a law firm specializing in that type of thing—whatever it was. I suggested she have Gordie call me with a few details first.

"As it turned out, it wasn't necessary for me to provide a recommendation. I was able to supply the information he needed myself—in five minutes, right over the telephone. To be honest, it was such a simple matter that just about any attorney could have done the same. At any rate, afterwards Gordie made some reference to my fee. I said there wouldn't be one. I wouldn't have been comfortable charging him for my services, Desiree, considering that he'd required so little of my time. Well, to show his appreciation, he insisted on taking both Melanie and me to Le Cirque for dinner the next week. And the rest, as they say, is history."

"Um, I'm not sure that Melanie's steering Gordon

to you for professional advice is any indication that she intended for the two of you to become romantically attached."

"She's always maintained that it *was*. That he was all set to consult with someone else when she prevailed upon him to come to me for a referral, contending that I was acquainted with all of the top legal practitioners in the city. Besides," Rhonda said firmly, "when Gordie phoned the evening following our dinner to ask me out, I checked with Melanie before accepting his invitation. She assured me that if she had any designs on him, she wouldn't have put us in contact. I had no doubt this was so, too. Otherwise, Melanie would have expended every effort to keep Gordie and me apart. Take my word for it." Then with an unmistakable flash of pride: "I'm afraid I was regarded as something of a predator in my younger days. Anyhow, now I'm even more convinced that she was telling the truth."

"What do you mean?"

"About a year and a half ago Melanie fell madly in love. She confided to me that she'd never felt about anyone else the way she felt about this man. She needn't have bothered saying it, though. On the two or three occasions I was in their company, I could tell that from the way she looked at him. Trust me, she didn't look at Gordie that way—ever."

"Are they still a couple?"

"Unfortunately, no. They broke up at the end of last summer."

"Would you have any idea why?"

"Excuse me, Desiree, but I can't imagine what bearing this could have on my husband's murder."

"I can't, either, not at the moment, anyhow. But it may have some significance down the road."

Rhonda took a few seconds off to scowl at me before responding grudgingly, "All right. Hal was anxious to have children, but as crazy as she was about him, Melanie couldn't see herself as a mother."

"And that ended it?"

"That ended it."

"One other thing," I lied. "I was informed that after you and Gordon married, your friendship with Melanie cooled—and that this coolness between the two of you lasted until fairly recently. I also understand that the marriage affected Melanie's relationship with your husband, resulting in an estrangement that continued until he died."

"Where did you *hear* those things? There *were* long stretches when Melanie and I didn't see each other. But this was only because we both have such demanding professions. As for Gordie and her, there was never any problem between them. It's just that when Melanie and I get together, it's usually for lunch and girl talk. So not only wasn't Gordon invited, but he wouldn't have been at all interested in joining us if he were."

"There's something I'm curious about, Rhonda. Is the name Francis Lonergan familiar to you?"

Now, I did not regard this as breaking my promise to Fielding. I mean, I wasn't tying the man in with the shooting, was I? The thing is, I had the idea that it might be worthwhile to put this to all the suspects to gauge their reactions. Plus, there was a chance, too, that someone might have knowledge of a link between the killer and one of the other suspects on my list—or perhaps somebody else altogether.

"No-o . . . I don't believe so," Rhonda responded thoughtfully. Then a moment later: "Should it be?"

"Probably not. This is a little awkward," I said sheepishly, "but I myself can't remember where I heard the name. I was hoping that maybe you could help me out. But let's move on; I don't want to keep you too much longer. Uh, there was also some talk about your husband and stepson not being on the best of terms."

"That, at least, has a grain of truth to it. But just a grain. A long while ago Danny was jealous of his father's closeness to my son, Chip. I didn't mention that to you when you asked me about grudges before because it simply didn't come to mind. And the reason for this is that the friction occurred when Danny was a teenager. He's presently in his early twenties—a grown-up—with a successful Wall Street career in the offing. Frankly, I can't envision this adolescent envy's suddenly erupting into murder after all these years. Especially since Chip is gone now—he died as the result of an auto accident last winter." And, leaning over to the coffee table, Rhonda grabbed a handful of Kleenex from the tissue box.

"Yes, I know. And I'm very, very sorry. It must have been terrible for you."

"It was," she whispered, turning her face and dabbing at tear-filled eyes.

"Um, please forgive me for what I'm about to ask you next," I said when she was looking in my general direction again. "But it's something I can't *not* ask if I'm to conduct the type of investigation I should. Did you hold Gordon responsible for what happened?"

"The answer is yes. I did. But I was positively distraught when Chip was so badly hurt. And then when he passed away . . ." Swallowing hard, Rhonda plucked what was most likely an imaginary piece of lint from her skirt. "Eventually, though, I came to realize how unfair I was being. After all, Gordie wasn't responsible for the awful road conditions that day. Besides, he loved Chip, too. Very much."

"How about your former husband? What were his feelings about Gordon's involvement in that accident?"

"He, too, blamed Gordie—initially, at any rate. But you have to understand how grief stricken he was.

Like me, Luke had to find an outlet for his pain. But if you're thinking that he either killed Gordie or had him killed to avenge Chip's death, forget it. My former mate has the spine of a jellyfish."

"To get back to Danny for a moment, though . . . what sort of relationship did he and your husband have lately?"

"Well, they didn't actually see each other very often. But that was to be expected. First Danny was busy with his studies. After that, he devoted every free moment to locating an apartment. Following which he was occupied with finding a job and then establishing himself in this new position. If you want to know if there was any animosity between them, though, the answer is no."

I had just about run out of questions at this juncture, and I started to get to my feet. "Well, I guess that about covers it. I thank you so much for your time, Rhonda."

"Before you go, there's something *I'd* like to ask *you.*"

"Sure. What is it?"

"The man they arrested for Gordie's murder—do the police have any more information on him yet?"

"I don't believe so," I told her.

"But they're convinced he *was* the shooter?"

"I think so, yes."

"I assume that you'll get in touch with me as soon as there are any new developments."

"Of course. And if anything should come to mind after I leave here, you'll contact me, won't you?"

"Certainly."

"Let me give you my card. Call me day or night."

I dug into my handbag in search of the card—which listed my office, home, and cell phone numbers. And then I continued to dig—and dig and dig.

Happily, I managed to produce it before the sun went down.

# Chapter 24

In the taxi on the way downtown, I conducted my usual postmortem after a meeting of this kind.

And, as is also usual in these circumstances, I was frustrated.

Rhonda had rejected all of the suspects on my list, torpedoing the possible motive of every one of them.

Danny's beef against his father went back too far, she'd maintained; it was no longer valid now that he was an adult.

Her ex didn't have the spine to avenge his son's death.

And Melanie had never been in love with Gordon and had never been estranged from either him or Rhonda herself. (These assertions directly contradicting what I'd heard from Blossom.)

I had to wonder if my client's widow truly believed everything she'd told me, or if she'd been shielding one or more of these people—either because of her affection for them or because she was convinced they were innocent of the murder.

And then there was Rhonda's claim that her own bitterness against her husband had been transient, born of her anguish at Chip's injuries and subsequent death and dissipating when she was able to acknowledge to herself that Gordon, too, was in pain. But had she actually forgiven him for the accident? Or had this apparent change in her been part of a careful plot to remove herself from suspicion once she'd made the decision to hook up with a hired killer?

And speaking of that, which of my suspects would be likely to have access to one of these admirable citizens, anyway? This was something I'd have to check into. I mean, it isn't as if there's a section reading "Hit Men" in the Yellow Pages.

Instead of heading directly for the office, I instructed the cabdriver to drop me a few blocks away, at Little Angie's. This destination having been mandated by my stomach, which at least had had the good sense not to carry on until it had exited Rhonda's posh premises. Since then, however, it had been protesting its lack of sustenance at a steadily increasing volume.

Now, I don't know about you, but my idea of heaven is the thinnest, crispiest pizza crust that ever was, topped with a delectable combination of zesty tomato sauce, mozzarella, and anchovies. Or—depending on my mood—mushrooms, onions, and pepperoni. Today was definitely an anchovy day.

There aren't any tables at Little Angie's—the place is so tiny there's barely enough room for Little Angie. And, as always, it was jammed. Luckily, I managed to get a seat at the counter. For this, I can thank the fact that the woman who was all set to race me for the one vacant stool had to stop to pick up her umbrella. (But I certainly didn't knock it out of her hands on purpose.)

Anyhow, three pizza slices later (or maybe it was four), I was ready to get to work.

Once I was holed up in my cubicle, I decided I'd devote what remained of the afternoon to transcribing my notes. And I had every intention of doing this at breakneck speed. I can't imagine how I thought that might be possible, however, since I don't type at breakneck speed. Or any speed at all, for that matter. What's more, I can rarely resist attempting to absorb the material as I go along, which slows things down even further.

Naturally, I wasn't accomplishing nearly as much as I'd (foolishly) planned to. Nevertheless, at around four o'clock it occurred to me that as long as there was nothing pressing to keep me here, I might as well call it quits and get in some shopping for Sunday night's dinner.

Jackie, of course, wasn't satisfied with my "See you in the morning" when I passed her desk.

"Is anything wrong?" she demanded, glancing at her watch.

"No, I just have some things to take care of at home, that's all."

"You're feeling all right?"

"I'm feeling fine."

"Are you *sure?* You really don't look too good."

"Thanks. Just what I needed to hear," I grumbled.

"Well, maybe you're coming down with the flu."

Now, Jackie and Ellen aren't anything alike— except in one respect: They're both among New York's premier *nudges.* So in the interest of expediency, I leveled with the woman. "I figured I'd cut out a little early to get in some food shopping for my dinner with Nick on Sunday."

"Oh. Listen, I hope you've reconsidered."

"Reconsidered what?" Go ahead. Ask me why I asked. A reflex, I suppose.

"I still think you should make the chicken."

"Maybe next time."

"Yeah, right." Judging from the exasperated look on Jackie's face, you'd have thought I was feeding *her.*

\*　　\*　　\*

I spent close to an hour at my neighborhood D'Agostino's, then made a brief stop at the liquor store.
When I finally walked into my living room, the answering machine was blinking furiously at me. There
was one call.

"I *have* to talk to you, Aunt Dez," Ellen said. She
sounded so distraught that I immediately tried reaching her at Macy's.

A man answered her extension and told me she was
with a customer. I was in the process of leaving word
that I'd phoned when he said hurriedly, "Wait. Here
she is; she'll be right with you."

"Hi, Ellen," I got out. "Is there—"

"Oh, Aunt Dez!" she wailed.

"What's wrong?"

"It's my mother. She bought a dress for the wedding today."

"But that's good—isn't it?"

"The dress is black."

"It's *what?*"

"*B-L-A-C-K*. Black! B-but she's trying to assure me
that it looks navy in most lights."

Now, it's not that I'm so big on tradition. But it was
incomprehensible to me that someone—even someone
as insensitive as Margot—should elect to walk down
the aisle at her daughter's wedding wearing black.
"She must have been teasing you," I ventured.

"Uh-uh. She was serious."

Well, it was a little late for my sister-in-law to be
going through a midlife crisis, and I couldn't come up
with any other rational reason for her behavior. Then
it occurred to me, knowing Margot, that it might simply be her way of commanding attention. "I assume
you told your mother how you feel about her choice."

"Naturally. But she claims she's been to every shop
in the Miami area, and this is the only gown that's
flattering to her. And she says that, anyhow, nowadays

there are no set rules for what sort of apparel's appropriate—even for weddings. She made me feel a little selfish for even suggesting she try to find something else."

"Have you thought of asking your father to talk to her about this?"

"It wouldn't do any good. He can never persuade her to do anything."

"What about Joan?" I suggested, referring to Ellen's sister-in-law, who also lives in Florida. "She and your mother have always gotten along well."

"Yes, but they're not on speaking terms right now."

*Swell!* I tried again. "Steve?" This was Ellen's brother.

"My mother hates Steve's taste in clothes. She's constantly lecturing *him* on what to wear."

"Oh."

"Um, Aunt Dez? I was wondering. . . ."

It took so long for her to relate her wonder that I finally said, "What about?"

"Um, maybe if *you* talked to her . . ."

*"Me!"* I practically screeched. It just slipped out. Then, in a more moderated tone: "Listen, Ellen, I don't think I'm the right person to do that. Your mother and I have never been really close." (Which was a euphemistic way of stating that we hate each other's guts.)

"But she *does* respect your opinion on things. Honestly. Besides, I've heard her mention a number of times how well dressed you are."

Yeah. Except that considering this was Margot, she probably added, "For a fat lady."

"Please say you'll ph-phone her and at least try to get her to change her mind."

Well, I'd rather have all my glorious hennaed hair pulled out by its black roots than endure a conversation with my sister-in-law—*any* conversation. Right now, however, my main concern was that my intervention could result in a dramatic increase in Margot's determination to keep the damn dress. But the problem was, if I pointed that out to Ellen, it was likely she'd regard it as an attempt to worm my way out of this dreaded assignment.

So what could I do?

"All right, I'll take a shot at it," I agreed with what must have been a noticeable lack of enthusiasm. "And I promise you, I'll do the best I can. Only, please, don't count too much on my being successful."

"I won't," Ellen murmured.

"But is it all right with you if I get in touch with your mother tomorrow? Gordon's son is coming over tonight, and I'd like to give some thought to the questions I want to ask him."

"Of course. And Aunt Dez? I don't know how to thank you."

"I do. By letting me go, so I can grab a bite before he shows up."

# Chapter 25

Danny declined my offer of something to drink.

"No, thanks, Ms. Shapiro," he said. "My roommate and I had dinner out tonight, and we polished off a carafe of wine between us. Then, after that, I had two cups of coffee with my chocolate mousse. It's a wonder I'm not floating at this point."

"All right. But let me know if you change your mind—there's coffee, tea, Coke. . . . And it's Desiree, by the way." I almost tagged on, "And you don't have to call me *Aunt* Desiree, either." But of course, not having had my mother to supervise his upbringing, he wouldn't have had the slightest idea what I was talking about.

We were seated in my living room, with Danny in one of the club chairs while I was settled on the sofa directly opposite him.

Now, from the moment this nice-looking boy had crossed the threshold, my impression of him had been favorable. But maybe some of that was a carryover from our phone conversation. Certainly not all of it, though.

Danny Curry was both friendly and polite. And he had this truly melting smile. The smile, as far as I could see, being Danny's only resemblance to his murdered father. Otherwise, where Gordon was of medium height, Danny was tall—six feet or more. And where Gordon was on the chunky side, Danny was lean. His features were more regular, more refined than Gordon's, too. Also, he had thick blond hair. And if my client's hair had ever been that shade, by the time we met it had surrendered all of its color, along with a good deal of its body, to the passing years. There was one attribute of Gordon's that his offspring lacked, however: the blue eyes I'd found so compelling. (Danny's eyes were dark brown.) Nevertheless, when you took everything into consideration, the son was more than a match for the father. Appearance-wise, at least.

"What did you want to ask me?" he was saying now.

"For starters, Danny," I put to him gently, "do you have any idea who might have had something—*anything*—against your dad?"

"You don't believe the fellow who's in jail now was responsible for his murder?"

"It's pretty definite that he fired the gun. But he may have been acting on someone's behalf."

"You mean he was a hired killer?"

"Could be. Or it could be that the man was close to someone your father had supposedly injured, and he took it upon himself to avenge that someone."

"What would be your guess?"

"I lean toward hired killer."

"I do, too. So does Aunt Blossom."

"To get back to my question, though, can you think of anyone at all who didn't care much for your father?"

"I've been going over and over that same question in my mind since . . . since it happened. And I haven't come up with a single soul. People *liked* him, Desiree; they really did."

"Um, I was told that for a while your stepmother blamed him for the death of her son."

"Only at first. She finally came to recognize that it wasn't Dad's fault."

"How positive are you that she didn't fake her forgiveness? I mean, suppose that at some point she decided to have your father killed. Rhonda's bright enough to appreciate that in order to remove herself from suspicion, it would be wise to pretend that things were sweetness and light between them again."

"I don't buy into that theory at all. Rhonda's not like that," my visitor declared emphatically.

"You're fond of your stepmother, aren't you, Danny?"

"Yes, I am. She's a very decent human being, and she's always treated me well."

I was impressed. Most kids wouldn't have been too tickled about the remarriage of one of their parents so soon after the death of the other. But if Danny here was displeased with Gordon for taking a new wife, it didn't appear that he'd extended his anger to the wife herself. And this was even more admirable when you consider that it was Rhonda who'd given birth to the boy he'd once feared was replacing him in his father's affections.

"I understand that you and her son didn't get along too well, though.

"We were fine—honestly. But a few years ago—and no doubt you know all about this—I was sort of ticked at my dad because I had the notion he favored Chip over me. I didn't hold that against Chip, though—I never felt it was his doing."

"What made you believe your father was more attached to his stepson than he was to you?"

"It was my own insecurity at work there. But back then it seemed to me that my dad was totally involved with Chip. If he wasn't helping him with his homework or attending one of his school functions, he was busy teaching him how to bowl. Or anyway, this was how

I saw it. When I got older, though, I realized that it wasn't that my father preferred Chip; it was just that he'd developed a bond with him, too. Which was only natural, especially since I was away at school so much of the time."

*My God! I wish I had this kid's maturity!*

"Oh, let me ask you this before I forget. Does the name Francis Lonergan ring any bells?"

Two deep parallel lines suddenly materialized over Danny's nose—and vanished almost as quickly. He shook his head. "Doesn't sound familiar. Is this someone you think might have had some involvement in my dad's murder?"

"I wish I could answer that. I probably shouldn't admit this, but the name was recently mentioned to me, and I have no idea who did the mentioning or why. I was hoping you might be able to fill in the blanks for me."

"Sorry," Danny responded, his tone apologetic.

As was true of his stepmother, he didn't give me the impression he was at all perturbed on hearing the name.

"Well, it was a long shot. Anyhow, you'll be thrilled to learn that I have another question for you now—and this one's *definitely* related to the investigation."

The boy grinned.

"How well do you know Chip's father?"

"I used to see him when he came to pick up Chip for the weekend. He—" Danny cut himself off. "You're suggesting that Luke may have been the one to avenge Chip's death, right?"

"I'm only suggesting that it's conceivable."

"I can't be of any help to you there, I'm afraid. I've never so much as had a conversation with the man. And about the only thing I can recall being said about him in the house was that he and Rhonda hadn't been too happy together." Danny grinned again. "Of course, that's fairly obvious, considering that they divorced."

"*Very* obvious," I agreed with a little titter. "Okay, then let's talk about Melanie Slater. Tell me about her."

"She was my mother's nurse. She's also related to Rhonda—they're cousins."

"What was your impression of her when she was caring for your mother?"

"I didn't really have one. We seldom spoke more than a couple of sentences—she was always so busy with Mom."

And here I treaded carefully. "Um, what about her relationship with your father?"

"Evidently she had a thing for him. I once heard her talking on the phone to someone—a girlfriend, probably—and that was pretty clear from what Melanie said to her."

"So, as far as you're aware, the interest was all on Melanie's side, then?"

"I can't say that for sure. My dad was always kind of . . . well, a flirt. But listen," Danny added hastily, "that doesn't mean he cheated on my mother." There was a brief silence before he hunched his shoulders, conceding, "On the other hand, though, I can't swear that he didn't."

"I, uh, don't suppose you would have been too pleased with him if you discovered he'd been having an affair."

"I'd have despised him for it," the boy said flatly.

"There's one thing more I'd like to discuss, Danny."

"No problem. That's why I'm here."

"I, um, understand you and your dad weren't on very good terms when he died."

Danny frowned. "Who told you that?"

"I can't remember." (It was Blossom.) "Is this true?"

He didn't immediately respond. And when he did, his eyes were moist. "Yes, it's true. I wish to God it wasn't, but it is," he murmured.

Anxious to prevent the threatening tears from gathering any momentum, I threw in here, "All right, whatever the problem was, we've eliminated that it was caused by your father's supposed partiality toward Chip."

"I told you; I got past that a long time ago."

"And I'm also going to assume that it had nothing to do with his being unfaithful to your mother."

At this, Danny flashed even white teeth. "Particularly since I'm not at all certain he *was*."

"Then would you mind telling me what did happen between the two of you?"

"My father didn't approve of me."

"May I ask why?"

"My lifestyle."

It finally jelled: *Danny was gay!*

I think it must have been quite soon after he walked in here that it struck me—on some level—that this might be so. Maybe in part because his chinos were so neatly pressed and his white shirt was so crisp and immaculate and his brown tweed jacket was such a superb fit. But of course, there are straight men who take that sort of pride in their appearance, too. (Although, if you ask me, not nearly enough of them.) Maybe another, larger basis for this conjecture was the boy's mannerisms. They weren't feminine, you understand; they just weren't particularly masculine. In retrospect, however, I suppose the main reason I entertained this possibility had little to do with anything tangible; it was mostly something I *felt*.

At any rate, do you want to hear what popped into my head at that moment—idiot that I am? The thought that there was some twenty-year-old girl out there who would be deprived of marrying a lovely young man like Danny.

"My father couldn't accept my being gay," Danny was saying.

"When did he find out about this?"

"I talked to him last April. I actually figured that if he loved me, it wouldn't matter."

"But it did."

"Oh, it did, all right. And how I could have been stupid enough to think— He didn't even attend my graduation from Yale. Rhonda drove up there by herself. She said he had food poisoning."

"I suppose there are two possibilities," I speculated. "Either this is what he really told her. Or this is what *she* told *you* to spare your feelings."

"You didn't know my father. He'd rather I'd have been a rapist or a murderer. I assure you he'd never have admitted to anyone—and this includes his wife— that his only son was a *fag*." As he blurted out the word, Danny's entire face turned brick red and that nice mouth of his contorted into a sneer.

I was searching for an appropriate response, but I'm sure I'd only have managed to come up with a silly platitude. So I was relieved when Danny spoke before I had the chance to embarrass myself. "Do you want the truth, Desiree? I wasn't crazy about how he lived *his* life, either. Harmless or not, I couldn't stand how he came on to every woman he met."

"I imagine his wife wasn't too crazy about that, either—or was he more circumspect when she was around?"

"Hardly. But Rhonda didn't seem to mind. In fact, she may have been amused by it. My stepmother's a very confident woman."

"I gathered that."

"There were other things that bothered me about him, too—like his passion for hunting. He even went *doe* hunting."

"*Doe* hunting?" Now, I can't explain why I should

have been any more disturbed at the thought of a female deer's being targeted than I was when a buck was the prey. But for whatever reason, this was apparently the case. Maybe it was a Bambi thing.

"That's right. My father went hunting in the Poconos the second week in October this year. I understand this was doe-hunting season up there."

"Oh, my."

"That's what I say." And then on noting my expression: "Anyway, I guess he shouldn't be blamed too much for the hunting thing. It's how my grandfather brought him up." There was no anger in Danny's voice now. Only sadness.

"Yes, he mentioned that to me."

"My dad's reaction to my sexual orientation—that really hurt, Desiree. I didn't approve of some of the things he did, either, but I loved him regardless."

"And I'm certain he loved you, too, and that if he were still with us, he'd have come around eventually. It just takes some people longer than others to accept what they can't understand."

"That's something I'll never know, will I?" Danny said dejectedly. Moments later, however, his lips curved in a kind of half smile. "But I'd like to believe you're right."

# Chapter 26

I couldn't help it. That night I went to bed really impressed with what a terrific kid Danny Curry was. After all, how many boys wouldn't have resented the stepbrother who—or so they'd decided—was now the recipient of the giant share of their father's affections? Plus, what about those very kind words Danny had for the woman who'd become his stepmother practically on the heels of his own mother's passing? And listen, while the boy was understandably angry at being summarily dismissed from Gordon's life (and for something he couldn't control, too!), he, nevertheless, appeared to be deeply affected by the loss of his father. Certainly more so than the widow did. But then again, *I* seemed to be taking Gordon's death harder than Rhonda was.

When I woke up the next morning, however, it was with a totally revised mind-set. Almost from the moment I opened my eyes I began lecturing myself. *You are* such *a pushover,* I scolded.

The thing is, was I willing to swear to Danny's sincerity? Maybe I'd been treated to a premier performance last night. Think a younger, taller, thinner, blonder, Americanized Anthony Hopkins (that actor, in my opinion, being kind of like a male Meryl Streep). But only minutes later I did a complete about-face again. I mean, there *were* three other suspects on my list, and with any luck, Gordon's killer could turn out to be one of *them*. I wasn't fussy about which one, either.

Well, it was evident that, in spite of myself, I was back to hoping that Danny was the innocent he'd presented himself to be.

I intended to perform the dreaded chore of contacting my sister-in-law, Margot, when I got to the office. (I couldn't so much as *contemplate* talking to her first thing in the morning.) But the second I arrived, Jackie began waving a pink slip in front of me. And before I could make a grab for it, she proceeded to reveal its contents.

"Your niece said that if you haven't already gotten in touch with her mother—don't. Call Ellen at home, Dez—she's off today—and she'll explain."

Relieving her of the slip, I muttered a reluctant "Thank you."

"What's this about?" Jackie demanded.

"Nothing very interesting."

"You're not going to tell me?"

"Uh-uh," I informed her with a pleasant smile. Following which I turned and marched down the hall to my cubbyhole.

I still had my coat on when I lifted the receiver. Was it possible I'd be getting a reprieve?

At the sound of my voice, Ellen inquired anxiously, "You haven't spoken to my mother yet, have you?"

"No. In fact, I was planning to try her now."

I could actually hear her exhale. "Well, you're off the hook. But I really appreciate that you were willing to intervene, Aunt Dez. I realize how difficult that would have been for you."

"What's going on?"

"My dad took care of things."

*God bless that sweet, darling man!* "See? And you didn't feel he has any influence with her."

"Oh, he doesn't. What happened was, he overheard

my mother talking to me on the phone yesterday. So
he immediately got in touch with this neighbor—May,
her name is, and she and my mother are good friends.
He told May how aggravated I was that Mom planned
on strolling down the aisle in black. Apparently, May
didn't regard this as being so terrible, but since I was
upset about it, she promised to see what she could
do."

"And this neighbor convinced your mother to take
the gown back?"

"That's right. Only not in the way you'd suppose.
She called my mother and asked if she'd found anything to wear to the wedding yet. And when my
mother said yes, May claimed she was dying to see
what she'd bought. So then Mom invited her to stop
by if she felt like it.

"At any rate, my mother tried on the gown for her.
And instead of mentioning anything about its being
an inappropriate color—which would probably have
resulted in an argument and ended up with my mom's
still keeping the dress—May said it was very nice except for one thing." Ellen paused for dramatic effect.

"What thing?"

"She told my mother the dress made her look flat
chested."

Another dramatic pause. "Mom took it back to the
store this morning."

What a deliciously devious woman! I was practically
in awe of the clever May. Listen, if there's one quality
that's worthy of admiration but is, unfortunately,
much underrated—it's deviousness.

As for my brother-in-law, I silently blessed him
once again.

"You're aware, I'm sure," I pointed out to Ellen,
"that if it weren't for your father, this story might not
have such a happy ending."

"Oh, I know. He phoned me before—right after my

mom left the house—to fill me in on all this. And I kept wishing he was there in the room with me so I could give him a big hug and about a thousand kisses."

I figured the conversation was just about over now, but then Ellen let this little "Oh" escape her lips.

"What's wrong?"

"Nothing, really. I was just thinking."

"About?"

"Uh . . . well, wh-what if Mom c-comes home with another b-b-black dress?"

# Chapter 27

I did my best to convince Ellen that Margot wouldn't be buying another black gown for the wedding. ("She'll get something suitable this time; you wait and see.") The thing is, though, I wasn't so sure myself.

Following the conversation with my niece, I settled down at the computer to transcribe my notes—for a change. At around one I allowed myself a brief break for some nourishment: ham and Brie with honey mustard and a Coke. Then I was back at the computer again.

It was five after two when Jackie—evidently still smarting from my refusal to explain Ellen's message—notified me in a chilly tone that "There's a Ms. Slater to see you."

Melanie Slater made no attempt to conceal her displeasure at being here. And while she shook my hand, it was with obvious reluctance.

I relieved her of her parka, and she sat down alongside my desk.

As I was slipping the parka on a hanger at the back of the door, I considered the lady's appearance. She was large boned like her cousin, only slightly slimmer and a couple of inches shorter. And if I'm any judge—and I admit I'm not a very good one—the two were approximately the same age. But although pleasant looking, the nurse wasn't nearly as striking as the widow. Of course, one reason for this may have been that Melanie wasn't decked out in Armani (or Versace or Prada or anyone else of that ilk); she was sporting a beige wool turtleneck and slightly baggy brown wool pants. She wasn't what you'd call elegantly coiffed, either—her medium brown hair having been pulled back into a not overly neat ponytail and fastened with a plain rubber band. She could have been a little less stingy with her makeup, too. I mean, those light eyelashes were practically screaming for a generous application of mascara. Still, that wouldn't have altered the fact that Melanie hadn't been gifted with her cousin's gorgeous turquoise eye color, her own being a paler and far less arresting shade of blue.

I asked if I could get her something to eat.

"No, thanks," she responded in a voice that seemed too small for the rest of her. "I had a bite just prior to coming here."

"Some coffee?"

"I had my fill of that, too."

"Let me know if you change your mind," I offered, taking a seat at my desk.

"All right." She seemed to have difficulty getting out the "Thanks," not throwing it in until a second or two later.

"Then I guess we should get started, Melanie," I announced. "Uh, do you mind if I call you Melanie?"

"Go ahead," she answered, shrugging.

"I'm Desiree, by the way. Anyhow, on the phone you insisted that you didn't have any information that could be of assistance to us in our investigation." (Note the "us" and the "our," which I felt gave the interrogation more of an official air.) "But I've been hoping something might have occurred to you since we spoke. Wasn't there anyone—even going back to the time you were living with the family—who exhibited any sort of hostility toward Gordon Curry?"

"No one. Everyone was very fond of Gordie. He—"

Breaking off, she wrinkled her brow and repeated the "No one" with conviction.

"You've thought of something, haven't you?" I pounced.

"Not anything that could be helpful to you."

"Please. Tell me what's on your mind."

"Well, there may have been some sort of conflict between Gordie and his father-in-law—Edie's father. But that *really* goes way back—to the days when Papa Charlie—this is what we all called him—was my patient. In fact, it wasn't until after he died that I moved in with the Currys to take care of Edie."

"Why did Papa Charlie dislike his son-in-law?"

"Did I say he *disliked* him?" Melanie snapped. "If anything, it was more that he didn't trust him."

"Why is that?"

"Okay. I heard talk—but who can say how reliable it was?—that at one point Gordie was planning to leave Edie for another woman. But then Papa Charlie wrote out a nice fat check to persuade whoever she was to end the relationship."

"And how was Papa Charlie with his son-in-law after this?"

"Cordial, from what I could see. According to the rumor, he read Gordie the riot act, and Gordie swore to him that nothing like that would ever happen again."

"And did it? Happen again, I mean."

Melanie fastened her eyes on mine, and her voice seemed to acquire extra body when she replied crossly, "I seriously doubt it."

"And you can't think of anyone other than Papa Charlie who might not have been that enamored of Gordon?"

"He's the only one I can come up with. But of course, he's been dead for years." *She didn't have to rub it in.*

"Um, I understand you introduced Gordon to Rhonda?"

"That's right."

I proceeded with caution, hoping I'd handle this next matter so tactfully that even the peevish Melanie wouldn't be offended. But I didn't—and she was.

"You . . . er . . . weren't romantically interested in the victim yourself before he remarried?"

Melanie's eyes almost doubled in size, and a vein at her left temple was now jumping up and down. "Me?" she squealed. "I would never have introduced him to another woman if that had been the case!" Following which she mumbled in disgust, "God, how do you people come up with this stuff?"

"I'm sorry if I've upset you, Melanie. It's the last thing I wanted to do, believe me. But I'm trying to find out who killed Gordon Curry, and, well, I've never been able to figure out how to go about something like that without asking a lot of irritating questions."

Seconds ticked by as I waited for Melanie's response. And when she spoke again, to my surprise, she was contrite. "I apologize for reacting so strongly—and for behaving like such a bitch this afternoon. It's just that I didn't see any reason for this meeting. The fact is, I still don't. But I realize you're only doing your job, and I'll try to be more cooperative from here on in. About Gordie, though. I did like him—but as a friend."

"And the friendship remained intact until he was killed?"

"Yes, although we didn't really see each other that often once Edie passed away."

"But you kept in close touch with Rhonda."

"That's right."

"How did she and Gordon get along?"

"Fine, as far as I could tell."

"If there'd been something amiss, do you suppose Rhonda would have talked to you about it?"

"Well, if she confided in anyone, I'm sure it would have been me."

"Then you don't believe she held her husband responsible for Chip's death? Accident or not, with something like that, most of us look to blame *somebody*."

"If she blamed Gordie, she never said anything to me about it."

Obviously, this was a crock. The toll the tragedy initially took on that marriage was confirmed by everyone else I'd spoken to—including Rhonda herself. But I didn't hold it against Melanie for attempting to shield her cousin from suspicion. (Actually, I gave her a couple of points for this.)

And she wasn't through yet. "If Rhonda *did* feel that what happened was Gordie's fault, though, it wasn't for long. I saw them together toward the end of August at a relative's anniversary party, and they were very lovey-dovey."

Now, *this* was pushing it. I absolutely could not picture Rhonda displaying that much emotion toward her husband—not if the emotion she allotted to him following his demise was any indication.

"Oh, by the way, do you recognize the name Francis Lonergan?" I brought up here.

Melanie sucked in her cheeks in apparent concentration, after which she slowly shook her head. "I don't think I ever heard it. Is he involved in the murder in some way?"

"Probably not. But someone mentioned the name recently, and I can't remember what it pertained to. I wasn't exactly counting on your being able to help me out, but it was worth a try." I reminded myself to look embarrassed.

"I wish I had the answer for you—that sort of thing

can be awfully frustrating," Melanie said, a hint of regret in her tone. Like the others, she had seemed more puzzled than disturbed by this mention of Gordon Curry's assassin.

"Well, if you have no more questions," she told me now, "I'll be on my way." She smiled wanly, and I was instantly aware that this was the first time she'd managed a smile since coming here. "Assuming, that is, I can find the energy to move."

"Losing someone you really care for can take a lot out of you," I murmured sympathetically.

"Don't you *listen?*" the woman retorted, springing to her feet. "I *told* you; I *liked* Gordie, but that was the extent of it."

"You misunderstood me. I was referring to your patient—Sissy McCann. I recall your saying that she was like a sister to you."

"Oh." A shamefaced Melanie sat down again. "I am so-o sorry, Desiree. Lately my nerves aren't what they should be. I realize that's not much of an excuse, but it's all I have.

"You know, I've been a nurse for many years, and more than a few of my patients passed away during the period I was with them, but none of those other deaths affected me the way Sissy's did."

"She must have been a very special person."

"She was unbelievable—so bright and thoughtful and funny. So *brave.* If Sissy told you she was in a little pain, you knew she was in *agony*—that's how she was." Melanie's face contorted for a moment in what appeared to be an attempt to control her tears. "The whole family is wonderful."

"You mentioned that she had eight-year-old twins."

"Yes, Mark and Matthew. They're adorable." And beaming now: "They call me Aunt Melly."

"Um, did Sissy have a husband?"

"Yes. One of the most considerate people I've ever

met. But before you get any ideas, I am no more in love with Jason McCann than I was with Gordon Curry."

"The thought didn't even occur to me."

"The truth is, though, that he's a great guy. I had this . . . this personal situation at the beginning of September, and Jason—with Sissy in agreement, naturally—insisted I take as much time off as it required for me to . . . to deal with the matter. He said not to worry and not to push myself, that they'd get someone in temporarily until I felt ready to come back. Imagine. With the troubles *they* had, they were concerned about me."

"I hope everything's all right now. I mean, with you."

"It's fine. Actually, it was the sort of thing that happens every day—even to the best of us. We women can be such fools, can't we, Desiree?" I would have responded in the affirmative, but I didn't get the chance. "I'd fallen in love with someone—or thought I had—and he turned out to be the wrong someone. At least for me. I just needed to hole up for a short while and lick my wounds. So I went home, got things sorted out in my head, and I was back with the McCanns about a week later."

"That break you took was obviously helpful."

"Oh, it was. Incidentally, you said the magic word: 'break,' " Melanie apprised me, grinning. "A couple of days after that, I was roller-skating with the twins—right in the driveway—and I broke my arm."

*"Roller-skating?"*

Melanie chuckled. "It's hard to believe of someone my size, huh? And forget my age! Sitting in front of you is a prime example of arrested development. At any rate, fortunately it was my left arm that got busted up—and I'm right-handed. Still, there were occasions when caring for Sissy called for someone with two functioning arms. Sissy and Jason wouldn't hear of my leaving, though. They said that Nattie—Nattie's the housekeeper—would help out during the day whenever I needed her to, and Jason would be there at night."

"Evidently they had a very high opinion of you. Have you been in touch with any members of the household since Sissy passed away?"

"I was at the funeral, of course. And I'll be seeing Jason and the twins on Sunday. Jason's taking the boys into Manhattan for a show. Did I mention that the family lives on Long Island? A little town called Ashbrook. Anyhow, I'm meeting them for dinner afterward. Don't look at me like that, Desiree." (I had no idea what sort of look she was referring to, but I certainly wasn't thinking what *she* thought I was thinking.) I didn't get the opportunity to protest, however, because Melanie went on matter-of-factly, "For your information, Jason's mother lives in the city, and she'll also be joining them at the restaurant."

And now my visitor got to her feet. "I should get going. Again, I apologize for giving you such a hard time."

"I've had worse," I assured her, smiling beneficently.

She laughed. "Then I must be out of practice."

# Chapter 28

I wasn't just being polite when I'd responded to Melanie's apology as I had. I mean, in my years as a PI I've been on the receiving end of comebacks that were a lot more hostile than anything I'd experienced today. Actually, although there were a couple of instances where Melanie Slater had been a royal pain in the whoosis, eventually I'd even warmed up to her. Kind of.

Anyhow, Melanie had no sooner left my office than I began picking over our meeting. Obviously, she hadn't been leveling with me when she insisted she'd never had a romantic interest in Gordon. Not if I believed what Danny told me he'd overheard her saying years ago on the phone—which I did. The fact that the widow was also maintaining that Melanie's relationship with the victim had always been a platonic one meant zilch, of course—neither lady impressing me as being a strict adherent to the truth. And I certainly didn't place any stock in their both claiming that the nurse wouldn't have introduced Gordon to Rhonda if she'd had a thing for himself. After all, considering how close the two women were, Melanie might have had the misguided idea that Rhonda would abandon her acquisitive ways in this instance.

Still, I had to ask myself the same question I'd

posed when Blossom first broached the possibility of an ill-fated affair between Melanie and my dead client: Even if she *had* felt that the man had betrayed her, why wait five-plus years to do him in? Another thing: If Rhonda *had* stolen him right out from under her cousin (so to speak), wouldn't Melanie's bitterness extend to her, as well? Yet the cousins gave every appearance of getting along famously—these days, at any rate.

And now I wrenched my thoughts away from all this speculating. I had to get in touch with my favorite attorney and find out how she'd fared with the police.

As I'd come to expect with Blossom, her cough preceded her voice.

"Blossom Goody," she was finally able to announce.

"Hi, Blossom. This is—"

"Yeah, yeah. I *know* who it is, for crissakes! Well? Got something for me, Shapiro?"

"I wish."

"Wonderful. I was halfway out the door, and I had to run back on accounta the telephone. Hey, there was always the chance it was somebody interested in acquiring my services, right?"

I echoed the "right," after which I inquired casually, "Kelly isn't in?" (Kelly being Blossom's secretary or receptionist or whatever.)

"Girl didn't bother showing up this morning."

"Oh. Listen, am I keeping you from an appointment?"

"An *appointment?*" the lawyer said derisively. "What's that? Business sucks, so I'm closing up shop early today."

"This will only take a minute, Blossom. I'm just checking on whether or not you've heard from the police."

"Two cops graced these premises yesterday afternoon. One of 'em—a Sergeant Fiedler—yesterday afternoon."

"Fiedler? Oh, you must mean Fielding."

"Yeah, that's it. Anyhow, he started asking me about Edie's nurse, and I told him I had no idea what he was talking about."

"Do you think he believed you?"

"Why wouldn't he? When it comes to liars, kiddo, they don't make 'em any more convincing than this old broad."

"Uh, just one more thing."

"Oh, Christ," Blossom muttered. "Okay, but hurry up. I'm melting in this goddam coat."

"Any idea which of the suspects we discussed would have some kind of access to a hit man?"

"Let me see. . . ." She said the words slowly, obviously turning this over in her mind. Then, in a firm voice: "Every one of 'em."

*Swell.* "Could you explain that?"

"Look, Rhonda's practice put her in contact with all sorts of undesirables."

"I'm surprised. A divorce lawyer, particularly one of her stature—"

"The woman specialized in criminal law when she started out. As for Luke, he was married to her back then. So it's a pretty good bet he was familiar with the names of some of the thugs she used to represent."

"And Melanie Slater?"

"She once lived in the same house as Edie's father—Papa Charlie—for crissakes! The old man was big—*very* big—in organized crime. You shoulda seen the lowlifes who used to march in and out of that place."

Blossom didn't mention Danny, although it was possible she was already aware that I'd questioned him the previous evening. And I didn't bring him into the conversation, either. I didn't have to. As Papa Charlie's grandson, the boy no doubt had a whole bunch of "uncles" who weren't even related to him—most of whom were unlikely to have been too conscience stricken when called upon to blow away a fellow human being or two.

I was about to say good-bye then, but all of a sudden I somehow found the courage to risk Blossom's wrath. Stiffening my spine, I resolved to slip in another question.

"Give me a ring the minute you learn anything," she was instructing.

"I will. But there's something else I really need to check out with you, if you don't mind."

"*Mind?* Naturally, I mind. I told you, I'm *melting* in this damn coat. Weighs a ton." An exaggerated sigh. "But go ahead. Only make it snappy, or I'll end up being a puddle on the floor."

"Well, those rumors you mentioned about Gordon's cheating involve the period when he was with his first wife. Can I take it there wasn't any similar gossip during his marriage to Rhonda?"

"None I know of. Want my opinion?"

"Naturally."

"Gordie was in awe of Rhonda. She's an unusually sharp lady. She's also good-looking—very well put together. But you've seen her. And she has classy friends, too—a lot of 'em regularly show up on the society pages. Gordie enjoyed hanging out with those people; he was definitely impressed by 'em. And don't forget that Rhonda's a *muy* successful attorney who pulls in huge bucks. Anyhow, I think he behaved himself with her."

"But he was still quite a flirt."

"That was second nature to ole Gordie," Blossom murmured with obvious affection. "Besides, I always had the impression he thought he was doing all of us a favor. Making us feel good." It was an impression I'd entertained myself.

"I noticed that you didn't use the word 'love.' "

"Love, schmove. You can't put a label on everything. Whatever it was Gordie had with Rhonda, it seems to have kept him in line." Then directly on the heels of this I was provided with a reminder: "Although no one can say for sure that he stepped out on Edie, either."

"You're right. Tell me about Rhonda, though. Do you think *she* was in love with Gordon?"

"I guess so."

"She doesn't appear to be shedding too many tears over him."

"True. But maybe she's the kind who does her grieving in private."

"Maybe," I conceded, but without a lot of conviction.

"Or could be his feelings for her were stronger than vice versa."

Now, *that* I could buy.

A couple of minutes later I was considering Blossom's report of her conversation with Fielding (aka Fiedler), when it occurred to me—belatedly, I admit—that as yet the man hadn't made an attempt to bawl me out for misleading him like that. At least, not that I was aware of.

I buzzed Jackie on the intercom. "Um, by any chance, has Tim Fielding tried to contact me in the last two days?"

"If he had, wouldn't I have given you the message?" she all but snarled.

Chastened, I answered meekly, "Yes, of course you would."

Well, it was plain that the woman was in a snit, but for a moment I couldn't figure out what was bothering her. Then it occurred to me. "I'm sorry for not going into the reason for Ellen's phone call before, Jackie. I was just being perverse—I don't know why, either. I *have* had a lot on my mind lately, but that's still no excuse. Anyhow, Ellen wanted to talk to me because—"

"You don't have to tell me if you don't want to."

"But I do want to." And I presented a quick synopsis of the tale of the black dress.

When I'd finished, Jackie's response was, "That's it?"

Would you believe I almost felt guilty about disappointing her?

It took a little time for me to work up the courage to lift the receiver. Then while I was dialing Fielding's number, I was actually hoping he wasn't in. But he was there, all right. And on hearing the familiar voice, I was afflicted with an instant case of dry mouth.

Tim's response to my cordial (although slightly tremulous), "Hi, Tim, it's Desiree," was an extremely *un*cordial, "Well, well."

"I, er, understand you spoke to Blossom Goody."

"You do, do you?"

"I just had a conversation with her, and she said that when you asked about Edith Curry's nurse, she played dumb. She thought I might object to her giving you that information."

"Really?" (You can't imagine how much sarcasm a motivated person can manage to squeeze into that one small word.) "And why would she think that?"

"Apparently, she, um, got it into her head that I could be worried about its hampering my own investigation."

"Which, of course, is far superior to any probe the police might be conducting," Fielding commented dryly.

I considered it advisable to leave this alone. "Anyhow, it was really foolish of her." (Forgive me, Blossom.) "But I can fill you in now myself. And, incidentally, I didn't have to get Blossom's help to do it, either. As it happens, I came across that piece of paper with the nurse's name and number on it this morning. It was in the wrong folder." I followed this with a short, insipid titter.

"Well, what do you know."

"The woman's name is Melanie Slater." I spelled out the "Slater," then recited the telephone number.

"You wouldn't, I'm sure, have held out on me in order to delay our interrogation of Ms. Slater."

"Why would I do that?" I asked, sounding—or this was my intention, anyway—like the very essence of the falsely accused.

"Just tell me. Have you met with her yet?"

"Well . . . um . . . I contacted her this morning— as soon as I found that slip of paper. And she stopped by my office a little while ago."

"Lucky she was available on the spot like that, wasn't it?"

My "Yes" was practically inaudible.

"Listen, Shapiro, I *do* have an IQ over sixty. This was all about your wanting first crack at the woman. And you convinced that shyster lawyer to go along with you."

"You're wrong, honestly."

"Sure." Fielding laughed. And it wasn't a pleasant laugh, either.

"Really, I—"

"I'm kind of concerned about *your* IQ, though."

"What do you mean?"

"I'd have thought you'd wonder why I wasn't immediately on your neck about this nurse business. And the truth is, I would have been—if something else hadn't taken precedence."

"What was that?" While I didn't expect much of an

answer, there was no way I could stop myself from asking the question.

"Why don't you watch the eleven o'clock news tonight and find out."

# Chapter 29

What was going on, anyway?

Now, the chances of my wheedling anything out of Tim had ranged between "highly unlikely" and "not on your life," skewing heavily toward the latter. Nevertheless, I'd tried my damnedest to persuade him to open up—although I can't claim that I'd been shocked when he wouldn't budge. Listen, I regarded it as a major coup that I'd gotten him to tell me what channel to tune in to.

At any rate, the fact that this whatever-it-was would be making the eleven o'clock news was a pretty good indication that it was weighty stuff.

Could the murder weapon finally have surfaced? I mused. Or maybe the DA had made the shooter an irresistible offer, and the man had proceeded to identify the individual who'd hired him. And then it occurred to me that Tim might actually have managed—on his own, I mean—to discover who'd set this whole tragedy in motion.

I'm ashamed to admit that I experienced a twinge of envy the instant I considered this last possibility. I had to remind myself that it wasn't important who solved this damn thing. What *was* important was that the guilty parties—both of them—be held accountable for my client's death.

\* \* \*

Necessity forced me to abandon the topic. It was now 4:33 on the nose. Time for somebody planning to entertain one's (hoped for) future significant other— or whatever they're called nowadays—to make a speedy exit. That is, if she had any additional shopping to do for the meal she was planning to seduce him with that weekend.

Which she did.

I managed to sneak out when Jackie was away from her desk, thus sparing myself a final round of the boeuf-bourguignon-vs.-orange-chicken-with-almonds debate.

After picking up a bunch of ingredients I needed for Sunday's dinner, I headed home. I was unpacking my purchases when I decided that nothing in the refrigerator could tempt me to serve it to myself for supper. So I went downstairs again and walked over to this new pizzeria in the neighborhood, having totally forgotten about those three—or was it four?—slices I'd consumed the day before. (Although it probably wouldn't have made any difference even if this hadn't slipped my mind.)

A short while later I reached the conclusion that while the pizza here wasn't half as tasty as Little Angie's (but whose is?), it wasn't half bad, either. Besides, Mama Gina's was less than two blocks from my building. And besides *that,* you didn't have to leave your scruples at the door to get a seat at the counter. (I might as well own up to it; yesterday, at Little Angie's, I *did* provide a slight assist in separating that woman's umbrella from her person.)

During my twenty-minute stay at Mama Gina's, I was able to banish any thought of the eleven o'clock news from my head. The subject was still verboten when I got home, so I figured I'd busy myself with making telephone calls.

First on my agenda was my old and much married friend Pat Wizniak (formerly Martucci, formerly Altmann, formerly Green, formerly Anderson). It seemed husband number four might be a keeper, though. The couple had recently returned from a trip to Outer Mongolia (!), and they had a perfectly *wonderful* time. "Burton always comes up with the most unusual vacations," Pat raved. Well, who could argue with that?

We spent the next ten minutes or so chatting about all sorts of things, and then I wound up telling her about Nick. Pat considered the dinner invitation a very positive step. "I'm glad you're taking the initiative," she pronounced. "Some men just have to be kick-started." I smiled. Leave it to Pat to put it like that. Still, if *she* considered this a good idea . . .

A moment later I reminded myself of the woman's track record. In between all of those disastrous previous marriages had been a bunch of even more disastrous affairs. And I'm talking *cataclysmic*.

Pat Wizniak's stamp of approval was almost enough to get me to consider canceling Sunday's dinner. (I did say "almost.")

At any rate, after the conversation with Pat, I thought about Christie Wright, a close college buddy from Minnesota. We hadn't spoken in what must have been a couple of months, and it was time we touched base. I was looking up her number in the proverbial little black book (which in my case happens be red) when the phone rang.

"Ms. Shapiro?" the man inquired.

The voice was so nondistinctive that this in itself made it distinctive—if you follow me. "Mr. Garber?"

"Oh, you recognized my voice. Er, I hope this isn't too late to call—you weren't asleep, were you?"

I glanced at my watch. It was only about nine fifteen. "No, no. I'm lucky if I make it to bed before twelve. But how are you feeling, Mr. Garber?"

"Pretty good. As it turns out, I didn't have the flu at all. It must have been one of those twenty-four-hour viruses. But thank you for asking. The reason

I'm telephoning, though, is that something's come up, and I have to go into work for a while tomorrow morning. I thought that as long as I was in the city anyway, maybe I could meet with you then. Would that be okay?"

"Absolutely. Any time that's good for you."

I soon learned that this was not the wisest answer. "Well, why don't I stop by your office first?" Luke proposed. "That way you won't get stuck hanging around for hours if I'm tied up longer than I anticipate. Would eight o'clock be all right?"

Did he say *eight o'clock?*

It was a rhetorical question.

Inwardly I began screaming curses at the man. I mean, first it was Fielding, and now Luke Garber was suggesting this same obscene hour for my get-together with *him*—and don't forget that in this instance it was for a Saturday! Still, I didn't dare ask if we could make it later. After all, suppose Garber wound up having to devote the entire day to completing whatever business was bringing him into Manhattan. That could result in his canceling with me entirely!

"Eight's fine," I responded graciously. Like the hypocrite I am.

After Luke's call I began to get really antsy. I no longer had the patience to chat with friends, so I took a shower and put on my pajamas. Then I stretched out on the sofa with a book. But after going over the same paragraph a half dozen times, I realized I couldn't rely on reading to keep me occupied. Luckily, there was still some Häagen-Dazs in the freezer.

Finally, at 10:50, I switched on the TV and waited. . . .

The news seemed to go on forever, and in spite of my best efforts, my eyelids were in imminent danger of closing. Then all of a sudden, I perked up.

"Last Sunday night," the anchorman was saying, his

near perfect features in tight close-up, "business executive Gordon Curry was shot three times on a quiet street in the city's Chelsea section when leaving the apartment of a friend. Two police officers who were in the area at the time chased down and apprehended the alleged shooter a few blocks from the crime site. But the suspect—whose identity is being withheld by the authorities—has continued to maintain his innocence, and the NYPD has been unable to locate the weapon that could tie him to the homicide. Now, however, there appears to be a major breakthrough in the case. Our Lurene Bolton has the news on this latest development. Lurene?"

The scene cut to a dimpled, dark-haired female reporter on a Manhattan sidewalk. To her immediate right was a gawky boy of about thirteen or fourteen. And on *his* right was a pudgy bald man I estimated to be somewhere in his late forties. A small group of curious onlookers milled around in the background.

"Thanks, Curt," Lurene said, acknowledging the introduction. Then to the TV audience: "I'm outside the station house in Manhattan's Twelfth Precinct. With me are young Ronnie Gulden and his father, Harvey." She made about a thirty-degree turn toward the boy—ensuring that at least one of her dimples would still be on camera. (And who could blame her?) "I understand that you, Ronnie, just delivered to the police here what was very probably the weapon involved in last weekend's fatal shooting." She shoved the microphone in the kid's face.

"Yeah," he responded, looking startled.

"How did you come into possession of the gun, Ronnie?"

"Uh, me and my friend Shorty was walkin' home from the movies that night, and this guy comes barrelin' down the street and bumps into us. That's when he musta slipped it in my pocket." There was a slight hesitation, after which the boy elaborated, "These two cops was running after him, but they were almost a block away then."

"And this man you're referring to is the one who was arrested for the crime?"

"Yeah."

"You were able to identify him for the police?"

"Yeah."

"You're certainly a wonderful example of what it means to be a good citizen, Ronnie. But was there a reason you waited five days before stepping forward?"

"At first I didn't even know he planted the thing on me. And later—"

The pudgy bald man, having found his opening, leaned across his son now, blocking him from view. "He was afraid he'd get in trouble with me; that's the reason," he supplied.

"This is Harvey Gulden, Ronnie's father," the reporter announced unnecessarily. After which she reluctantly thrust the microphone under Harvey's chin.

He favored the television audience with a fatuous grin. "That's right. My wife and me, we was at a wedding in Jersey that evening, see, and Ronnie was supposed to stay in and do his homework. Instead, he goes to the movies. Only I didn't know nuthin' about that, see? Not till last night when he's talkin' on the phone to his friend, and I hear him say the word 'gun.' "

Harvey's half-open mouth was a fairly reliable sign that he was about to continue, but the reporter appropriated the microphone. "And you persuaded Ronnie to tell you what happened?" she asked before giving the eager father access to it again.

"You bet your a—" A shamefaced Harvey Gulden broke off but quickly recovered. "I mean, you bet I did. And I got him to come down to the station here, too."

"Well, New York is very grateful to you both, Mr. Gulden. Now back to you, Curt and Dolly."

The broadcast reverted to the studio again. "Great job, Lurene," the anchorman said (rather patronizingly, if you ask me). Then the camera angle widened to reveal the pretty anchorwoman seated alongside him. "Well, Dolly, it looks as if the authorities could finally have the evidence they need to bring charges against the suspect in that terrible murder."

"Yes, it does, Curt," she agreed. And to the viewer: "Curt and I will be following this story closely, folks, and we'll keep you advised of future developments as soon as they unfold."

Apparently unwilling to let his partner have the last word on the matter, the anchorman nodded, threw in, "That we will," then smiled broadly to put his gleaming, perfectly shaped teeth on display.

My God! This *was* a major breakthrough! If the weapon that killed Gordon was definitely established as Lonergan's—and there didn't seem to be much doubt that it would be—the hit man could very likely be persuaded to roll over and name the individual who'd hired him. That is, if the district attorney's office promised him a reduced sentence in exchange for his cooperation. Which it probably would.

Still, what if the DA refused to offer him a deal? Or Lonergan refused to go along with one? *You'd better not start counting your chickens yet,* I warned myself.

As it turned out, I'd rarely received sounder advice.

# Chapter 30

I find it really distressing to rise before the sun does. Considering the pace at which I move, however, it was either that or greet the world with a naked face. Something the world was hardly ready for.

Anyhow, it took a while for both eyes to open fully. But once they did, I put on my makeup, engaged in a prolonged battle with my glorious hennaed hair— which was, as usual, determined to go its own way— and got into some clothes. Then after a wake-up cup of coffee accompanied by a corn muffin, I grabbed a taxi to the office. It was just before eight when I arrived, and I waited in the reception area for my visitor, who followed me by less than five minutes.

Luke Garber looked pretty much as I'd pictured him. He was quite tall and on the thin side. His hair was a medium brown, with what little remained of it in dire need of a trim. And while the man had nice hazel eyes, you really had to peer at him closely to appreciate that fact, since they were mostly obscured by thick, rimless glasses. "Ms. Shapiro?" he inquired.

"It's Desiree."

His smile was almost shy. "Okay, but in that case, you'll have to call me Luke."

We shook hands, and I preceded him down the hall to my cubbyhole. Stepping aside so he could enter the room, I mumbled what was only too apparent: "It's tiny."

"I like it—it's cozy," Luke responded tactfully. Then rejecting my offer to hang up his jacket ("Oh, I won't be here that long"), he draped it on the back of the "visitor's chair" and sat down.

"Why don't I send out for breakfast?" I suggested as soon as I'd planted my own bottom in its customary location.

"That's very nice of you, but I've already eaten."

"Well, then let's just go over a few matters, if you don't mind."

"No, I don't mind. Although as I warned you on the phone, I'm afraid I don't have anything to tell you. And I *am* pressed for time."

"I'll keep it brief. Uh, you mentioned that you didn't see very much of Gordon."

"That's true."

"Still, you must have heard some things *about* him over the years."

It took a few seconds for Luke to reluctantly admit that, well, Gordon *did* have a reputation as a ladies' man.

"Do you believe he cheated on Rhonda?"

"I have no idea. I do remember that there was some talk about Gordon's running around on his first wife. But whether or not this was an actual fact, I couldn't say."

"Were Gordon and Rhonda happy together? As far as you know, that is."

"They appeared to be. Rhonda may have been too dynamic and too much the socialite for me, but she and Gordon—" Luke stopped cold. "I'm afraid that sounds as if I'm being critical of her, and this isn't how it was meant. Basically, Rhonda's a good person; it's just that we were completely wrong for each other."

"In what way?" I asked, anxious for a little insight into both these people.

"In every way. My ex is always in overdrive. Me,

on the other hand—I'm a pretty laid-back guy. While
Rhonda enjoys going to fancy restaurants with her rich
friends, I prefer sitting home with a book or watching
TV. It's not that I'm faulting her for her lifestyle, you
understand; it's only that I was never comfortable with
it. When Bobbie—my present wife—and I do venture
out for an evening, we like to have dinner someplace
in the neighborhood, maybe take in a movie later."

"There must have been more," I put out there,
fishing.

"Sure there was. To be honest, I wasn't crazy about
Rhonda's insistence on going by her maiden name.
No, let me be *really* honest; it used to bug the hell
out of me. We were even at odds when it came to
clothes. Rhonda pays a fortune for hers—which is
okay; she has the money to do it. But she was constantly nagging me about letting her outfit me, too—
in the kind of stuff I couldn't afford on my own. And
even if I could, well, as you can see," he pointed out
with a grin, "I'm not exactly a slave to fashion."

I quickly appraised Luke's slightly large-in-the-seat
brown slacks and heavy red wool sweater. They were
certainly presentable enough, but you can bet your
firstborn that neither garment carried a designer label.

"Evidently, though," he continued, "Gordon had no
problem with any of this. Actually, I imagine it was
all part of the attraction."

I stated the obvious—and for no particular reason,
except that I felt I should say *something* at this juncture. "I guess it boils down to everyone's having different needs."

"I can't argue with that." And now, with a self-
deprecating smile: "Hey, I'm a schnooky accountant
from Brooklyn who's satisfied with just earning a
decent enough living to provide for my family. As for
Rhonda, she was determined to make it big. And, God
bless her, she has."

"So I've gathered. Listen, Luke, considering that

you and Gordon knew many of the same people, there's a possibility you heard something else about him that's since slipped your mind. So please try to think. Are you aware of anyone who had a grudge against Gordon? Or anyone who quarreled with him? And I'm talking about even the tiniest spat."

"I'm sorry, but no, I'm not."

"Well, if something should occur to you, you'll contact me, won't you?"

"Of course." There was some brief hesitation before Luke put to me, "Er, would you mind if I asked you a question?"

"Please do."

"You mentioned on the phone that Gordon had been in fear for his life."

"Yes. There'd been two earlier, failed attempts to kill him."

"And he didn't know who was responsible?"

"Gordon was positive the perpetrator was a bitter former employee he'd found it necessary to fire."

"Rhonda tells me that the fellow the police arrested was most likely a hired killer. Is there a possibility that this employee was the one who hired him?" He sounded hopeful.

"Sorry, but no. I've since learned that Roger—he was the employee—committed suicide even before the previous attacks."

"What if this Roger had set something up beforehand?" Luke still sounded hopeful—but a little less so.

"That doesn't make it, either. Roger couldn't have afforded a hit man; he was totally broke. Besides, from what I know of him, I'd be willing to place a good-sized wager on his being the type who'd want to do the job himself. Oh, before I forget. Is the name Francis Lonergan familiar to you?"

"Lonergan . . . The family wouldn't be from Georgia, by any chance?"

"I couldn't say."

"Wait," a plainly embarrassed Luke murmured almost immediately. "I just remembered. The people I had in mind are the *Lenihans*. And come to think of it, they may not even be from Georgia; they could be from Tennessee. Is this person important to your investigation?"

"Probably not. Somebody mentioned the name to me, and I can't recall in what context this was. I just thought you might be able to help me out." And here I took a deep breath. "Umm, I have one last question, and then I'll let you leave for work."

I shouldn't have phrased it like that, because Luke glanced at his watch and grimaced. "I had no idea it was so late. I really have to get going."

"I'll make this fast. I promise." My tongue, however, wasn't willing to cooperate—not unless I exhibited a little sensitivity first. "I'm so sorry to bring this up, Luke; I'm sure it's still extremely painful to you. But I do have to ask—for my records." Anticipating what would follow, the man's face turned ashen. "Uh, I understand that your son died as a result of injuries he sustained in an automobile accident and that Gordon was the driver of the car."

"You're wondering if I murdered him because of Chip—is that it?"

"No, I—"

"Well, I didn't. Although I won't deny that at first—right after Chip passed away—the idea of Gordon Curry's winding up six feet under wasn't unappealing to me. But I didn't kill him; I couldn't kill anybody. Or pay anyone to do it for me, either. And eventually I came to accept what happened for the accident it was." With this, Luke inched forward in his chair, obviously preparing to get to his feet.

"Just one more thing," I said hastily.

"All right. But please, Desiree, let's do this

quickly." And with a look of resignation, he moved back in the seat—but not very far.

"In your opinion, how likely is it that Rhonda hired the shooter?"

"I can't see her even considering a thing like that."

For a few moments, neither of us said a word. I watched, mesmerized, as a single tear trickled slowly down Luke's cheek and onto his chin. "Oh, God," he uttered in a voice that was nothing short of wrenching. "If only he'd listened to her when she pleaded with him to cancel those plans. If only this woman who can usually convince anyone of just about anything had been able to do that when it mattered most."

"You mean Rhonda tried to persuade Gordon not to go up to Vermont that day?"

"Oh," Luke said, "I was under the impression you knew. She begged him to make it another time. She'd tuned in to the weather reports that morning, and the road conditions in that area were said to be hazardous. But Gordon insisted he was an excellent driver and that he'd be careful. He couldn't disappoint Chip, he told her. And in the end Rhonda gave in."

*So Gordon had gone against his wife's wishes in making the trip that cost Chip his life.* Suddenly I understood why Rhonda had initially held him responsible for the loss of her son. And why, despite her assertion to the contrary, she may never really have forgiven him.

And glancing at Luke's stricken face, I realized that it was equally possible he never had, either.

# Chapter 31

My apartment wasn't exactly in eat-off-the-floor condition. That's not to say it was dirty. It's just that it no longer gets completely overhauled twice a month now that Charmaine—my every-other-week cleaning lady—is gone. Oh, I don't mean that she's dead, God forbid. But she took a powder on me some years back, and since then you'd be wise to have your meals at the table.

Anyhow, as soon as I got home from my meeting with Luke, I allotted myself twenty minutes for lunch. And after this I began tearing the place apart.

I mopped. And I vacuumed. And scrubbed. And dusted. And polished . . . There was barely an inch in that place that escaped my scrutiny—and manic right arm. I wasn't through with my chores until almost four o'clock. And let me tell you, I was exhausted to the point where it was a strain to lift my pinkie. But, I swear, that apartment was so clean you could hear it squeak! Sooner or later Nick might decide to end the relationship (if you'd care to regard it as that), but there was no way he'd be able to blame the split on my being a lousy housekeeper.

At any rate, the tough stuff behind me, I made myself a cup of coffee, then sat on the sofa to relax for a few minutes. . . .

It was close to an hour before I woke up—and dis-

covered I was one giant ache. Nevertheless, I'd promised myself I'd put in a call to Fielding this afternoon,
and it was about time I got around to it.

It was, of course, crucial that I have an update on
the police investigation. And I certainly didn't want
to keep getting my information filtered down through
Lurene and Curt and Dolly—attractive as they were.
Currently, though, Tim Fielding would most likely
hold a cockroach in higher esteem than he did his
old friend Desiree. But while I'd had to work up to
contacting him yesterday, thanks to that warm reception I'd received, it was ten times more difficult for
me to pick up the phone today. I kept telling myself
that with any luck the man had had a good lunch and
that this would improve his disposition. Possibly to the
extent of his forgiving all the transgressions I'd managed to rack up lately.

At any rate, I finally took the plunge—only to be
apprised by some woman at the precinct that Sergeant
Fielding wasn't in and wasn't expected until Monday.
Could someone else help me? she wanted to know. I
refrained from saying "Detective Melnick." Listen, if
Fielding considered me persona non grata now, all I
had to do was to try pumping his partner. I could just
picture him making a replica of this pudgy little torso
of mine and sticking a few sharp pins in its most sensitive parts.

Besides, with THE DINNER coming up tomorrow,
I was too busy at present to follow through on anything anyway. I'd wait until Monday morning to find
out what was what.

Supper that night was macaroni and cheese (my recipe), along with four or five fish sticks (Mrs. Paul's),
followed by an extra-generous helping of Häagen-
Dazs macadamia brittle. After all, it had been a very
demanding day, and I deserved a reward to accom-

pany that cup of my positively horrendous coffee. (The latter, incidentally, being something absolutely no one deserves.) Anyhow, once I'd finished the meal, I was ready—more or less—to tackle tomorrow's menu.

I prepared the ingredients for the boeuf bourguignon. Then while the meat and wine and those lovely vegetables were simmering on the stove, I whipped up the cold lemon soufflé, which I'd decorate in the morning.

That night, I went to bed achy and exhausted. I had every intention of sleeping until noon—or, at any rate, somewhere in that neighborhood. But it wasn't to be.

The phone rang at nine a.m.

The "Hello" I muttered into the mouthpiece came out sounding—even to my ears—like "Halumf."

"Desiree?"

I sat up slowly, my poor, abused body protesting every little movement. (Who did I think I was yesterday, anyhow—Mrs. Clean?) "Nick?"

"I hated to call this early, Dez, but I wanted to catch you before you started fixing dinner."

*Uh-oh.* "That's okay—I was awake. In fact, I just finished breakfast. Is something wrong?"

"Well, no . . . and yes. I heard from my ex a couple of minutes ago. It seems that she won't be escorting our son to any party this afternoon. Derek's little cousin—the birthday girl—has come down with the measles. The problem is, though, that right after Tiffany learned about that, some new fellow she's interested in phoned to invite her out tonight. And of course, Tiffany accepted. She said she was certain I'd be only too happy to have Derek stay over until Monday. And the fact is, normally that would have been true. But not this time. I told her I'd already made arrangements of my own and strongly suggested she rearrange *her* plans for a change. Only Tiffany insists that she can't get in touch with the guy, that he's staying with friends while his apartment's being redecorated, and she has no idea of their last name. I don't regard myself as the suspicious type, but Tiffany was trying to convince me that the man's cell phone just happens to be broken, so she isn't able to reach him that way, either. How's that for a coincidence? At any rate, I had no choice but to agree to keep Derek with me until tomorrow.

"I'm really sorry about this, Dez," Nick said, sounding, well, really sorry. "I was looking forward to this evening. I hope you haven't done any cooking yet."

"Uh, no. Not yet." (Better not to give him the idea that I was making any big deal about having him over for a meal.)

"That's a relief, anyway. Listen, I'd like the three of us to go out to dinner later—if you're agreeable, that is."

"I'd prefer it if you both came here. I've already done all the grocery shopping, and I even have some hamburger meat in the freezer for Derek." (I figured a burger would probably be more appreciated by a nine-year-old palate than boeuf bourguignon.)

"Are you sure you want to do this, Dez? Derek can be a pain in the rump when it comes to food."

"Thanks for the warning, but I'm positive."

"Well, okay. I hope you won't regret this, though."

*I hope so, too,* I retorted silently.

And now, just when I thought everything was all set, Nick sheepishly informed me that the previously agreed-upon seven thirty might be a little late for his son, who was used to eating at least an hour earlier. So we rescheduled for six. (Listen, far be it from me to throw the little darling's constitution into a tizzy.)

\*   \*   \*

The instant the receiver was back in its cradle, I got out of bed, slapped on a little makeup, slipped into some clothes, and then—without stopping for so much as a swallow of coffee—hurried over to D'Agostino's, where I acquired the ground beef I'd claimed was in the freezer. Before long, keeping the meat company in the shopping cart were such other Derek-related items as hamburger buns, coleslaw, potato salad, macaroni salad, pretzels, tortilla chips, a can of diced chilies, a two-liter bottle of Coke, and three flavors of ice cream. After arranging to have my purchases delivered, I left the supermarket and headed for this little appetizer store, where I bought three varieties of cheeses. Next, it was on to the greengrocer's for the salad fixings. And finally, I stopped off at the bakery for a French bread and a pound of cookies.

It wasn't until I was back in my apartment again that I took the time to question my sanity.

*Are you crazy?* I asked myself. *Who knows what that little bastard could pull tonight?*

I rallied to my defense with the reminder that I'd already prepared practically the entire meal. Plus, I'd gotten myself into that cleaning frenzy, which had left every bone in my body in trauma and from which I would probably never recover. I mean, the result was the same as if I'd been deliberately *exercising*—the very word being anathema to me. And to let these things be for naught? Not on your life!

Besides, now that I knew what I was dealing with, I'd just love to see him try something!

# Chapter 32

With most of the advance preparation on the fare for us grown-ups having been finished yesterday, all that remained was to cut the vegetables for the salad and make the dressing, then whip up some heavy cream and pipe it onto the top of the lemon soufflé in a decorative pattern. Not being any great shakes at "decorative," however, I'm always a bit antsy about what the soufflé will look like when I'm through. But this time I did myself proud. If I say so myself, the results were not unappetizing.

And now I turned my attention to feeding The Kid from Hell (this designation hereafter frequently used in its abbreviated form). Fortunately, all I needed to do there was to shape and season a hamburger patty and mix up some salsa for the chips. His dessert required no effort at all. It would be ice cream—in a choice of three flavors—along with an assortment of very delicious bakery cookies. (I can personally attest to the delicious part, having sampled a few of the cookies myself—the kind of thing I consider to be the duty of a good hostess.)

After taking a few minutes out to swallow an egg salad sandwich and a cup of coffee, I set up the folding table in the living room—which, incidentally, is also my dining room, my guest room, and my office. I covered the table with the only really nice cloth I own and set out the good china, glassware, and silver.

At that point I decided I'd better devote a fair amount of attention to seeing to it that I was presentable, too.

I began by immersing my aching bones in a lovely, almost relaxing bubble bath. The "almost" stemming from my finding it impossible to unwind completely, knowing that before long I'd be in the company of TKFH—and that there was no predicting what might be on his diabolical little mind tonight. Not that I permitted myself to speculate about this. I instantly banished the thought whenever it threatened to enter my head.

The downstairs buzzer sounded just as I was about to dry myself off. Wrapping the towel around me and leaving a trail of puddles in my wake, I hurried over to the intercom. There was a delivery for a Ms. Shapiro, I was advised. I buzzed the man into the lobby and made a dash for my bathrobe.

A short while later a very small individual carrying a very large floral arrangement was standing on my doorstep. I mean, this arrangement was so huge that the poor fellow seemed to be in danger of collapsing under its weight. I had never *seen* such a magnificent display! The entire bouquet was in shades of pink and purple, with at least a dozen pink roses, as well as purple irises and scattered lavender asters (I think), plus some other blooms I couldn't identify. All set into a handsome lavender basket.

As soon as the deliveryman left I grappled with the hernia-inducing chore of setting the flowers on the folding table—although slightly fearful that the table might not hold up as well as the deliveryman had. When I was pretty much satisfied that it would remain upright, I reached for the card. "Can't wait to see you. Thanks for having us over." It was signed, "Nick."

Of course, "Love, Nick" would have been nice. Okay. Go ahead—say it: Some people are never satisfied. But, actually, I *was;* the truth is, I was delighted.

I didn't allow Nick's being a florist to detract one bit from my appreciation of this thoughtful gesture, either. Listen, my friend Pat—you know, the one who gets married a lot—was going out with a butcher a few years back. And he never gave her so much as one lousy little lamb chop!

Getting myself decked out for an important evening (which was certainly how I regarded this) is normally fraught with minor disasters. But for some inexplicable reason, tonight the task was completely problem free. For starters, my makeup went on without a hitch: Not a smudge of mascara wound up on a cheekbone; not a trace of lipstick migrated to my chin; and I didn't drop the eyebrow pencil down the drain. (Yes, this really happened—twice.) Even my incorrigible hair behaved itself—quite possibly a first. I also didn't misplace my earrings. Or discover a run in my panty hose. As for my dress, it had taken a week of agonizing, but I'd finally settled on the pale green A-line (probably because when I last wore it, someone commented that it did nice things for my coloring). And wonder of wonders, I actually stuck to this decision. In fact, everything went so smoothly that I was able to take my sweet time when tending to some last-minute touches for the dinner itself.

I heated the mushroom croustades and grouped them on a platter, which I set on an electric hot tray. Then I arranged the cheeses on a board with an assortment of crackers. Put out the nibbles and salsa. And removed the boeuf bourguignon from the refrigerator and placed it on the stove.

The bell rang as I was on my way to the bathroom mirror to verify that nothing had gone awry since I'd checked myself out only a few minutes earlier.

When I opened the door to Nick and son, the first thing I noticed was the brightness of their smiles—one of these genuine, the other plainly forced. (I don't suppose I have to tell you which was which.)

As the pair entered the room, Nick bussed me on the cheek. TKFH stuck out his hand. "Hi, Desiree. It's nice to see you again," he lied.

I took the outstretched hand gingerly. "It's nice to see you again, too, Derek," I lied right back.

"You refused to tell me which you preferred, so I brought red *and* white," Nick informed me, handing me a plastic bag.

"First, this gorgeous bouquet—and I want you to know I'm totally overwhelmed by it—and now wine, too? I thank you, Nick, but I have to ask you something."

"What's that?"

"Are you *crazy?*"

He chuckled. "Probably. But not because of the flowers or the wine."

Derek sat down on the sofa then and, at my invitation, helped himself to a couple of tortilla chips and dipped one in the salsa. "Mmm, this is very good salsa," he said.

"I'm pleased you like it. Would you care for a Coke?"

"Yes, thank you." The kid was like the poster boy for politeness, for God's sake! *Can it be he's no longer intent on disappearing me from his father's life?*

*No way!* the more intelligent side of me responded. *Have you forgotten how well behaved, how positively darling he was that other time you broke bread together? And then he dumped his frozen hot chocolate in your lap!*

Anyhow, I brought him his Coke, following which Nick accompanied me to the kitchen to open the wine—both of us selecting the Pinot Noir over the Chardonnay. As I handed Nick the corkscrew, he was so close to me (of course, it was hard to be anything *but*—considering the size of my kitchen) that for a moment I entertained the ridiculous notion that he might be about to kiss me. The moment passed. But once he'd uncorked the wine, he did say, "You look beautiful tonight, Dez."

"So do you." And it was true—I swear! He was wearing a really classy outfit—a hand-knitted (I believe) charcoal gray sweater and coordinating light gray tweed pants. Both of which fit him perfectly.

Nick laughed. "Me? *Beautiful?*" He rolled his eyes heavenward. "And this woman called *me* crazy!"

Nothing more was said, and we were soon back in the living room with our wine, Nick joining his son on the sofa, while I perched on one of the club chairs. Nick reached for one of the wild-mushroom croustades, and it took only a single bite for him to declare it "the best hors d'oeuvre I've ever eaten." I beamed, although I had to admit to myself that he might be engaging in a slight exaggeration.

At his father's urging, TKFH also sampled a croustade and immediately exclaimed, "Wow! This is delicious, Desiree." A second later he added, "So's everything else."

But I wasn't about to let myself be fooled—after all, we had a history, Derek and I.

For fifteen minutes or so the three of us sat there, sipping and stuffing ourselves silly, while engaging in polite conversation—much of it revolving around TKFH's theatrical debut, which was to be in his school's December production of *Our Town*. "Derek's pretty nervous about it," Nick said.

"Yeah, I am," the boy admitted, "even though I don't have a very big part."

"Everyone's nervous when they perform—especially for the first time. But I'm sure you'll do fine," I told him. (I wasn't just saying that, either. Listen, hadn't I already witnessed his acting talent? Wasn't I, in fact, being treated to another example of it tonight?)

"Thanks, I hope so," he murmured, getting to his feet. "May I be excused to use your bathroom, Desiree?"

"Certainly you may. Do you know where it is?"

"I'll find it." And with this, he left the room.

When he was out of earshot, Nick thanked me again for having them over. And I said how pleased I was that they'd come. We'd been chatting for another five minutes at most when I reminded myself that it might be a good idea to get dinner ready—I still had to broil the burger, reheat the boeuf bourguignon, and put the salad together. So at that point I, too, excused myself.

Now, I'm not claiming I had a premonition. On the other hand, *something* made me walk to the kitchen on tiptoe.

At the entrance, I stopped cold. TKFH had a bottle of black pepper in his hand and was in the process of dumping its contents into the boeuf bourguignon!

I felt as if Mike Tyson had punched me in the stomach! Plus, my heart was thumping so loudly in my ears that I could barely hear myself think. I wasn't sure how long I could count on my legs to hold me up, either. I thrust my arm against the wall for support.

Too stunned to move or even speak, I remained frozen in the doorway. Mutely I watched Derek hurriedly screw the top back on the bottle and return it to my spice rack, then pick up a wooden spoon from the stove and thoroughly stir the pepper into the stew.

Finally, I found my voice. "What are you doing, Derek?" I said quietly.

TKFH wheeled around and, on seeing me, turned chalk white. But in a flash his color quickly returned. "Nothing. I just thought I'd help out and mix the stuff up. I hope that's okay, Desiree." He looked so innocent that I almost doubted my own eyes. But not for long.

"I *saw* you pouring the pepper into that pot."

For perhaps ten seconds Derek just stood there, biting his lower lip. Then he put his hands on his hips and stretched his lips into what might have been a smile. Only it wasn't. "Why don't you go running to my dad about this?" he challenged. "I bet you won't, because you know he wouldn't believe you."

In that instant I wanted nothing more than to place my hands around that scrawny neck of his and squeeze. But I realized that indulging in this luxury would not merely have been physically impossible in my present condition; it would have been extremely foolish, as well. (Besides, my palms were so wet they'd probably have slid right off the kid.) I also decided against tattling to Nick. And not because of Derek's pronouncement.

There was a chance—maybe a pretty good one— that Nick would accept my word for what had transpired. But look, suppose he did. I'd have forced him to go against his adored only child and take the side of a woman he was only dating casually. (What else would you call a kissless relationship *but* casual?) And how long could I expect that we'd continue to see each other once he became aware of his son's real feelings toward me?

It seemed clear that in light of TKFH's determination to undermine me, I'd wind up an also-ran—no matter how I handled this latest episode. Nevertheless, I refused to make things that easy for him. So I decided to keep my mouth closed and my options open—for the present, at least.

All of this raced through my mind in what must have been less than a minute. But I was left with a towering problem: how to explain this inedible dinner to Nick.

The solution occurred to me in a flash.

And now I strode purposefully into the kitchen and, in imitation of my abominable little adversary, stretched my lips into a smile that wasn't. Elbowing him aside, I picked up the contaminated pot, went over to the sink, and, with a shriek, pitched in its entire contents. (Listen, I wasn't about to let that whole mess land on my nice clean floor.)

Nick came rushing in. "What's happened?"

"I wanted to pour off some of the fat, but I lost my footing," I told him, looking I'm sure, appropriately stricken. (Which, considering what had just transpired, required no effort at all.) "I can't believe I was that clumsy."

"I am *so* sorry, Desiree. All that work down the drain. It— God, did you hear what I said? I wasn't trying to be funny. Honestly."

"I know that."

"And it smells delicious, too," he mumbled awkwardly, sniffing the air. He glanced at his son, who was still standing by the stove. "Derek didn't get in your way or anything, did he?"

"I wasn't—" Derek started to protest.

"He had nothing to do with it," I broke in, fixing my eyes on the kid's face.

"Listen, there's a Chinese restaurant that just opened up about four blocks from here, and I've heard some nice things about it. How about our going over there for dinner?"

Forget that I didn't care to be within shouting distance of young Satan here. There was another consideration, as well. I was convinced that in addition to all my other physical responses to Derek's treachery, my throat had begun to close up, and I'd be unable to swallow so much as the tiniest morsel. This condition most likely being a permanent one. "I think I'd better pass, Nick. I'm really not hungry—I suspect it was all those hors d'oeuvres. And anyhow, I'm anxious to clean up and put everything away."

"I'll help you with that as soon as we come back.

It'll do you good to get out of the apartment for a while, Dez."

"Thanks, but—"

"You don't go; we don't go," Nick insisted. "And there's a growing boy here who needs his nourishment. So do it for Derek."

I suddenly realized how delighted the "growing boy" would be if I stayed home.

So I said all right—for Derek.

# Chapter 33

A little glass of wine can do wonders for your appetite. Particularly when it's followed by another little glass of wine.

In light of my limited tolerance for alcoholic beverages, however, I'm a little fuzzy regarding much of that evening at the Black Pearl. But while I probably couldn't quote a single word of our dinner conversation, there are other things that did stick in my mind—including one exchange it's unlikely I'll ever forget.

I have a vague recollection of Derek and me wearing false smiles and being extremely polite to each other. I remember, too, that he stood up when I went to the ladies' room and pulled out my chair for me when I returned. I also recall having the impression that although he managed to put on a good show, he wasn't actually that much at ease. But then, I may have concluded this because I didn't feel he had a right to be. Anyhow, the fact that I was more relaxed than he was—or, at least, so I believed—pleased me no end. (My own placid state you can, of course, attribute entirely to that second glass of wine.)

As for Nick, I'm certain he failed to pick up on the underlying tension surrounding him. Listen, the kid wasn't the only talented actor he was feeding that night.

At any rate, later—and this incident I can relate

precisely as it occurred—when we were finished with our meal and waiting for the check, an elegant silver-haired couple who'd been sitting across from us stopped at our table as they were leaving the restaurant.

"We couldn't help noticing how well behaved your son is," the gentleman commented. Then addressing Derek: "We have a grandson about your age, and he could definitely take some lessons in manners from you."

"He's such a handsome young man, too," the woman put in. She glanced at me and smiled before looking at her husband. "I think he favors his mother. What do you think, dear?"

"Dear's" response was aborted by Derek, who, jumping up—and overturning his water glass in the process—screeched, "She's not my mother! My mother isn't fat and ugly and she doesn't have yucky hair and a big nose." (This last knock was a new one on me.)

As the mortified pair hurried off, Nick reached up and pulled his pride and joy back in his chair. "What's gotten *into* you, Derek?" he demanded, plainly traumatized. "Have you suddenly lost your *mind?*" He touched my arm. "I'm so sorry, Dez, so terribly sorry. I can't understand this, either. Derek's always telling me how much he likes you." (I noted, with a small degree of satisfaction, that TKFH's eyes were already filling up.)

By now I had retrieved my handbag from the floor and, hoping that everyone in the place was extremely hard of hearing, was on the verge of fleeing the premises. "It's okay, Nick. But it would be best if I left," I told him, getting to my feet.

"Wait until the check comes," he pleaded, rising, too. "I don't want you to walk home alone."

"I'll be fine," I assured him, already in motion.

"I'll speak to you tomorrow," Nick called out to my rapidly retreating back.

I didn't get much rest that night. I was too busy bawling. I dozed off sometime after five and woke up about ten, having slept through the alarm.

The first thing I did was to ring Jackie to inform her I wouldn't be in, that I'd be doing some work at home today.

"How did the dinner go?" she inquired eagerly.

"That's not something I want to talk about." And before she could take offense: "The truth is, it was one of the worst evenings of my life. I'll tell you about it when I see you."

"Maybe you'd feel better if we talked about it now," she wheedled.

"I really wouldn't, Jackie."

"Uh, it's up to you. But look, whatever happened, it can't be *that* bad. Will I see you tomorrow?"

"Sure. If I don't kill myself in the meantime."

I spent the next few minutes assuring the woman that I was only joking. After that I devoted an hour to straightening the apartment, which I'd totally ignored when I got back last night.

My plans to contact Fielding this morning had flown right out the window. I just wasn't up to the abuse—however well deserved—that I had no doubt was in store for me. Besides, I was focused on that call I was expecting from Nick. I figured he'd try reaching me at the office and that Jackie would tell him I was at home. So for I-don't-know-how-long I sat almost on top of the phone, cursing evil little boys and, after a while, the parents who'd made them.

It was past one o'clock when I put down the book I'd been attempting to read and turned off the TV that I'd simultaneously been attempting to watch.

I had a killer to catch here.

I got the file on Gordon from my desk and began to study it. Not all of my notes had even been transcribed yet, but I waded my way through the entire mess.

When I closed the manila folder a few hours later, I'd reached two conclusions: (1) I knew who had hired Gordon Curry's killer; (2) getting Tim to accept *how* I knew this was going to be one helluva job.

# Chapter 34

I decided that when I took on Fielding, it would be advisable to provide him with some verification of my conclusion.

Picking up the receiver, I made three phone calls—and had my judgment confirmed three times.

Satisfied now, I dialed the Twelfth Precinct.

When he realized who was on the other end of the line, my old friend wasn't too friendly.

"How are you?" I inquired politely.

"Living."

"Uh, I saw the news on Friday, and I was so excited I could hardly breathe. Finally, huh?"

"Yeah."

"Has the ballistics report come back?"

"Yeah."

I gnashed my teeth. Granted, I hadn't exactly played fair with the man. Nevertheless, this was hard to take. I felt my best bet would be to react as if he wouldn't have been delighted to perk up my Cheerios with a little strychnine. "And?" I prompted.

"And what?"

"And, um, it *is* the gun that killed Gordon, isn't it?"

There was a pause, during which Fielding was, I'm certain, deliberating about whether or not to share this information with me. He decided on the not. "Keep watching the news," he said tersely.

I pressed on. "What about the Gulden kid? Was he able to identify Lonergan?"

"Hey, what is this? Sorry, but I'm afraid I'm too busy to just sit around and allow you to interrogate me all day."

"The *main* reason I called wasn't to ask you anything, Tim; it was to tell you something."

"Suppose you spit it out, then."

"I know who hired Lonergan."

"Who?"

"I have to talk to you about that in person. The explanation's kind of complicated."

"And you want to drop by." Then, in a voice that practically *leaked* sarcasm: "You figure it would be a good idea if we worked on this together, right?"

"Yes," I answered sheepishly.

"Gee, why does that sound so familiar? When did I hear it before?" Fielding's tone hardened. "I tried to overlook how you inveigled your way in here last week. But then you do it to me again; you withhold the name of a suspect until after you've had the opportunity to question her yourself." Before I could manufacture some lame excuse, he added, "You persuade your shyster lawyer buddy to go along with you, too. I'd call your actions interfering in an official police investigation. What would you call them, Shapiro?"

Well, of course, I didn't dare touch that one. All I could say was, "I'm leveling with you now, I swear."

"That won't work anymore. You've blown what little credibility you had left."

"Unless I'm mistaken, you instructed me to keep my ears open, Tim. So this is what I did. That's how I found out who was behind the murder. Look, don't you think you should at least listen to what I have to say?"

I almost dozed off waiting for a response. "All

right," Fielding agreed at last. "I expect to be here until late—there's a bunch of stuff I have to clear up. But I'll probably want to take a break. Let's see. . . ." And after a few more seconds of dead air: "How's six o'clock." It wasn't really a question.

When I approached his desk, Fielding didn't bother getting to his feet—something that's almost like second nature to him. And I had to regard this as a pretty good indication of just how far from favor I'd fallen. "Sit," he instructed firmly.

I took off my coat and slung it over the back of the chair before complying. Then glancing over at Melnick's desk, I noticed that the young detective wasn't at it. "Norm isn't in today?"

"He left."

"Is he all right?"

"He's dandy," an exasperated Fielding answered. "He had a podiatrist's appointment. Can we get on with this?"

"Sorry. To begin with, I should tell you that I mentioned the name Francis Lonergan to all the suspects." Before Fielding had a chance to turn purple, I put in quickly, "But I didn't identify him as being the shooter. I just asked them if the name was familiar."

"Why?"

"I wanted to gauge how they'd react when I said it—whether any of them would seem nervous. Also, there was always the possibility that one suspect might link the name to another of the suspects—you know, maybe come out with something like, 'Somebody named Lonergan called so-and-so once when I was at the house.' Or 'I believe so-and-so was friendly with a Lonergan.' "

"And what did you claim was your reason for bringing up the name?"

"That I'd heard it somewhere but that I couldn't be

certain this was in relation to the case. I told them I was hoping they could help me out.''

Fielding eyed me skeptically. "And that was how you learned who was responsible for Curry's murder?''

"As a matter of fact, it was. But not in a way I'd anticipated. You see, one of them made a slip.'' To increase the suspense, I delayed elaborating on this, first uncrossing my legs, then pulling down my skirt. I had just given my hair a couple of pats when Fielding spoke up.

"Okay, Sarah Bernhardt, let's have it," he said, unsuccessfully attempting to hide a smile. "What kind of a slip?''

"In my phrasing of the question, I'd never identified Francis Lonergan as being a 'he'—and, incidentally, that wasn't on purpose, either. Anyhow, this person said, and I quote, 'Is *he* involved in the murder?' "

Fielding shook his head in disgust. "Hell, Shapiro. It was a good guess, that's all.''

"That's what I attributed it to originally—I mean, it wasn't that this went over my head. But the thing is, it kind of lay there in the back of my mind. And then when I went through my notes today, the 'he' jumped out at me. I was suddenly struck by how strange it was for anyone to simply *assume* that I was referring to a male in this instance.''

"It was a fifty-fifty shot, for crying out loud.''

"That's where you're wrong. Most often that name is spelled *F-r-a-n-c-e-s*, and it's given to baby *girls*.''

"I take it you have data supporting this contention.''

"Oh, come on. I can think of a number of women with that name, but offhand, I can't think of a single man.''

Looking smug, Fielding stated wryly, "I gather you've never heard of Francis Albert Sinatra.''

"You've just helped me make my point. Sinatra called himself Frank—like most men who've been saddled with 'Francis.' But please. If you want proof of how the name is normally perceived, do what I did."

"Which was what?"

"I conducted a little survey. I called three people: my secretary, Jackie; Harriet Gould—the woman who lives across the hall from me; and Gabe, this young guy who clerks at Gilbert and Sullivan. I asked each of them if they'd ever met anyone named Francis Lonergan.

"Jackie said that if she did meet her"—I came down hard on the "her"—"she didn't remember it. Now, Gabe's answer was a flat no. So I questioned him as to which gender he thought I was referring to. Well, it appears that it hadn't occurred to him that this could also be a man's name. As for Harriet, she'd met a Frances at some party recently, but she had no idea of the last name. Then I asked her the same thing I'd asked the law clerk. Her answer was—and this is exactly what she said—'I assumed you meant Frances with an *e,* naturally.' After that, she threw in that the only Francis with an *i* who came to mind was Ron Francis, who's a hockey player."

"You arrived at this monumental conclusion of yours by polling *three people?*"

"It only bore out something I was already certain of. That's why I suggested you ask around yourself; you'll find out that I'm right."

"I imagine you're doing this for effect," Fielding declared now.

"Doing what?"

"Withholding the identity of the individual who made what you regard as a slip of the tongue."

My face must have turned crimson. "Oh, God! What an idiot I am! I never did say who it was, did I?"

"No, you didn't," Tim replied quietly with what, if

I wanted to be charitable, I'd have termed a grin. But feeling particularly vulnerable just then, I viewed as a smirk.

"Melanie Slater."

"You've got to be joking! It's been at least five years since that affair between the victim and Slater, right? Assuming, of course, there was ever anything between them to begin with. Which, incidentally, is something the lady vehemently denies."

"You've talked to her?"

"Norm and I paid her a visit this morning."

"The time lapse troubled me, too. Then I considered something Norm had said when I was here last Wednesday. We were discussing how the motives of both Melanie and Danny—Gordon's son—dated back too far to be really viable, remember? And Norm remarked that something might have happened recently to set one of them off."

"And you know of an occurrence like that?"

"I believe so, yes. During my conversation with Rhonda, I discovered that Melanie had been seriously involved with someone recently and that the romance ended around September. Melanie was pretty hard-hit by the breakup, too. The reason for it—according to Rhonda—was that the man wanted to have children, and her cousin didn't. But then, when I was questioning Melanie, we got on the subject of a former patient of hers, and she spoke very lovingly about the woman's young sons. Well—"

"That doesn't necessarily translate into her wanting kids herself," Fielding pointed out.

"Granted. But on the other hand, it isn't as if she dislikes them. On the contrary, actually. At any rate, when Blossom originally filled me in on all that gossip about Melanie and Gordon, she mentioned—and I almost forgot this—that there was also a rumor that the affair led to Melanie's having an abortion.

"Now, what if something went wrong during the procedure, and the woman is no longer able to bear a child? It's not too much of a stretch to imagine that she would have blamed Gordon for destroying her chance at happiness with the man she loves. Especially if Gordon was the one who pushed for the abortion."

"You're scrambling for a motive to justify your suspicion," Fielding accused.

"If Melanie had Gordon Curry killed—and I'm sure she did—the abortion thing makes sense. What doesn't make sense is that she'd have given up the love of her life because she didn't care to have children—particularly when you take into account her comments to me about that patient's twin boys. Ergo, she let this guy go not because she *wouldn't* agree to have children but because she *couldn't.*"

"Look—"

I wasn't through yet. "Besides, I was under the impression you didn't put much stock in coincidence."

"What's that got to do with anything?"

"Those two unsuccessful attempts on Gordon's life occurred just weeks after Melanie's boyfriend took off."

Fielding placed an elbow on the desk now and cupped his chin in his hand. "I'm not going to say you're wrong about any of this, but I'm not convinced that you've got this thing figured out correctly, either. You have to be aware that there's no concrete evidence at all to support your theory that it was Melanie Slater who hired Lonergan."

"I realize that. But I was hoping you could check out whatever bank accounts she might have to see if she'd made any substantial withdrawals in September. I don't imagine hired killers go for peanuts."

"I'd need a subpoena from the DA's office to do that. And I can just picture somebody there issuing a subpoena on the basis that Melanie Slater knew that the shooter's name was spelled with an *i* instead of an *e*. Christ, Shapiro! I'd be laughed right outta there if I asked for one!"

"Maybe not. Um, do you suppose you could at least give it a try?" I suggested meekly.

"Oh, sure. And have some pissy little assistant DA go around telling everyone that my brain short-circuited? Trust me, Desiree, there is no way I can gain access to those accounts on the basis of what you've told me."

I guess I didn't do such a great job of hiding my dejection, because moments later, when he spoke again, Fielding's tone was softer and not unsympathetic. "If you want that woman behind bars, you'll have to give me something that has a few more teeth than what you've given me tonight."

I stood up. "All right, Tim. Then that's what I'll do."

# Chapter 35

When I announced that I was leaving, Fielding actually got to his feet and helped me on with my coat. And it wasn't because he was hustling me out of there, either—at least, I didn't get that impression. The way I saw it, while all was not yet forgiven, it was fairly safe to assume that our long-term friendship hadn't totally unraveled.

"I'll walk you to the door," he offered. Then, as we were making our way to the station house entrance, he *really* mellowed. "The gun the Guldens brought in is the same one that killed Gordon Curry," he announced.

"Hallelujah! Uh, I don't suppose it was registered to Lonergan."

"Don't tell me you considered that a possibility," Fielding scoffed. "There aren't even any serial numbers on that thing—they've been filed down."

"But anyhow, the kid ID'd him."

"Well, Ronnie Gulden never did get a look at his face. When the perp planted the weapon on him, they were in an area that was pretty poorly lit. But as Lonergan was running away, he passed under a streetlamp, and the boy caught a glimpse of him—although it was only for a couple of seconds and from the back at that. Fortunately, however, this was long enough for the youngster to establish that the man's hair was blond, that it was tied back in a ponytail, and that he was wearing a brown leather bomber jacket and light pants. Lonergan has *his* blond hair in a ponytail. And he was decked out in a brown leather bomber jacket and tan slacks when the officers brought him in."

"Has Lonergan been informed of any of this yet?"

"He has. Once the ballistics report came in, we weren't worried about the guy's walking anymore—we've got ourselves a pretty decent case. So we told Lonergan what we had in an effort to persuade him to roll over on the individual who hired him. But he insisted that the gun wasn't his, that the kid made a mistake when he identified him. I still figured he might change his mind once he thought things over, though. Only that was this morning, when Lonergan was being represented by a public defender. As of this afternoon, however, it looks like Sebastian Grinkoff will be taking over—I hear he visited Lonergan in prison right after lunch today. And I wouldn't bet my hard-earned pension that Grinkoff would advise his client to cop a plea. But then again, who knows?" And resignedly: "I guess we'll have to wait and see."

When we reached the entrance, Fielding and I stood there facing each other for a minute or two. "Anyhow, I thought you'd like to be brought up-to-date," he apprised me gruffly.

"Thanks, Tim. Thanks very much. I'm really sorry that I misled you. The truth is, I feel I have a personal obligation to my dead client to find out who ended his life. That's the reason I—"

Fielding held up his palm to signal for silence, and I obediently cut myself off in midsentence. "Let's forget it, huh?"

"All right. But I can't tell you how much—"

"If you thank me again, I'll have to deck you." And with the merest hint of a grin, he held open the door for me.

*    *    *

For some perverse reason, I couldn't convince my-self to hold off until I got home to establish that Nick hadn't tried to get in touch with me. So retrieving the cell phone from my handbag, I dialed my own number—only to have the damn machine bear out something I was 99.99 percent certain of.

There was a message from Ellen, though. She was off today and was asking if I'd like to come over for some Chinese food.

Well, after last night, that Chinese-food invitation almost made me gag. But on the other hand, I wasn't anxious to hurry back to the apartment and have the answering machine verify that Nick still hadn't been heard from. Which would, of course, result in my spending a large portion of what remained of the eve-ning sitting around and waiting for a call I wouldn't be getting. That is, when I wasn't driving myself crazy attempting to figure out how to nail Melanie Slater. No, I definitely did not look forward to returning home. If Ellen hadn't already eaten, maybe I could talk her into meeting me somewhere.

"Hi, Ellen, it's me. Have you had dinner yet?"

"Oh, Aunt Dez. You're just in time. One of my neighbors dropped in a while ago to borrow my hair dryer, and she stayed for so long I had to remind her why she was here." Ellen giggled—as only Ellen *can* giggle. "She finally left, and I was about to order from Mandarin Joy. What would you like? You *are* coming over, aren't you?"

"To tell you the truth, I ate Chinese food yesterday, so I was hoping maybe we could go for Italian or burgers or something. I'm right in your neighborhood—I had to stop by the Twelfth Precinct." I imagine that Ellen regarded the fact that I'd had Chinese the day before as a pretty lame reason for my suggesting an alternative cuisine, since I suspect she could eat Mandarin Joy's fare seven days a week—and frequently does. But she obliged me nevertheless.

"There's a really nice Italian restaurant—family owned, very homey—on East Twenty-fourth. Some friend of Mike's recommended it, and we were there last week."

"Sounds good to me."

She recited the address, and we agreed to meet at Casa Mia in a half hour.

Now, while I'm always going on about how I try to avoid bringing my murders to the dinner table, there are occasions when I feel compelled to make an exception. This was one of those occasions.

My declaration to Fielding that I'd be digging up the necessary evidence against Melanie Slater to justify a subpoena had been, I confess, part bravado and part transient insanity. I was at a total loss as to what my next step should be.

If I had any hope of moving ahead with the investigation, I needed to have my self-confidence bolstered. I was also desperate for somebody to listen while I aired my thoughts about the case. My generous and supportive niece could always be relied on for both these things—and fortunately, here she was, sitting across from me. (And in the unlikely event you're wondering, while a homicide discussion doesn't exactly stimulate my appetite, it, nevertheless, failed to deter me from enjoying my meal.)

At any rate, while we were sipping our Merlot, I asked about Mike. I was advised that he was fine, health-wise. Sensational, character-wise. And working tonight. (Which I'd already surmised.) Then Ellen wanted to know about Nick.

Well, I would definitely not be going into *that* this evening. I was too unnerved to talk about it. Besides, at present there was something more urgent on my agenda. "He's okay," I told her—I even managed to produce a smile. But the effort was wasted.

"You're upset," Ellen declared.

"I didn't think it showed."

"It shows, all right. What's wrong?"

I caved at once. (So much for my unshakable resolve.) And Ellen was soon treated to an only slightly abridged version of yesterday's debacle. I concluded with a half-sobbed, "Nick promised to call today. But I checked my answering machine a little earlier, and he hasn't."

I'll say this for her: Ellen didn't start spouting platitudes. She was silent for close to a minute, her forehead deeply furrowed, her hand covering mine. At last she murmured, "I'm sure Nick cares for you, Aunt Dez. But he has to realize that as long as his son has the attitude he does, there isn't much hope that . . . that anything will come of it."

"I understand that this can't possibly go anywhere. Regardless, though, Nick should have kept his word and picked up the telephone—even if it was to tell me that it would be advisable if we stopped seeing each other."

"He does seem to have taken the easy way out," Ellen agreed. "Still, he might call again. But suppose he does. And suppose you go out with him. It won't change the fact that his kid's a horrible little creep who's intent on ruining things between you two. Listen, I'm aware of how taken you are with this man, Aunt Dez. But don't you . . . that is, wouldn't you be better off if—" She tried again. "What I'm saying is, the longer this goes on, the more unhappy you're liable to be when it ends."

She was repeating exactly what I'd been telling myself. But somehow, when I heard it verbalized like this, I was forced to accept—*really* accept, I mean—that it (whatever "it" was) was over.

All at once I felt surprisingly calm—relieved, almost. Maybe tomorrow or the next day—or even in a couple of hours, when I was back at the apartment—I'd wind up crying my eyes out. But it wouldn't change anything. Clearly, the time to put a period to the relationship was now. Whether Nick phoned again or not.

Over our appetizers—clams oreganato for Ellen and a very tasty portobello mushroom dish for me—we chatted about a variety of things. One of these being the latest crisis to arise out of the impending nuptials. Some relative of Mike's was pressing for permission to schlep his twenty-something girlfriend to the wedding, although the SOB's estranged wife—to whom he'd been married for thirty-plus years—would be attending.

"What are you planning to tell him?" I asked.

"I'm not. Mike's mother—thank goodness—promised to talk to him."

Of course, while we were on the subject of mothers, it was a natural segue to Ellen's female parent. "Mom called yesterday," my niece notified me, looking agitated. "She . . . uh . . . said that she still hasn't found a suitable dress."

"At least she's now in the market for something *suitable*," I quipped. "That's progress."

Ellen actually laughed.

Our entrées were served soon afterward. On Ellen's recommendation, I had joined her in ordering the veal with prosciutto and fontina cheese. She peered at me closely as I took my first bite—although she was kind enough to allow me to swallow before eliciting my critique.

"Well, do you like it?"

"Very much."

With a satisfied smile, Ellen sampled her own dish.

I decided to wait until *she* swallowed before broaching the subject I'd been anxiously waiting to introduce.

She beat me to it. "Oh, I almost forgot. You said on the phone that you were at the Twelfth Precinct before."

"That's right. I went to see Tim Fielding. You remember Tim." (They'd met during the course of my first homicide case.)

Ellen nodded. "How come?"

"Because I discovered who hired Gordon Curry's killer."

*"You did?"* she squealed. "Who? I'll bet it was the wife."

"Wrong. It was a woman named Melanie Slater. She was Gordon's first wife's nurse and is also his second wife's cousin."

Ellen giggled. "Let me get that straight in my head." Then after a moment's reflection: "Okay. I've got it. Why would this Melanie want to have him murdered?"

And here I acquainted her with some of the particulars: the purported affair between Melanie and Gordon, the rumored abortion, and my deceased client's trading in the nurse for Rhonda five years earlier.

"And Melanie held out all this time before paying the guy back?" Ellen's tone bordered on skeptical. *"That's* what I'd call patience."

"She didn't have him murdered because he threw her over. I believe Melanie took out that contract on Gordon because she considered him responsible for the grief she was experiencing now—*today*." Which led me to relay Rhonda's information about her cousin's recent love affair and the supported reason it had ended as it did.

"The thing is, though, Melanie mentioned to me that this deceased patient of hers—the woman she was caring for when the breakup occurred—had two young sons, and it was obvious that Melanie dotes on those boys. She was positively beaming when she said that they call her Aunt Melly. Uh-uh, Ellen. This business about her refusal to have kids? I don't buy it. I'm convinced that Melanie's affair with this fellow Hal went down the tubes because she wasn't able to conceive—not because she didn't choose to have children. I'd bet almost anything that she had an abortion when she was involved with Gordon and that it left her sterile." And in response to Ellen's doubtful expression: "Listen, just because abortions aren't done in back alleys anymore doesn't mean something unforeseen can't happen during the procedure. There's always that risk with any type of surgery."

Ellen chewed this over for a few moments. "You could be right," she murmured at last. "Anyhow, do you think Melanie told Hal about the abortion?"

"I have no idea. Why?"

"Just being nosy, that's all." Sometimes it's hard to believe that Ellen and I don't share the same gene pool.

For a short while after this Ellen devoted herself to the food. Then, putting down her fork, she stated solemnly, "I can understand her hating your client."

"Particularly if he pressured her into that abortion," I contributed.

"That's part of it, naturally. But I was also factoring in that later he did her dirty again—by ditching her and marrying her own cousin. Maybe if I'd been in Melanie's shoes, I'd have toyed with hiring a hit man myself. Although if I did make up my mind to go for it, I doubt that I'd have been lucky enough to be able to locate one."

"*Lucky* hardly applies to Melanie Slater. She even managed to break her arm not much more than a week after that traumatic split with her lover."

Ellen leaned toward me. "You have to tell me,

Aunt Dez. How did you reach the conclusion that Melanie was the person responsible?"

"I won't tell you; I'll demonstrate it for you. Did you ever hear of someone named Francis Lonergan?"

"No-o-o. Unless it was this woman who worked briefly in the shoe department at Macy's. What was her last name anyway? . . ."

"Did it occur to you that I could have been referring to a man?"

Ellen was momentarily taken aback. "Um, I guess not. But it really should have. A few weeks ago I read an article about silent-movie stars, and one of them was named Francis X. Bushman. Do you remember him?" she inquired just prior to revisiting her veal.

I revisited mine, too, after which I informed her stiffly, "Francis X. Bushman was quite famous in his day. But contrary to your opinion, he and I did not attend grammar school together." (The only explanation I can offer for reacting with such ridiculous sensitivity to this innocuous question is that this very morning I'd concluded that my posterior—never exactly perky—seemed to have dropped a good two inches recently.) "At any rate," I went on before she could attempt to defend what required no defense, "Francis Lonergan is the hit man. And when I asked Melanie if she was familiar with the name, she wanted to know whether *he* was involved in the murder—and I hadn't specified the sex."

"Oh."

"Yes, 'oh.' Tim Fielding doesn't see this as being any big deal, but I regard it as a *major* blunder on Melanie's part."

"I agree with you," Ellen said.

And now I posed the all-important question: "The problem is, though, where do I go from here?"

"You'll come up with the answer; you always do. Besides, you've already doped everything out—and that was the hard part. You just have to find something to tie Melanie and Francis together."

*See? I was certain I could count on my favorite—and only—niece to pump me up.* "Yes, but how?"

"I wish I could help you," she murmured. "I—"

Suddenly I had an epiphany. "Hold on a sec. Melanie needed to get the money to Lonergan, didn't she? Now, she and the boyfriend split in early September. And right after it happened, she took a week off from her nursing stint on Long Island and went home to Manhattan to glue herself together again—by her own admission, the breakup had hit her hard. It's likely that sometime during that week, the woman determined that the person she considered responsible for ruining her life should pay for it with his own. But not being too keen on doing the deed herself, she decided to farm out the job. I don't suppose that scrounging up an assassin would have been too difficult for someone with Melanie's connections—she was once the live-in nurse of a major crime figure. Nevertheless, it would probably have required a few phone calls.

"Anyhow, she's subsequently put in touch with Lonergan. She tells the man what she wants done, and he agrees to handle the matter. Well, if she doesn't have a rich uncle who's willing to bankroll this venture, she then has to withdraw some cash from one or more bank accounts to at least give Lonergan a down payment on his services. I can't imagine that someone in this profession would be willing to take a check.

"It's conceivable that Melanie took care of all this while she was still recuperating at home. But unless she started things moving the instant she walked through the door—which is doubtful—and everything progressed one-two-three—also doubtful—it would be pushing it to assume that she got to hand over the money to Lonergan during that interim. And then only two days after she returned to work she broke her arm—when she was roller-skating with her patient's twin boys, by the way. Which means she couldn't have driven anywhere to meet with Lonergan."

"Maybe she met with him before she injured herself," Ellen suggested.

"I guess I can't really rule that out," I conceded reluctantly. "But don't forget, Melanie had just come back to Long Island after being away from her seriously ill patient for a week. And I assume she'd have been inclined to stick pretty close to that house for a while—certainly for the first couple of days. My feeling is that she'd have arranged to get together with Lonergan on her day off. Only in the meantime she smashed up her arm."

"Couldn't she have brought the payment to him after she healed?"

"Uh-uh. Listen, Ellen, these people who own a deli in my neighborhood—their little boy broke his arm last summer. It was a simple break, too, and the doctor told the mother those things take a month to heal—minimum. I recall Mrs. Binder's remarking one day that her Seymour was still walking around with a cast almost six weeks after his accident. And remember, those motorboat and hunting incidents occurred when Gordon and his wife were on vacation in the Poconos—which was late September, early October."

At this moment I was struck by something else. "At first Melanie must have wanted Gordon's death to appear accidental."

I'd made the comment more to myself than to Ellen, but she responded with, "Apparently she changed her mind."

"Yes, but why?" I mused.

Ellen beat me to the punch. (I'm pretty sure I was only seconds behind her, however.) "Could Melanie have learned that this Roger had threatened him?"

"You bet your tush she could! Rhonda heard all

about Roger Clyne's threats just prior to leaving on that holiday, and at some point after she returned she must have mentioned them to her good friend and relative. Of course, what she didn't mention—because she wasn't aware of it—was that Roger was now deceased. So under the impression that she had the perfect fall guy waiting in the wings, Melanie evidently got in touch with Lonergan and amended her instructions. He no longer had to bother making it seem that it was simply the victim's bad luck that he ceased to be among the living. Lonergan could just get the hit over with."

"Nice lady," my niece remarked sarcastically. "It's one thing to have someone killed because he screwed up your life. But to be willing to let an innocent man take the blame for it . . ." Ellen's expression adequately conveyed her disgust.

"And she couldn't even be sure Clyne wouldn't have an alibi for the time of the shooting," the practical side of me observed. "Actually, I'm a little surprised, though. I wouldn't have thought Melanie was the type of individual to do something like that. The only thing I can come up with is that she must have been terribly frustrated by then, desperate to put all of this behind her. Keep in mind that it had been more than a month since her hired gun's previous efforts."

"Still, this doesn't—"

"Hold on a sec. You know, Roger Clyne might not have had anything to do with Melanie's changing her mind about the accident business. Who can say if she was even aware he existed?" I gave myself a mental shake. "Boy, have I digressed. What I was trying to determine before was how Melanie managed to pay the man in time for him to do his thing in the Poconos. And it strikes me that the two most logical scenarios are (a) she hopped on a train or a bus to deliver the cash to him—in which case it would be extremely tough to establish any connection between the two of them: or (b) Lonergan drove out to Ashbrook—the town Melanie was working in. And I really do think that's more likely in light of her physical condition. But it could be I just prefer to think that's how it went down. At any rate, I'm going to ask Fielding to fax me Lonergan's picture, and then I'll take a little trip out to Ashbrook." And before Ellen could say a word: "Thank you, Ellen. Thank you, thank you, thank you."

"But I didn't do anything."

"Yes, you did. By our talking things over like this, I was able to get a fix on my next move. Maybe if I cross my fingers—and also my eyes and my toes—I'll find someone in that place who can identify the man who shot Gordon."

With things now settled in my mind, Ellen and I were able to devote our complete attention to our tiramisu.

All in all, it had been a very productive evening. With Ellen's help, I had established a direction with regard to my investigation. And I was more accepting of the fate of my relationship with Nick, as well.

She even deserves most of the credit for the restaurant's finally agreeing to share one of their recipes with me. As I've said before—and she proved once again—along with her other fine qualities, my niece is one of New York's premier *nudges*.

# Chapter 36

There was no message from Nick on my machine when I got home. Which was just as well—or so I tried to convince myself. At least it spared me from having to inform him that I wouldn't be seeing him anymore. Although, doubtless, he would have survived the sad news.

Nevertheless, based on my record, it was practically preordained that I'd do considerable blubbering that night. And I did, finally falling asleep when it was almost time to get up.

I was jolted into consciousness in the morning by a screeching alarm clock. A short while later—without even waiting until I'd brushed my teeth—I phoned Jackie to let her know I wouldn't be at work today.

"You're still depressed over Sunday's dinner, aren't you?" I'm sure she meant this to sound sympathetic, but it came out more like an accusation.

"That has nothing to do with it. I'm driving out to Long Island later—it's about the case."

"What's in Long Island?"

Mercifully, I was able to avoid an explanation because Jackie had to take another call. "I'll give you all the details tomorrow," I promised before quickly putting down the receiver.

Right after this I tried to contact Tim Fielding. He wasn't in, I was told, and the officer who answered his phone couldn't say when he was expected.

I wolfed down my breakfast, then dialed the number again. I was in luck. Following the briefest of amenities, I worked myself up to, "I need a favor, Tim."

"*You?* A favor? I can hardly believe it."

I ignored the dig—good-natured as it was for a change. "This is really important."

"Naturally. Okay, let's hear it."

"I'd appreciate it if you'd fax me a mug shot of Francis Lonergan."

"That's against regulations; you should know that, Shapiro."

"It could help us wrap things up. Honestly."

"How?"

Well, not having managed to dream up a plausible excuse for the request, I had to settle for the truth. "I'm driving out to Ashbrook, Long Island. That's where Melanie was working when she hired Lonergan to do my client, and I want to show the picture around town to see if I can find someone who recognizes the guy. I have an idea that he went there to collect his down payment from her."

"How did you come up with that?"

"I'm not positive, of course, and it's kind of a complicated story, but I don't mind going into it—that is, if you're not in any hurry." I broke into a smile, anticipating Fielding's reaction.

"No, no. That's okay," he answered so hastily that he all but tripped over his tongue.

"You'll fax me the photo?"

"Christ, Shapiro," he groused. "One of these days you're gonna get me busted."

I took this as a yes.

"Um, one more thing. You wouldn't be able to give me directions for getting out to Ashbrook, would you?"

"I wouldn't, but I'll check it out and fax them to you."

"I was hoping—" I stopped cold. The man's patience did have its limits, as I'd already discovered—time after time.

"Go on."

"It's no big deal."

"Say it anyway," he pressed. "You were hoping—what?"

"Uh . . . that you might be able to fax me that stuff this morning. If possible, I'd like to go there today."

"That shouldn't be a problem."

"Thanks, Tim. Thanks a million. I realize I've been getting in your hair lately, but—"

"*You?* Get in my hair? Now, why would you think a thing like that?"

At a few minutes after eleven I was on my way to Ashbrook, having dressed with what, for me, was breakneck speed.

Fielding's directions had included the P.S. that the drive should take about two hours.

I was there in three.

It's remarkable how frequently I manage to get lost, even when the instructions are crystal clear—as they were in this instance. I tell myself that with all the weighty matters I have on my mind, it's no wonder I'm forever taking the wrong exit or miscounting the number of traffic lights or turning left when I should have turned right.

One of the things that kept me occupied during that protracted trip was trying to figure out what made Rhonda Curry—oops, *Leonidas*—tick. (Although I had a feeling that wasn't actually doable.)

The woman projected this aloof persona, yet she'd apparently been a devoted mother to her son, Chip. And there was no disputing the fondness she inspired in her stepson. Or her closeness to her cousin—at whose expense it's likely she'd acquired her second husband. Which led me to ponder an extremely per-

plexing question: Why would Rhonda persist in denying that Gordon and Melanie had ever been
romantically entangled? True, this was academic now;
nevertheless, I was intrigued by the motivation behind it.

Had Melanie pressured Rhonda into making this
claim? I mean, she might have persuaded her that
regardless of its being ancient history, if the affair
came to light, the police could view her—Melanie—
as a suspect. Or, I speculated, perhaps Rhonda, confident that her cousin had had no part in the murder,
volunteered to withhold the information herself. It was
also conceivable that the two women had entered into
a pact, whereby Rhonda would declare that Melanie
and the victim had never been more than good friends.
And for her part, Melanie would remain mum about
Rhonda's having implored Gordon not to drive up to
Vermont on that fateful day.

At last I abandoned Rhonda and Melanie—and the
"Why?" that would probably always be a mystery to
me—and reacquainted myself with Danny and Luke
for a while. Then I moved on to Ellen's wedding (but
I refused to devote a single second to Margot's dress).
I also remembered about Thanksgiving at some point.
I'd been invited to spend it across the hall with Harriet
and Steve and, unfortunately, their Pekinese, Baby—
the most malevolent little creature you'd ever be apt
to meet. And I'm not just saying this because he deliberately peed on my brand-new faux-crocodile Italian
pumps, either. Anyhow, I suddenly realized that the
holiday was only two days away, and I still hadn't
asked Harriet what she'd like me to bring over for
our dinner. I vowed to call her as soon as I got home.

It was what I didn't think about, though, that was
really noteworthy. I had survived that very tedious
drive without allowing Nick to enter my mind even
once—at least, not for more than a minute or two.

Ashbrook was much smaller than I'd expected. Actually, it was much smaller than I'd have expected *any* town to be.

I'd barely passed the sign proclaiming that I was now entering Ashbrook when there I was, right at its hub (if you could call it that)—which was all of about three blocks long. Or, to be more accurate, three *short* blocks long.

The place looked as if it had jumped off a picture postcard, with treelined cobblestone streets and charming old buildings, most of them Tudor-style. These housed a grocery, a coffee shop, a pizzeria, a pharmacy, a dry cleaner, a shoemaker, a liquor store, a beauty parlor/barber shop, and—incongruously—an insurance agent.

I was buoyed by what I saw here. In a town this size, I reasoned, there was really a pretty good chance that someone would notice a ponytailed stranger.

An hour later, however, I found myself thoroughly disabused of this notion.

My first stop had been the pizzeria. I said I was a PI and that an attorney had hired me to locate a man who'd recently inherited some money. To explain away the obvious mug shot origins of the faxes I'd be showing around (Fielding had, in his wisdom, sent me two views—one of them establishing the killer's ponytail), I'd come up with the story that the man was once arrested for drunk driving.

"I was fortunate enough to obtain these from a friend in law enforcement," I told the tiny, gray-haired woman behind the counter.

"He doesn't look familiar," she asserted while studying the pictures.

"It's possible he was with Melanie Slater," I suggested in an attempt to jog her memory. "She was the nurse who used to care for Mrs. McCann."

"Nice girl, Melanie. But I still don't know him. Maybe the kid who works for me can help you." And with this she bellowed, "Maurice! Come out here!" I was so startled to hear that booming voice emerge from someone of this lady's stature that I must have jumped three inches off the floor. A moment later a teenager joined us from the back room, and she thrust the pictures at him. "You ever seen this guy?"

The boy's head swung back and forth, back and forth, from one likeness to the other. I was beginning to think they were exercising some sort of hypnotic spell over him when he finally grunted, "Nah."

"He was maybe with that nurse who used to work for Mrs. McCann," Maurice's employer informed him, sparing me the effort.

"Nah," the boy said again.

And so it went as I proceeded to trudge up and down those three short blocks.

My last stop was the shoe repair shop. Salvatore, the proprietor, regretfully shook his head. "I'm very sorry," he murmured, returning the photos to me.

Now, after spending so many hours behind the wheel, I was hardly willing to abandon Ashbrook yet. I'd pay a visit to the McCanns next. Could be I'd learn whether Lonergan had contacted Melanie there—or vice versa. It occurred to me then that the nurse might have hired a car service in order to meet with the hit man somewhere. I'd check into that, too. "Would you be able to give me the McCanns' address?" I asked Salvatore.

"I go look up for you." He hurried toward the rear of the store. A couple of minutes later he was back with a slip of paper and verbal instructions for getting to the house.

After saying good-bye to Salvatore, I retraced my steps to the coffee shop. Here, in preparation for the second part of my agenda, I fortified myself with an overstuffed club sandwich and a large mug of coffee—along with a generous wedge of apple pie à la mode.

Oak Lane was a quiet street of large, graceful homes a few miles from Ashbrook's main street. (Which, incidentally, was actually *named* Main Street.) Number 32 was a well-kept, white-shingled house that loudly proclaimed there were children in residence here. Two beat-up bicycles and a shiny red wagon cluttered up the walkway, while on the front porch, a baseball bat leaned against a chair, and a pair of ice skates sat in a corner of a glider strewn with comic books. Being from New York (the city, I mean), I found it almost inconceivable that no one had immediately—and permanently—"borrowed" all of these things from the McCanns.

Praying that someone would be in, I pressed the bell. I'd barely taken my hand away when the door was opened by a formidable-looking woman with a stern, squarish face. I judged this to be Nattie, the housekeeper Melanie had mentioned. I put Nattie's age at about sixty—but it was a very hardy sixty.

"Yes?" she demanded, arms folded across her ponderous bosom.

"Umm, my name is Desiree Shapiro, and I'm a private investigator—" I showed her my license. "I've been engaged to locate someone, and I wonder if you'd mind looking at a couple of photographs and telling me if you recognize the man."

"What do you want with him?" She was definitely eyeing me with suspicion.

I realized at once that unless I was anxious to have that door slammed in my face, it might be advisable for me to provide her with a more compelling story than the one I'd dispensed on Main Street. "My client believes he may be involved in some kind of scam," I improvised.

Nattie began to pepper me with questions. "*What* kind of scam?"

"Bilking senior citizens with a phony get-rich-quick scheme."

"Who's your client?"

"She's . . . uh . . . the daughter of one of the victims."

"You say the fellow you're looking for is from Ashbrook?"

"No, he isn't. But apparently he's been seen in the company of someone who resembles a nurse that used to work here. In this house, I mean."

"You're referring to Melanie Slater?"

I was quick to offer reassurance. "Yes, but my source isn't at all certain the individual in question *is* Miss Slater. And besides, the man's companion isn't under suspicion."

"You should have told me right at the beginning this had something to do with Slater," she scolded. "Come in."

I followed her into a small study off the central hallway. Once I was seated, she asked, although with very little enthusiasm, "Would you like some tea or a cup of coffee?"

"I stopped off for coffee in town. But thanks very much, Ms.—?"

"I don't go for that 'Ms.' business. It's Mrs.—Mrs. Finster—I'm a widow. But you can call me Nattie—everyone does. I'm the McCanns' housekeeper," she added as she closed the study door. Then almost in a whisper: "There are eight-year-old twin boys doing their homework in the kitchen, and I thought it would be best if we talked where they can't overhear us. I wouldn't want to upset them—they're fond of Slater."

The wrinkled nose that accompanied this statement was extraneous. It was obvious from the way she pronounced the name that Nattie didn't share the boys' favorable opinion of their dead mother's caregiver. Which, it occurred to me, could work to my advantage.

As soon as she'd settled into a chair, Nattie held out her hand. "Okay, let's see your pictures."

After stating that they were a result of the man's having had a prior brush with the law, I turned them over to her. She examined them closely, then shook her head. "He doesn't look familiar."

"His name is Francis Lonergan. Does that ring a bell?"

"No, it doesn't."

"Nobody by that name ever phoned here to speak to Miss Slater?"

"Not that I'm aware of. You say Slater wasn't involved in the scam, though?"

"It isn't likely."

She wasn't quite able to conceal her disappointment.

"I understand Miss Slater was very fond of this family," I commented.

"Of course she was. Wouldn't you be if they gave *you* a week off so you could run home and stick your head under the covers and feel sorry for yourself? The way she acted, you'd have thought she was the first female to ever get dumped by her boyfriend. I've got my suspicions that Mr. and Mrs. McCann paid Slater while she was away, too, even though they had to hire someone else to look after Mrs. McCann in her absence." The housekeeper screwed up her face. "Then as soon as she deigns to get back here and attend to her patient, what does that stupid girl do? She goes roller-skating with a couple of eight-year-olds and breaks her arm. Naturally, she wasn't able to lift poor Mrs. McCann by herself anymore, but the McCanns *still* kept her on. And don't get the idea I was given any added compensation, either, for all the extra work that fell on me because of her foolishness."

I responded with a few clucks of the tongue, follow-ing up with an appropriately sympathetic, "It must have been very difficult for you."

"That's putting it mildly," Nattie mumbled sourly.

"So, uh, did Miss Slater have any visitors while she was working for the McCanns?"

"Before he ditched her, the boyfriend used to pick her up on her days off quite often. Oh, and every now and then a friend of Slater's who works at a hospital somewhere on the island would drop by. Vanessa somebody, her name was."

"There were no other visitors?"

"No." But a moment later: "Wait. I'm wrong. There *was* this fellow who came here once. Slater acted like they were strangers, but I had my doubts." And now she spoke slowly, obviously putting the facts into place as she recounted the incident. "As I remember, he showed up on what was supposed to be my free day— only at the last minute I decided not to go out after all. Mrs. McCann had had a particularly bad night, you see, and I didn't feel right leaving her alone with a girl who had just one functioning arm." And here Nattie's eyes widened. "You know, it seems to me he could have been that crook in the photographs you showed me."

"You weren't able to identify him from the pictures, though," I pointed out.

"That's because I didn't get a look at his face that afternoon." She gave me this smug little smile. "I was in the living room, dusting, when the doorbell rang. And before I could make a move, Slater hollered, 'I'll answer it!' and right away she was at the door. The man couldn't have been here more than a few seconds, and as soon as he left, Slater called out to me that he was trying to find some street in the area. But I thought that was, well . . . *peculiar*. There hadn't been enough *time* for him to get directions. Also"—and Nattie wriggled a finger for emphasis—"Slater never used to answer the door if I was anywhere around. She considered that my job.

"Now, I'm no busybody—ask anyone—but I was curious. So I peeked out the window. I only saw the man from the back, but I did notice that he had light hair."

"What about a ponytail?"

"I couldn't tell—his collar was turned up. But I wouldn't be surprised."

"Anything else—anything at all—that you remember about him?"

"He had on blue jeans and a dark jacket—brown, I believe, but it might have been black. And he was wearing athletic shoes: Nike or Adidas or one of those—I can't tell one from the other. There was a package covered in brown paper tucked under his arm. And even at the time I had a suspicion that this was why the man was here: to pick up that package. Naturally, I can't be a hundred percent sure of that, but my friends say I'm a very intuitive person. Anyhow, a minute or two later he hopped into his car and drove off." Nattie had barely finished her recitation before asking eagerly, "So what do you think? Think he could be that scammer you're after?"

"It's very possible. Listen, Nattie, do you have any idea when this was?"

"I don't know the exact date, but if I'm not mistaken, it was fairly soon after Slater busted up her arm."

At this juncture I posed a question that was bound to result in an answer I'd be unhappy with. But I had to put it to the woman anyway. "Did you happen to notice his license plate number?"

"No, why would I?"

"I don't suppose you paid any attention to the car, either."

"That's what you say."

It's hard to speak once you've stopped breathing. But I managed. "What make was it?"

"I don't know anything about cars, but my brother has one just like it. Same color, too—black. I'll check with him around ten—which is when he usually gets home from work. Is that too late to call you?"

"You can call me at three in the morning, Nattie, if that's when your brother gets in. And I can't thank you enough for your trouble."

"You don't have to thank me. If this man's been preying on the elderly, I'm anxious to help."

I believed her about being anxious to help. I imagine she was also hopeful that, in spite of my denials, her information could get Melanie in hot water, too. And this, I had no doubt, was an opportunity Nattie Finster wouldn't have wanted to miss.

The phone rang at just after ten. My right hand immediately began shaking so badly that I had to steady it with my left in order to lift the receiver.

"It's Nattie. I spoke to my brother. He has a 2001 Nissan Altima."

"And you're positive this is what Melanie's visitor was driving?" (After all, by her own admission the woman knew nothing about cars.)

"I certainly am. It has these big, round taillights. And according to Fletcher—my brother—it's the only model that does."

# EPILOGUE

In the two weeks since my trip to Ashbrook, things have, for the most part, finally been resolved—although there's one matter that's, well, kind of in limbo. But let me fill you in on what's happened. . . .

To start with, even before I notified Fielding about what had transpired on Long Island, I got in touch with the one person I knew would be as happy as I was that Gordon's nemesis has been identified. I made the call on Tuesday night, right after my conversation with Nattie.

Blossom greeted me with her customary graciousness and warmth. "For crissakes, Shapiro! It's past ten!"

"I'm sorry, Blossom. Did I wake you?"

"Never go to bed till one. But you didn't know that, did you?"

Presented with this challenge, I had to concede that I didn't.

"Well, what do you want? And make it fast. I'm watching *NYPD Blue*."

"I just thought you'd be interested in finding out who was behind Gordon's murder."

For quite possibly the only time in her entire existence, Blossom Goody was rendered speechless for close to a minute. At last she got out a single word: "Who?"

"Melanie Slater."

"Why'd she do it?" Blossom asked in a choked voice.

I told her about the abortion and the impact it had had on Melanie's life. But I was careful not to reveal in any way that, despite her horrendous act, I couldn't help feeling some sympathy for the woman. Understandably, Blossom would hardly have appreciated my view of things.

"You're sure it was Melanie?"

"Positive."

She didn't ask for any details, and I didn't offer any. Not then, at any rate. "God," was all she said—right before hanging up on me.

For once, I didn't curse her for it.

The fact is, when we'd met for breakfast two days after Gordon's death, I began to suspect that Blossom's obvious affection for her cousin by marriage hadn't been of the strictly platonic variety. That morning her eyes looked to me as if she'd recently wept a bucket or two. Plus, while she's no Miss Sweetness and Light under the most pleasant of circumstances, she was unusually testy then—even for Blossom. However, I told myself I was being stupid. Listen, where is it written that in order for you to sincerely mourn someone's passing, this someone had to be capable of putting your libido in overdrive?

But talking to Blossom on the phone the day of Gordon's memorial service convinced me that I'd been right in the first place. As you may remember, she broke down when she spoke of the victim, then quickly apologized. I said for her not to worry about it, that I knew how fond she'd been of him. Her response, if you recall, was "No, you don't."

Anyway, I'd like to think that now that she's learned the truth about Gordon's murder—and has every reason to be confident that the responsible par-

ties will be brought to justice—she'll be able to put
the tragedy behind her. The thing is, in spite of that
less than lovable disposition of hers, I like Blossom
Goody. I realize this may sound like a cliché, but she
has a good heart. She slipped up once or twice, and I
got a peek at it.

I contacted Fielding the next morning and announced that I had new evidence against Melanie
Slater, which—as he'd requested—had "a few more
teeth" than what I'd originally presented to him. He
came back with, "You're kidding, right?"

Initially, I considered this comment to be a reflection on my sleuthing ability. But I later discovered
that the reason for Fielding's reaction was that he'd
pretty much settled on another individual as having
sponsored the homicide.

Apparently, Rhonda's former husband's present
wife (I hope you can follow that) had communicated
to the police that she'd overheard a conversation between Rhonda and Luke wherein the widow vowed
that Gordon would pay for the death of their son. Of
course, if there were so much as half a brain rattling
around in my head, Fielding's providing me with those
faxes would have put me on red alert. Now that I'm
aware of the truth, I can envision how pleased he must
have been to see me go off to Ashbrook and spin my
wheels (which is what he must have figured I'd be
accomplishing there). After all, any task that took me
out of town would enable him to conduct his investigation of Rhonda during that interim—brief as it might
be—unencumbered by some pesky little PI who was
forever sticking her nose into his case.

However, with Nattie's statement to the police (in
the persons of Fielding and Melnick), Fielding was at
last persuaded that he'd been slightly myopic in his
judgment. I mean, he could hardly disregard the

housekeeper's testimony that a male stranger driving a black 2001 Nissan Altima had turned up on the McCanns' doorstep in mid-September. And armed with this information, he must have been satisfied that no one in the DA's office would be splitting his/her sides when he requested a subpoena to look into the nurse's bank records. And evidently no one did.

The records revealed that on September 10 Melanie had withdrawn twelve thousand dollars from one of her accounts. Fielding also established, via phone records, that she and Francis Lonergan had been in intermittent contact from early September until a few days prior to Gordon's death. (I'd like to hear Lonergan's hotshot lawyer explain that one!)

The end result of all this is that Melanie, along with the killer she hired, has been arraigned and is presently facing a murder charge.

There are just a couple of other things I thought I'd mention, both of these being of a more personal nature.

One concerns Ellen's wedding and—yep—her mother's gown.

About ten days ago my niece, her voice clearly desperate, called to apprise me that Margot had made another purchase. "My mother just told me she found the perfect dress. Not only isn't this one black, she says, but it's not brown or gray, either. She claims it's a *happy* dress for a happy occasion. But here's the description she gave me: It's lime green with large fuchsia, Kelly green, and orange flowers. The thing sounds like a Hawaiian shirt for pity's sake," Ellen moaned.

Once again it was obvious that Ellen's father had to go into action. And he didn't disappoint. He contacted the same blessed neighbor who'd conned Margot into accepting that the black dress made her look flat chested. In this current instance, the woman—May, her name is—was somehow able to convince my sister-in-law that it's bad luck to wear a garment that has orange flowers on it. And then she offered to go shopping with Margot—who actually accepted.

I'm delighted to report that in a couple of weeks the mother of the bride will be walking down the aisle in a teal blue silk gown.

Just one final bit of news.

Last night I heard from Nick.

"I'm very sorry I haven't been in touch, Dez." He sounded so contrite that for a moment *I* was almost sorry for *him*. "The truth is, I didn't know what to say to you. For Derek to come out with those terrible things—well, sometimes I still can't believe he said what he did. It's really so unlike him."

I let that go—although it was all I could do not to shout that it was *just* like him. That, in fact, this wasn't the first time Daddy's little demon had attacked me. (Not to mention the fate he'd visited on my boeuf bourguignon.) There was something I did have to get off my chest, though.

"I understand what an uncomfortable position you were in, Nick. But, regardless, I thought I'd hear from you a lot sooner than this. Do you have any idea why?" I didn't pause long enough to allow for a reply. "Because you told me I would. Listen, I realized that with Derek feeling the way he does about me, we wouldn't be going out anymore. But I was expecting that you'd at least phone to commiserate with me a little, and then we'd say good-bye and wish each other well."

"There's no question that I should have called before—the next day, really. I wanted to, but it took me until tonight to work up to it. Frankly, I just couldn't face you. I was even a little concerned that you might hang up on me—and I wouldn't have blamed you. But this isn't a good-bye call, Desiree; I'm hoping you'll agree to see me again."

"Look," I explained, "I'm not blaming you for what happened that evening. How could I? But you have to admit that, under the circumstances, it would be best to leave things as they are."

And now Nick's voice was so soft it was like a caress. (I swear.) "I've missed you, Dez—a lot—and I want very much for us to spend more time together. Incidentally, Derek says he's sorry, that he can't understand what prompted his outburst. But that isn't enough for me, and I'm certain it's not enough for you, either. So, naturally, it would be just the two of us from here on in. Although I am optimistic that, with therapy, my son will straighten out one of these days and begin to act like a bona fide human being."

"But say that we do start going out again," I protested. "It's conceivable that one or maybe both of us could wind up getting emotionally involved. Think how much tougher it would be to break things off then."

"I can't speak for you, Dez, but I'm already involved."

My response was somewhat short of inspired. "Oh," was all I could manage before my throat closed (it had been doing a lot of that lately) and the rest of me became one giant tingle.

"Listen, why don't we have dinner some night? We can talk this over then. How is Saturday for you?"

Well, damned if my throat didn't open up again! And by the time I was aware that I had any intention of saying, "Fine," I'd already said it.

My relationship with Nick has about as promising a future as Melanie Slater has; I know that. I mean, I'm just asking for grief. Which is why, as soon as I put down the receiver, I laced into myself. "You idiot!" I yelled out loud. "How could you?"

The thing is, though, feeling as I do about the man, how could I not?

## Casa Mia's Funghi alla Graticola

*(This is so easy—and so good!)*

2 large portobello mushrooms (about 6 inches in diameter)
extra virgin olive oil
balsamic vinaigrette

6–8 leaves of radicchio
4 thin slices of fontina cheese (approximately ⅛ lb.)

*For vinaigrette:*

3T extra virgin olive oil
2T balsamic vinegar
½ tsp. Italian seasoning

1 small clove of garlic, minced
salt and pepper to taste

Stem mushrooms and cut into thin strips (about ¼-inch wide). Brush with olive oil and broil about seven minutes or until soft.

*Meanwhile:* Whisk vinaigrette ingredients together. Arrange a bed of radicchio leaves, torn into bite-size pieces, on a serving dish.

When mushroom strips are soft, cover with fontina cheese, and broil one or two minutes longer or until cheese is melted. Transfer to serving dish. Drizzle with vinaigrette and serve immediately.

SERVES 4

Turn the page for a
Preview of the next
Marvelously entertaining
Desiree Shapiro mystery
Coming in early 2006

I was frozen with fear.

I gulped. Then I gulped again.

But that didn't keep my stomach from doing sum-mersaults. Or prevent my heart from pounding so hard I thought it would burst out of my chest. That's not all, either. My mouth was totally dry, and my palms were so wet they slid off the armrests.

*God! I hate flying!*

I supposed I looked as terrified as I felt. Because the man seated next to me murmured reassuringly, "It'll be all right. We've just hit a couple of little air pockets, that's all."

Little *air pockets? I'd like to know what he'd con-sider* big *air pockets!*

A short time later, when the turbulence finally sub-sided, the man turned to me again. "Are you all right?" he said kindly.

I eked out what was meant to be a brave smile (but probably came across more like an insipid grin). "I'm fine. Thanks for asking, though."

"You don't seem to care much for air travel," he observed.

"How can you tell?" We both laughed.

Now, this gentlemen and I had been sitting side-by-side for over a half hour. But other than exchanging hellos right after we boarded, we hadn't communicated with each other by so much as a single syllable until our Boeing 767 started jumping up and down.

With those "little" air pockets behind us, however, we began making up for that prior lack of dialogue.

"Are you headed for New York on business or a vacation?" my companion—a tall, balding man of about fifty—inquired.

I told him I lived here, that I'd gone out to Minneapolis to attend the wedding of an old college friend.

"What do you do in New York? If you don't mind my asking."

"I don't mind at all. I'm a PI."

"As in private investigator?"

"That's right," I answered curtly, bristling at the incredulous tone. I mean, so what if I'm only five-two? Or that the scale—whenever I'm foolish enough to step on one—proclaims that my weight isn't precisely what the charts dictate it should be? And the fact that I'm slightly more mature than the phony celluloid version of the female PI doesn't say diddly about my ability to do the job, does it?

"I'd never have guessed," the man told me. "I'm an attorney—the name is Ben, by the way, Ben Berlin—and I've hired female investigators on occasion. Believe me, you don't resemble any of them—even remotely. You're so . . . so . . ."

*Watch it, buster,* I warned him silently.

". . . *soft.*" He wrinkled his forehead for a moment. "What I'm trying to say is that you appear to be much more feminine than the other women investigators I've met up with."

Well, I was okay with that, so patting my glorious hennaed hair, I decided to favor him with another smile. "I should introduce myself, too. I'm Desiree Shapiro. But please call me Desiree. Anyhow, what about you? Are you also from New York?"

"No, from Minneapolis. I'm flying in to attend the funeral of my favorite aunt," he informed me somberly.

"Oh. I'm sorry to hear . . . that is, I'm . . . um . . . very sorry for your loss," I commiserated, struggling for the words. (When it comes to anything like that, it's points when I'm even intelligible.)

Ben's "Thank you," was thick with emotion. "I still find it hard to believe she's gone."

"She died suddenly?"

"Yes. Aunt Bessie is—*was*—no youngster, of course, but she was in very good health." His eyes seemed to be on the verge of filling up, and he shook his head as if to will away the tears. "Her death was the result of an accident—a fall. At any rate, she's being buried tomorrow."

Unable to come up with an appropriate response, I relied on the all-purpose nod.

"Aunt Bessie was more like a surrogate mother than an aunt—I lived with her for awhile. Once I moved out to Minnesota I wasn't able to see her as often as I'd have liked, of course, but we kept in close touch. We . . ." He didn't finish. I suspect it had something to do with the lump in his throat.

It was just minutes later that this young flight attendant came down the aisle pushing a beverage cart. "Would you care for something to drink, ma-am?" she inquired in a voice that practically defined the word "perky."

"A Coke, please."

"And you, sir?"

Ben was wise enough to decline.

She poured my Coke and was in the process of handing it to me when the plane lurched. But ever so slightly this time—honestly. Still, you'll never guess where most of that drink wound up!

"I'm *awfully* sorry," the girl told me (anyone under thirty is a girl to me), her cheeks instantly becoming an identical match to my hair. As she was busy attempting to pat me dry, however, she evidently had second thoughts. "You really should be a little more careful, though, ma'am. And I do mean that for your own wellbeing."

"*I* should be more careful?"

"Well, you did jostle my arm a bit."

I was all set to protest. I mean, even my eyeballs had been immobile, for God's sake! But before I could say anything, Miss Klutz had moved on.

*Have I mentioned that I hate flying?*

I made a quick trip to the rest room to sponge myself off. I returned to find Ben fast asleep. He didn't wake up until we were circling La Guardia Airport.

Once we were on the ground and the plane had bumped its way to a stop, Ben rose and squeezed past me to collect his belongings. But before reaching into the overhead compartment, he glanced down at me. "Listen, Desiree, it's not too likely that we'll be running into each other again, so take care of yourself, huh?"

"You do the same." I fumbled under the seat in front of me for a few seconds before making contact with my "I Love New York" tote bag.

When I raised my head again, my soon-to-be-client was gone.

Signet

# Selma Eichler

"A highly entertaining series."
—Carolyn Hart

"Finally there's a private eye
we can embrace." —Joan Hess

**MURDER CAN BOTCH UP YOUR BIRTHDAY**
0-451-21152-9
**MURDER CAN RUIN YOUR LOOKS**
0-451-18384-3
**MURDER CAN SINGE YOUR OLD FLAME**
0-451-19218-4
**MURDER CAN RAIN ON YOUR SHOWER**
0-451-20823-4
**MURDER CAN COOL OFF YOUR AFFAIR**
0-451-20518-9
**MURDER CAN UPSET YOUR MOTHER**
0-451-20251-1
**MURDER CAN SPOIL YOUR APPETITE**
0-451-19958-8
**MURDER CAN SPOOK YOUR CAT**
0-451-19217-6
**MURDER CAN WRECK YOUR REUNION**
0-451-18521-8

Available wherever books are sold or at
www.penguin.com

S316

# GET CLUED IN

www.signetmysteries.com

**Ever wonder how to find out about all
the latest Signet mysteries?**

# www.signetmysteries.com

- See what's new
- Find author appearences
- Win fantastic prizes
- Get reading recommendations
- Sign up for the mystery newsletter
- Chat with authors and other fans
- Read interviews with authors you love

## Mystery Solved.

www.signetmysteries.com